ECHOES OF THE FUTURE

GARETH IAN DAVIES

CONTENTS

To my wife, Sherri.
Rosalind only wishes she could be as awesome as you.

CHAPTER ONE
HAVING FUN ALREADY

"Let's see it, then!"

I stood back as Jess extended her left hand toward Rosalind. The harsh lights of the O'Hare airport departure gate glinted off the diamond on her finger. The two women exchanged conspiratorial grins as Rosalind made a show of examining Jess's engagement ring.

I caught Martin's eye as I shrugged off my backpack, dumping it onto a spare plastic row seat as I adjusted my sweaty T-shirt. His smile was wistful, but he shook my hand and murmured congratulations. He looked exhausted, a foil for the nervous energy that caused me to shift weight constantly even when standing still.

Rosalind hugged me in turn, with an extra squeeze for good measure. "I was beginning to wonder," she whispered. "I'm glad Jess liked the ring. I'm so happy for both of you."

"I'm happy too," I told her. And I was. More sure about my decision - our decision - now than I'd ever been. The world may be descending into chaos, and a supernatural menace lurked in the shadows, but I'd committed myself to the woman I loved, and it felt right. Whatever was gonna happen, would happen. We'd face it together.

We all sank into surprisingly uncomfortable seats. I noted Rosalind and Martin wore loose-fitting, long-sleeved shirts and jeans, much more casual than their usual attire. Perhaps they knew something about the airplane or the late September British weather that I didn't.

"I'm sorry we missed you in St. Louis over Labor Day weekend," Jess told them. "We wanted to share our engagement with you then, but both our families wanted a piece of us. I don't think anyone really believed it until they saw the ring. Mom made D repeat the story of his proposal to everyone. I expect he'll get the movie rights soon."

"You're such a romantic, D," said Rosalind with a grin, but I didn't mind her good-natured teasing. I'd been nervous about showing and telling Jess's family, and positively terrified repeating it with mine, for no good reason. Everyone was happy that their family's respective black sheep had found each other. "Have you set a date?"

I caught Jess's eye and didn't miss the warning within. "Not yet," I confessed. "We've discussed some options. I think a lot depends on what happens during this trip."

Rosalind frowned. "Don't let the Henry Lyons Foundation dictate your life - especially this part of it. Whatever they promise or threaten us with, it's not as important as the two of you choosing what's best for yourselves."

"Have they threatened you?" Jess asked, indignant on her behalf. "How much have you talked to your new handler? Gutierrez, or whatever her name is."

"Maria Gomez. I've spoken with her no more than necessary. She's cordial, professional, and tight-lipped. Most of our conversation concerned logistics for this trip, as if Martin and I don't travel to England every year. How much have you talked to Jamal?"

I glanced around to check if Jamal and Izzy, our HLF trainers on probation, were here yet. I couldn't see them, but we were early. Rosalind and Martin's connecting flight from St. Louis had landed four hours before our London Heathrow-bound departure. Jess and I had arrived at Chicago O'Hare soon afterwards, intending to catch up with our friends before the others joined us.

"Talked? Quite a lot, actually. He's determined to understand what happened at the Themis Center. I think he's looking for any explanation other than the one we gave: that there's something out there, some vast intelligence, watching us imprint memories, or release them. He can't accept it. I guess he needs to experience it himself. Maybe that's why he's coming with us."

Rosalind glanced at her husband just as his phone rang. I couldn't miss Martin's flinch when he saw who was calling. Then he mouthed an apology, stood up and stepped away, cupping his mouth as he spoke urgently. Rosalind viewed him with a mix of concern and irritation.

"Work?" I asked, trying to project sympathy for her, and understanding for him. Day jobs could be so demanding.

"Possibly. It may also be Special Agent Carmella Jones. She has an annoying tendency to call outside business hours, when Martin could use some peace, and time with his wife."

"Carmella Jones?" Jess frowned as she stared after Martin. "The FBI agent who interviewed us the night we broke into the Themis Center?"

"The very same," grumbled Rosalind. "She's conscripted my husband to work with her task force investigating the Scales of Equilibrium, looking into their money trail. Allen Weston and that thug Lyall have gone to ground, but the urban sabotage continues, as I'm sure you know. I worried our flights would be canceled, especially as the main Paris and Frankfurt airports are still closed. Martin's bank has partnerships with many financial institutions worldwide. I understand his position makes him useful to the FBI, but he's been working twelve-hour days ever since she contacted him, the day we met her. Sometimes I wonder if it's her revenge for us getting her out of bed at four in the morning for nothing."

For a terrorist attack on Chicago that hadn't happened on August 1st. Daniel Hill, their estranged son, recruited by the radical, pro-environment organization/cult while in drug rehab, had broken years of silence to warn his mother, and us. We still couldn't decide if the threat had been real or not.

"It feels like we're waiting for the other shoe to drop," I said. "Daniel's warning didn't feel fake to me, not after what we saw and heard during our burglary."

"Do you mean the Scales' mention of removing evidence?" asked Rosalind, lowering her voice. More and more passengers crowded the gate area. A troop of blue-clad cleaners hovered nearby, as if waiting for us all to get on a plane before they swooped in behind. "Or are you talking about the Intrusion and your Presence?"

"The Scales," I said. I shared another unsettled glance with Jess. "We're still unsure what to think about the Intrusion, about Imprints or any of that. We haven't dared try again to tether an Intrusion or imprint its memory. We haven't found any, or any existing Imprints to erase if we wanted to, despite the HLF brass forbidding it. We're kinda scared that, well—"

"That we can't do it anymore," finished Jess, her impassive face belying the anxiety I knew she felt. "That we can't sense Imprints or Intrusions, much less do anything about them."

Rosalind looked from Jess to me, then offered a soothing smile. "I still don't understand what I did that day, after the Presence made itself known. I reacted by pure instinct. Maria intimated the Foundation was very interested in what happened, while evading my questions about what she called 'an Agency'. We shall see who is more stubborn! But I can tell you this: I don't know about Intrusions, but I can still sense Imprints, and I can still erase them."

I let out a breath I didn't realize I'd been holding. Jess and I had kept to ourselves in the two months since our Themis Center break-in, focusing on our day jobs, our dojo, and the handful of restaurants and stores we already knew. We shunned anywhere new, anywhere possibly harboring an Imprint, which we may or may not be able to detect. I couldn't decide which I feared more. "How do you know?" I asked at last. "When did you know?"

"Do you remember Nicole Kelly, the property manager? She called me last week about one of their corporate rentals, a house on Lafayette Square. Two residents in a month had left early, citing 'discomfort'. Nicole read between the lines and brought me in. I confess I was nervous, even after my research turned up a likely candidate memory. How would I look if the residents sensed something I could not? Yet, I felt it as soon as I walked through the front door, before I even set foot on the staircase upstairs. I erased the Imprint and left considerably relieved, with my reputation intact. I see no reason why you two shouldn't be able to do the same."

Rosalind didn't notice my nod of gratitude. She stared after Martin, who'd found a few feet of space for his phone call, next to a dark window through which I spotted the dim fuselage of our plane.

"You erased it?" Jess asked, puzzled. "You didn't re-tether the memory? Maria was okay with that?"

Rosalind sniffed. "We discussed it. In her judgment, it was a Level Four Intrusion. Not even you two superstars could handle that yet. My own training in tethering Intrusions has been lacking, as you're aware."

We were. Her previous HLF handlers, a couple called Alice and Robert Harrington, had been implicated in an attack on another HLF agent. Donovan Brooks, a former college buddy, karate teacher, and adversary of mine, was still in a coma. The same fate had met Conor McKee, Jess's old boss at Paragon Insurance, and several other Chicago agents. We knew the Scales of Equilibrium had perpetrated some of those attacks. Their leader, Allen Weston, had once been a top researcher for the HLF. One of my goals for this trip was to discover what links persisted between these two secretive organizations.

"Is Lana still creating leaky Tethers for Steven Rourke?" I asked. "Donovan's girlfriend. You said she was pretty upset about what happened to him."

"I don't know," Rosalind replied with a shrug. "The Foundation doesn't encourage agents to work together, except in a training capacity. And I will not countenance training from that woman! However, I suspect this Imprint predated her exploits. I can't see how Rourke profits from the deal."

"There could be other HLF agents in St. Louis we don't know about," speculated Jess, before I could voice my skepticism about Rourke's lack of involvement.

"Perhaps." Rosalind's expression turned more sour by the moment as she watched Martin's phone call.

I checked the gate monitor: still over an hour until boarding. Jess was absorbed by her phone, the ghost of a smile playing over her face as her thumbs tapped away. I craned my neck, searching for Jamal or Izzy among the hordes of travelers milling around the adjacent gates. I needed a distraction, something to take my mind off my first ever airplane flight. I wanted to pretend I wasn't terrified by the prospect of nine hours cooped up in a metal tube, thirty thousand feet high.

Be careful what you wish for.

"I'm going to the ladies' room," snapped Rosalind. "Can you watch our bags, D, since my husband is otherwise occupied?"

"Um, sure," I said to her, retreating back as she stalked off. I hoped Martin's call was over by the time she returned. Over thirty years of marriage should have taught him not to get on her bad side. I turned to say as much to Jess, to find her gazing after Rosalind. "Let's hope that doesn't blow up," I commented, immediately regretting my choice of words.

Jess didn't seem to notice. "How many cleaners were there?"

"What?"

"The cleaners. A bunch of them were hanging out by that Employees Only door a few minutes ago, but I don't see as many now."

Three women in blue overalls stood against the wall opposite the gate area. They huddled in conversation, and one cradled a walkie-talkie, which seemed quaint in an era when everyone possessed a cell phone.

"Maybe they went to clean something," I suggested. "More than those three are doing. The others took the cart with them, looks like."

"Yeah, they did." Jess's eyes narrowed. "I'll be right back." She set off in pursuit of Rosalind. I glanced at the cleaners in time to spot the one with the walkie-talkie speak into it. And that was when my spidey senses engaged.

A flustered-looking man wearing a white dress-shirt and suit pants hurried past, carrying a cardboard drinks tray supporting three coffees. I lurched into his path, colliding with and upending the tray. Cursing, we both recoiled from the scalding spray as the to-go cups detonated on impact with the floor.

"Sorry, sorry!" I yelled, palms raised to placate his fury, then I turned towards the cleaners. "Can we get some help over here?" They stared at me for a second, then huddled again. As they did, I glimpsed a dark smudge behind the left ear of walkie-talkie girl. Her wispy curls obscured some of it, but my eyesight was good enough to convince me it resembled a tattoo, one I'd seen before. A set of uneven scales, perhaps.

"Shit." I started in the direction Rosalind and Jess had gone, then paused to locate Martin. The chaos I'd caused had gotten his attention. I pointed at our bags as he strode over, phone still at his ear, a question on his face. "Watch our stuff," I barked, and with a defiant glare at the "cleaners", I hurried towards the nearest restrooms.

I had to weave and shoulder my way through the sudden throng of a just-arrived flight, all the while scanning the walls for the telltale stick figure sign. I'd used up a month's worth of apologies by the time I reached the women's restroom. A barricade of yellow nylon tape, suspending a "closed for cleaning" sign, blocked the entrance. I couldn't see Rosalind or Jess anywhere, and was debating whether to breach social etiquette when I heard a thump and a muffled shriek from within.

I took a moment to compose myself, and to ensure the cleaners back at the gate hadn't followed me - Sensei would be proud - then I plunged through the tape.

I almost tripped over the first cleaner, who groaned and clutched her stomach while coiled in a fetal position next to the banana yellow cleaning cart. Another blue-clad woman slumped inert against the far wall, but two others were upright, back to back between Jess, nearer me, and Rosalind. Everyone stood poised, weight centered, feet apart, arms spread for attack or defense.

The woman facing Jess, a short but fit-looking blonde - who might have been pretty but for her venomous expression and the trickle of blood from her split lip, noticed my entrance. Her eyes widened in alarm, and she barked something in a language I couldn't understand. Then she lunged at Jess, likely aiming to use her prone comrade to her advantage. Jess slithered to one side, grabbed hold of her attacker's smock, and pivoted, throwing her to me instead. Misplaced gallantry prevented me from doing more than wrapping the writhing woman in a bear hug, clamping her arms to her side. She kicked at my shins and tried to butt me with the back of her head, then Jess stepped up and slapped her hard across the face. Stunned, the blonde dangled in my grasp.

"Hi, hon," panted Jess, her hair half out of its ponytail. She poked the other cleaner with her foot, eliciting a groan. "Thanks for joining the party."

"Keep that one conscious," said Rosalind, rising from one knee and digging her phone out of her purse. She wasn't even breathing hard, and not a hair was out of place. The fourth cleaner lay spreadeagled, half under the row of sinks. Above her, a splash of blood smeared the edge of the counter top. "I'm calling security."

Jess grabbed the blonde's chin and turned her head. I had to lean back to see the tattoo behind her left ear.

"Do they all have it?" I asked. "At least one of those back at the gate did."

"Looks like it," said Jess, examining the woman at our feet. She turned back to our captive with a scowl. "Seems our scaly friends had a nasty surprise planned for Rosalind. Lucky for us, these chicks are clumsy as fuck."

The blonde muttered something incomprehensible and then spat at Jess. Fortunately for her, that's when airport security arrived.

They were efficient. Three well-built, well-armed men closed off the restroom, and took both conscious and unconscious cleaners into custody. Meanwhile, a stocky woman with a buzz cut and intense gray eyes recorded our statements. These were simple enough. The four cleaners had followed Rosalind into the restroom with their cart, surrounding her as she washed up. Jess entered as they closed in and helped Rosalind "defend herself". I arrived in time to mop up.

The officer appeared to enjoy the account and favored Rosalind with an admiring glance. She noted our contact and flight details - the flight whose boarding time rapidly approached - before asking the obvious questions. "Why? Why did they assault you? Do you know them?"

"I've never seen them before in my life," said Rosalind, without missing a beat. "As to why they attacked me, here in an airport restroom, before I boarded an international flight, I'm afraid I can only speculate."

The officer narrowed her eyes. One of her colleagues stepped forward. "Badges are fake," he told her, glancing at me, of all people. "Good ones. We have a security breach."

"You think?" muttered Jess, earning a scowl.

"And would you care to speculate?" the officer asked.

Rosalind hesitated, as if weighing how much she should say. "We've recently had unpleasant encounters with a group calling themselves the Scales of Equilibrium. Its members tattoo themselves behind their left ear." The officer turned towards the blonde, now in another colleague's custody. He looked and nodded in confirmation.

"I've heard of them," the officer said softly, expression darkening.

"There are more," I interrupted, suddenly remembering. "More cleaners, back at the gate. At least three of them."

Rosalind stared at me, and panic flashed across her face. "Martin!"

The officer escorted us, speaking rapidly into her own walkie-talkie as we hurried after Rosalind. Two more security guards converged just as we arrived, to find Martin standing over our luggage, his phone nowhere to be seen. Relief drove out his worry as Rosalind flung herself into his arms.

I couldn't see any sign of the other cleaners. But I noticed Jamal and Izzy had arrived. Rising from his seat behind Martin, Jamal looked sober and thoughtful, as immaculate as ever in a salmon pink polo shirt and khaki golfing slacks. Izzy, rocking a Siouxsie T-shirt and matching eye makeup, sported shocking pink hair and a broad grin.

"You guys are having fun already, without us?" she declared. "I hardly think that's fair."

Chapter Two
WHERE IS SHE?

The flight was no worse than I expected. We taxied to the O'Hare runway for what felt like an hour, giving my wild imagination ample opportunity to devise scenarios of disaster. A smooth takeoff suppressed those fears, but couldn't totally abate my unease. Most everyone aboard seemed uneasy, even the brave-faced attendants and more seasoned passengers. Malfunctioning air-traffic control systems, and the resulting near misses, had closed more airports worldwide than just Paris and Frankfurt - LAX had only re-opened the previous day - and while no accidents had yet occurred, there was a sense that it was only a matter of time. People still traveled, for business or pleasure, but our plane looked only two-thirds full. Rosalind assured us they were normally packed this time of year.

Yet, this undercurrent of apprehension was not the reason I regretted ever applying for my passport. The plane itself was incredibly uncomfortable. Our invitation to visit the Henry Lyons Foundation headquarters in England had not extended beyond tickets in Economy Class. Jess and I didn't have the funds to upgrade to Premium Economy, as Rosalind and Martin had done. My aisle seat felt cramped, and I couldn't extend my long legs under the seat in front of me. I tried poking my left leg into the walkway, but withdrew with a muttered apology after almost tripping our attendant. He looked like a CEO after being fired without a golden parachute, and he was decidedly grumpy the rest of the journey.

I couldn't sleep. Not even close. Jess, who'd also never flown before, popped in her ear buds and was already snoring softly before they took her dinner away. Jamal, on her other side, didn't sleep either, but kept tapping on his laptop throughout the flight. When I got up to stretch my legs and pretend to go to the tiny bathroom, I noticed Izzy had donned dark sunglasses, leaving me unsure if she was sleeping or just projecting her vibe.

I tried to watch movies, and couldn't. I tried to listen to music, and found myself skipping through my playlist, unable to settle on the right tunes to soothe my mood. It was dark and claustrophobic, the food was terrible, and by the time we bounced down the runway in London, I was thoroughly miserable.

I trudged through narrow, interminable and sometimes almost inexplicable corridors at Heathrow. The airport was a city all by itself, but Rosalind and Martin knew where they were going. I failed to detect the merest hint of an Imprint or Intrusion, but honestly I couldn't imagine this insipid environment could inspire any strong emotions. I tried to watch out for any threats from the Scales of Equilibrium, but perhaps the six of us together, led by a confident Rosalind, dissuaded any hostile action.

Outside the terminal, where our ride awaited, was where we'd be most vulnerable, I decided, and forced myself to stay alert as we emerged into cool, bright sunshine. Martin bid us a temporary farewell, off to visit his father in a nursing home. While he and Rosalind hugged, I tried and failed to rekindle the kernel of excitement at seeing an entirely new country. Maybe international travel was not for me.

I slumped into my seat in the back of the modest white SUV and was asleep before it even started moving.

"D. Hey, wake up sleepyhead! We're here."

I jolted awake. Tires crunched on gravel. Adrenaline pulsed as memory overcame my disorientation. Jess peered at me, grinned, then stretched as much as the cramped confines of the vehicle would allow. I rubbed my eyes and squinted through the tinted windows.

Neat hedges flanked a long, straight driveway, ushering us towards the type of house I associated with the British period dramas Jess occasionally binged on PBS. Two stories of brownstone spanned the end of the drive, punctuated by rows of dark windows the size of dining tables. The somber stone tiles of the steeply pitched roof drew the eye down to the imposing, black double-door front entrance, surrounded by classical columns and lintel.

Two people waited at the steps leading up to the doors. The taller one dressed in a sharp black suit, like those advertised in the airline magazine I'd resorted to in desperation. The other stood just behind and slid a phone into the back pocket of her jeans as we approached.

"They are keen to see you," said Jamal from the front passenger seat. Our car curled around a weathered marble fountain and parked facing away from the house. "That's Kara LeVault, our Field Director. They oversee all HLF field agents worldwide. They're mine and Izzy's boss, and yours too, technically."

Jess snorted at the same time as Rosalind murmured, "We'll see about that." Izzy turned toward me and grinned. I offered a weak one in return, but she still made me uncomfortable. Not just because of her mercurial brusqueness, but I hadn't forgotten her recent casual attempt to seduce me, and Jess too. Izzy had admired Jess's ring, but gave me a flirtatious wink anyway.

I all but fell out of the vehicle, my weary limbs refusing to coordinate properly. I stood and stretched, blinking in light much brighter than expected. The day had warmed considerably, with only a few white clouds scudding across the sky. A gentle breeze wafted a beguiling scent from the flower beds nestling between the hedges, birds twittered from trees sprinkled through the surrounding grounds, and somewhere an excited dog barked. The scene couldn't be more British if it tried.

"Welcome to Shotcombe House," said the person in the suit, in a deep voice with little accent. Midwest American, then. I struggled to tell if they were male or female, then recalled Jamal's careful use of pronouns. They appeared around Rosalind's age, silvering dark hair framing an olive-skinned face. Their chestnut brown eyes, set above a sharp nose and thin-lipped mouth, caught my gaze before skittering away. "I'm Kara LeVault, although I guess Jamal already told you that. Did you have a good flight?"

"No, but we never do on the redeye," grumbled Jamal, shaking Kara's hand. "You know Izzy, of course."

"Of course." Kara's eyes flicked towards Izzy's bubblegum hair, and they shook their head with an indulgent smile. "I believe you've both met Charli Simpson. Astbury is preoccupied, so sent her right-hand woman instead."

"Hello." Charli's vivid blue eyes inspected me, Jess, and Rosalind with intense curiosity as we said our hellos back. As the HLF lead researcher's "right-hand woman", it suggested she was smart, but I couldn't help but notice how attractive Charli was too. I guessed she was Jess's age, a couple inches shorter, but her T-shirt and jeans hinted at similar curves. Strands of turquoise threaded the blonde hair that dusted her shoulders and wound around long, intricate silver earrings. She gripped a thin laptop under one arm, and I noticed her fingers tighten when Izzy greeted her. A blush stole over Charli's pale face, and she gave her smirking colleague a tight nod in return.

"You and Charli might want to catch up, Miss Evans," Kara told Jess. "At least before Astbury sinks her claws into you. Charli's disrupted our operations almost as much as you have."

"Good for you," said Jess, studying Charli with renewed interest.

"That's hardly fair," Charli protested, her blush deepening. "But I'm def a fan of yours, Jess. You got our head of IT security proper rattled. He deserves it too, the pompous git." Jess grinned, while my brain caught up. I would have to concentrate to follow Charli's accent.

Kara coughed and raised an eyebrow, then turned to Rosalind with undisguised fascination as they shook her hand. "And this, of course, is the famous Mrs. Rosalind Hill! Your reputation has certainly preceded you."

Rosalind wore the kind of smile I imagined her reserving to greet school administrators and politicians. "I do hope my activities have not been blown out of proportion," she replied, with a sidelong glance at Jamal, whose lips twitched. She gestured at the façade of Shotcombe House. "I must say, I did not expect such a genteel and rural setting for the Henry Lyons Foundation's headquarters."

Kara smiled, the first genuine warmth I'd seen from them. "It's a Lyons family bequest. We own dreary office buildings in London and Birmingham too. And, of course, Astbury insists on keeping most of her researchers with her in Cambridge." Charli rolled her eyes, before appearing to remember herself. "I understood you were traveling with your husband, Mrs. Hill."

"Rosalind, please. He wanted to spend time with his family in London, though I expect you understand that as well."

"We do. Although, there are one or two matters we'd like to discuss with him, if he's willing."

"We shall see. He's not entirely comfortable with our visit. What do you have planned? Jamal has been vague on the details."

"I'm curious about the agenda myself," admitted Jamal. "'A few days to review recent events' is about as vague as you can get."

He and Kara locked gazes, and I caught an undercurrent of tension. I'd heard from many sources - including my former employer, nemesis, and mother's cousin, Steven Rourke - that the HLF was far from united in purpose and philosophy. Jamal had also been at odds with Chicago's supervisor of field agents, Faustyn Lazarowski. He'd claimed to be something of a maverick within the HLF, and I wondered how much of that was true, or what fractures lay beneath the surface of the organization.

Kara tore their regard away from Jamal and landed back on me, although their eyes never quite met mine. "D Rodriguez," they said softly. "The man at the center of it all."

I wasn't sure what to make of that, and judging by all the confused looks, neither were my companions.

Kara seemed to gather themselves and forced out a smile. "We have, as you know, followed your progress for a while. You're certainly not the first strong sensitive to hit our radar, but you appear to have done so at a pivotal place and time. The Foundation rarely gives out any more information than absolutely necessary, but I hope we can answer some of your questions - yours, Jess's and Rosalind's. And, of course, we have many of our own."

I nodded. We'd come for answers, and meant to get them. We'd trade our own for as high a price as we could. Before my sleep-deprived brain could formulate a reply, Rosalind interrupted.

"That sounds delightful," she said, stretching and rolling her head. "But perhaps we could do so inside, preferably somewhere with a pot of tea, and far more comfortable chairs than the airlines or your driver could provide. My companions may be young and hale enough to endure international travel without incurring a sore back, but mine is killing me."

Whether they bought into Rosalind's proclaimed frailty any more than the rest of us, Kara at least had the good grace to acknowledge the request. "Of course. We have a room prepared for our discussions, however," and their skittish eyes drifted in my direction again, "we do have something of an unusual situation that begs immediate attention. I'd like to borrow D and Jamal for a few minutes. Charli will escort you to the room, so you can freshen up."

"I don't get to freshen up?" I complained. The shenanigans had begun already, and Jess was having none of it.

"Where D goes, I go." Jess gripped my arm for emphasis, a little harder than was strictly necessary. "Whenever you people talk about 'unusual situations', the hackles on my neck rise. I'm fresh enough for you."

Kara's lip curled slightly, but they nodded. "Very well. Perhaps that's for the best. If the rest of you—"

"Enough." Rosalind didn't move, but Kara flinched at the cool authority behind that single word. "We haven't come all this way to be divided and conquered before we even step into the building. Show us this unusual situation of yours."

I imagined no-one had talked to Kara like that for years. Their lips moved soundlessly for a second, then they set them in a line and turned on their heel. "Follow me," they declared, and thrust open the entrance doors. Charli goggled after them, while Jamal caught my eye and raised his eyebrows. I'm sure he recalled his first meeting with Rosalind, and his first dressing down. He'd likely enjoyed Kara's taste of that medicine more than any of us.

"Whatever this is," grumbled Rosalind as she followed Kara inside, "it had better not unduly delay my first cup of tea."

We entered an entrance foyer far removed from the tall, airy and bright ones of PBS's country estates. If anything, it reminded me of the gloomy apartment building on Austin Boulevard in Chicago, where Izzy had first attempted to shield Jess and I from the Imprint we'd come to erase. A security checkpoint squatted in the near half of the dim space. We paraded through a full-blown metal detector, just like those back at O'Hare. The pair of black-clad guards manning the security post processed us with humorless and military precision.

"I didn't expect this," I murmured to Izzy, as Jess waited for her visitor badge. I had trouble clipping mine to my shirt, so Izzy did it for me.

"None of this crap was here last year," she muttered, close enough for me to smell the dark chocolate undertone to her musky perfume. "Just one guard checking IDs. I guess the Scales have the HLF spooked."

Jess stepped up, and I helped with her badge while she shared an unfathomable look with Izzy.

Peering over her shoulder, a dark wooden staircase dominated the remaining half of the lobby, flanked by open doors leading to hallways on either side. Bland cream paint covered the high walls, bereft of the gilt-framed portraits of nobility or hunting scenes I'd expected. Instead, security cameras nestled in every corner, covering all the angles. Suddenly, this felt very institutional, more like a prison than an English country house. I didn't like it.

Whether because of weariness, or my expectations of the organization devoted to studying the phenomena, I hadn't bothered scanning for Imprints. I didn't seek the strange sensations that had so disturbed me until Rosalind, then Jamal and Izzy, trained me to deal with them. I just trudged up the creaking staircase, following Kara around the switchback to the second floor - she'd called it the first floor - was she confused or was I?

They turned right at the top, then led us along a sparsely lit corridor that turned again to our right. We passed closed doors on either side, and heard nothing but the scuffling of our feet on threadbare carpet, which had long forgotten any pattern it once possessed.

I was unnerved even before a sudden chill prickled my skin, and I stopped dead. I licked my lips in a futile attempt to rid my mouth of the iron tang of phantom blood. So I could still sense the damn things after all. I stared at Kara, who'd halted at the next closed door to our right. Their expression was grim as they surveyed the rest of us. I wasn't the only one to have noticed.

"An Imprint? Here?" I rasped, and used the surge of adrenaline to marshal my forces in preparation. Jess took my hand, and I grew increasingly aware not just of her physical presence, but also her spiritual one, her consciousness, with which mine had somehow connected to handle such phenomena on multiple occasions.

"This is... odd," said Jamal, frowning at Kara. "I assume there is a reasonable explanation."

"Oh, I wouldn't assume anything of the sort," they replied. Their eyes bore into mine now, no skittishness at all. "I wanted only you and Mr. Rodriguez to see this, but if the rest of you must witness it too, fine. Please observe and don't interfere."

Jess stirred, and I squeezed her hand while stepping forward, but not so far that I couldn't sense her as well as the deepening cold. Rosalind muttered something I didn't catch as I passed her to join Kara and Jamal. I broke eye contact, and glanced at the closed door, its venerable wood panels interrupted by a brass nameplate bearing the inscription "Kara LeVault".

"Why is there an Imprint in your office?" I asked. "Or is this some other phenomenon you've neglected to tell us about?"

They grimaced. "'Imprint' is the word you use to describe an improperly tethered Intrusion, yes? That is what you sense, what we're all sensing. As to why someone in my position, and with my experience, failed to deal with the Intrusion that popped up yesterday afternoon in my own office, well, I'll let you be the judge. Why don't you tether it properly, Mr. Rodriguez?"

"What is it with you and last names?" I grumbled.

I stretched out a hand towards the door, and shivered, cocking my head at the echo of distant screams. The Catch, what the HLF called a Lock, linked to the handle. This was the focal point of energy that tethered the memory, and the mysterious Intrusion it manifested, to the place in which the real event had occurred. Theoretically, this prevented the Intrusion's spread, and even its detection by all but the most sensitive people. People like us, who perceived what others could not, for reasons I'd also come here to discover.

But first things first. "Is this a test? You want to observe firsthand what I'm sure Jamal has told you we can do?"

"It's a test, certainly," Kara murmured. "Jamal, you may wish to stand by, just in case."

Nice. Just what I'd traveled four thousand miles to hear. "Fine. Give me space, please. Is the door unlocked? Okay then." I drew in several deep, calming breaths, felt a pulse of concern from Jess, soothed it, and reached for the handle.

In the fractions of a second it took my hand to grip the dull, scratched brass, the cold and taste of blood intensified, and someone's scream grew into a deafening roar. I pinpointed the Catch as I turned the door handle and removed it with precise mental force.

My ears popped from a pressure change that had nothing to do with a descending airplane. The world lurched sideways an infinitesimal amount, and I was inside Kara's office without having stepped through the door. Sunlight leaked past the window blinds to illuminate a cluttered mahogany desk and bookcase-lined walls, but I couldn't appreciate the details. All my attention, and a growing sense of horror, was drawn to the two arguing people standing on either side of the desk. One was Kara LeVault, and the other was me.

My mind reeled, and it took all the self-discipline I'd learned from eighteen months of karate training not to flinch. I forced myself to watch and tried to understand. I'd never been here in my life. How could there be a memory of me in a room I hadn't visited until this moment? I couldn't answer that question now and risk getting wrapped up in the memory to the point where I lost myself in it, unable to return to the present world. I sensed other wills hovering nearby, observing the phenomenon and, I guessed, also trying to process it.

But the task had been given to me. This was my Imprint, mine to deal with. I watched myself argue with Kara while I marshaled my forces to re-tether the memory. Memory Me appeared angry, that much was clear. My fist slammed down on the desk, sending stray papers flying, and I leaned forward, shouting. As usual, there was no soundtrack to this memory, but I thought I could read my own lips, as I repeated my demand: "Where is she?" Kara held up their hands in placation, but whatever their reply was, it didn't satisfy me. Papers, then a monitor, flew as I rounded the desk.

Holy shit, what was I about to do?

The pressing of time, and an unwillingness to find out, spurred me to remember Jamal's and Izzy's training. This memory was what they might call a Level Three, roughly halfway up the scale of strength and difficulty. I hadn't tethered a Level Three before. The only chance I'd had was when Jess and I had ambushed two Scales of Equilibrium operatives, who were trying to trap our minds in the memory, to send us into comas like other Foundation agents before us. Our counterattack had stopped them, barely, but left us too weak to tether the memory, so we'd left that to Jamal and Izzy.

Not this time. I reached for Jess and she was there, the shape and potency of her will intertwining with mine, blending into one. We took the memory, the chaos unfolding in Kara's office—

When?

—and folded it, folded it fast, with care and precision, into a tiny sphere of staggering density—

Quick, it's coming!

—and fused it into a Single-Point Lock.

Done. Quick, simple, efficient, and terrifying. What the hell had just happened?

I let go of Jess's consciousness, but clutched her as we slumped to our knees. Our foreheads collided, and for long moments we just panted together. Our ragged breathing and my thumping heart were all I could hear.

I stared up at Kara's impassive face, searching in vain for hints of explanation, before they turned to Rosalind.

"Let's get you that pot of tea now."

CHAPTER THREE
A LOOMING THREAT

I thought I'd been exhausted before. My mind was a fog, and Jamal had to tap me on the shoulder and help haul me to my feet.

Rosalind again said something I couldn't catch, and she guided Jess as we stumbled after Kara, who led us back downstairs into what might once have been a dining room. Two sets of double doors opened into a space dominated by a marble stone fireplace on the far wall. Above it was the hunting scene I'd been missing, a massive portrait of dogs and horses and white men dressed in red, that stretched almost all the way to the high, square-paneled ceiling. Heavy drapes covered most of the tall windows on either side, leaking in the bare minimum of daylight to illuminate a surprisingly plain conference table through swirls of dust. A bank of screens and audio-visual equipment occupied one end to our left, and a buffet of refreshments beckoned to our right. Stainless steel coffee carafes squatted next to china pots presumably containing tea. I didn't recognize most of the selection of cookies and pastries.

I blinked in these details before slumping onto a chair halfway down the table, facing the doors of course. Jess groaned softly as she collapsed next to me, and held her head in her hands. Glasses of water appeared and we drank them. Rosalind brought plates of what she called sausage rolls, which we eyed with suspicion. Conversation hummed around us. Man, I needed sleep, but even more than that, I wanted answers. Waving off Rosalind's offer of "a nice hot cup of tea", I begged for coffee and roused myself to one last effort before succumbing to jet lag.

"Are we gonna talk about what the hell that was?" I demanded.

Rosalind took the chair to my left and, after a moment's hesitation, Jamal joined our side. Izzy and Kara sat while Charli hovered near the rightmost set of doors, tapping on her phone.

"We're waiting for others to join us," said Kara, as they propped up a tablet on the table in front of them. "Astbury should be down soon. Have you heard from her, Charli?"

"Five minutes ago. She said she's on her way."

"Who else is coming?" asked Jamal, as I counted the chairs. There were nine, although there was a sizable gap across from me.

"David Taylor, the Foundation director, and Carson Livingston, who heads up global operations. Their flight was due about the same time as yours."

"Flight made it, but they didn't," boomed a new voice. We all turned as a wheelchair rolled into the room with surprising speed. It parked at the table opposite me. Its occupant, an older woman with a shock of white hair and weathered features, tossed a laptop onto the table, then swept those of us across it with a calculating expression. "They were delayed in New York. They'll be here later tonight. You must be D."

I met her scrutiny with defiance. I felt like I was some sort of exhibit or curiosity, and I was tired of it.

Jamal cleared his throat. "Good morning, Astbury. Nice to see you too." The woman flashed an irritated glance at him, then her narrowed eyes resettled on me. "Emma Astbury, head of research for the Henry Lyons Foundation, let me introduce you to D Rodriguez and Jess Evans, two of our latest trainees in Chicago. Although it's safe to say they are no ordinary trainees, which is why they are here."

"No indeed," murmured Astbury, turning to Jess with a crooked smile. "I look forward to sitting down with you, young lady."

"Me too," said Jess, looking and sounding rather overawed.

"And this, of course," continued Jamal, "is—"

"Hello, Emma." Something about Rosalind's voice got everyone's attention. You could almost hear Astbury's neck muscles flex as her head swiveled towards our friend.

"Rosalind." The air didn't crackle, but we all held our breath as they surveyed each other. "I wondered if it was you, when I heard about a British schoolteacher with your name operating in St. Louis. Didn't recognize the surname, of course. Had to look you up. Glad you found a good man."

"I did," said Rosalind, then seemed, for once, at a loss for words.

"You know each other?" I prompted, not ready to believe yet another coincidence. They were piling up too fast to be credible.

"Indeed we do, or we did," Rosalind said. "Although the name 'Astbury' is new to me. I never took you for the marrying type, Emma."

The other woman snorted. "Never was. I took my mother's maiden name. Most people around here just call me 'Astbury'." There was more than a hint of challenge in her statement. Rosalind simply nodded, and we all relaxed.

Kara coughed. "Now we have introductions out of the way, and since David and Carson won't be here for a while, we can discuss the agenda for your time with us. We'll keep things light today, get you to your accommodations so you can get over your jet lag. However—"

"I want to get these two into the lab immediately," interrupted Astbury, gesturing at me and Jess. "The sooner we determine the physical basis for their connection—"

My fist thumped down on the table. That got everyone's attention. Astbury looked like she wasn't used to interruptions, nor impressed. I didn't care. "We didn't come here to be your lab rats," I said, keeping my fraying temper in check. "This isn't a one way street. We came here for answers too. You want to learn about mine and Jess's connection? You're gonna have to give up some information first, starting with what the hell we just witnessed in Kara's office."

Astbury returned my glare with one of her own, but kept her peace.

The silence stretched until Jamal's calm tones broke it. "I do think that's a good place to start. Just for confirmation, D, you have never set foot in this building before."

"Never," I snapped. "I've never even left the States until today. Yesterday, whatever."

"So that wasn't a memory." He turned back to Kara, who watched him warily. "The question is, what was it? And is there any precedent?"

Kara took a slow sip of coffee, then grimaced. "To answer your first question, we're not sure. It hardly seems possible, but—"

"Isn't it obvious?" Jess interjected. "It's a memory of a future event."

Charli stirred in her seat, but said nothing. Astbury steepled her hands and gazed at Jess with renewed interest. "That's hardly an obvious conclusion, girl," she murmured.

Jess shrugged. "Why not? You lot claim Intrusions drag memories from their origin in spacetime to the present day. What's to say it only occurs in one direction of time?"

I wasn't the only one who squirmed in their seat. As strange as the phenomena of Intrusions, Tethers, and Imprints were, I'd been able to rationalize others' explanations, based on my own experiences. But glimpsing the future was another level of strange, and I wasn't ready to accept it.

But what else could they be? I thought back to how angry I'd been, and the question I'd repeatedly thrown in Kara's alarmed face: *Where is she?*

"To answer Jamal's second question," Kara continued, "there does appear to be precedent. Very recent precedent. We've received two other credible reports of time-displaced Intrusions within the last week. We're working on it. In the meantime, D, you are not welcome anywhere near my office, ever." They caught my eye then. The tension in the room ratcheted up another notch.

"Does anyone know any party games?" said Izzy brightly. "Perhaps we could use an icebreaker." She earned frowns of irritation from Kara and Astbury, and a snicker from Jess.

"Can I assume your models predicted nothing of the sort?" Jamal asked Astbury in his usual measured voice.

She gave a tight nod in confirmation, but appeared unsettled. "We're entering the data now, but three points are insufficient to correlate. It's *possible* these new phenomena are future events, but there may be other explanations. We alerted field leadership. For now, we wait. Let Charli and the rest of my team do their jobs."

I glanced at Charli, but she appeared absorbed in her laptop.

"So that's it?" I said. "You show us this thing the moment we turn up at your door, then fob us off with 'we're working on it'?"

"Oh, there was more to it than that," murmured Rosalind. "They wanted to see how you would react, and how you would deal with the challenge - whether you would turn to your connection with Jess. They didn't wait to get you into Emma's lab. The testing began as soon as you walked into the building."

Astbury smiled in satisfaction, despite a flash of irritation at the use of her first name.

"We aren't fobbing you off," Kara insisted. "Less than a dozen people outside this room are aware of these new phenomena. As such, we'll keep you informed. What I know, you'll know. And in that spirit, I must ask you: have the three of you encountered anything like this before?"

"Not that," said Jess, and I could tell by the determination in her voice what she was going to say. I tensed, and felt, rather than saw, Rosalind and Jamal do the same. "But didn't you sense it? Right before we completed the Tether?"

"Sense what?" asked Kara, but I could tell from their sudden blank expression that they knew. They were waiting for Jess to say it.

Jess wasn't intimidated. "Another presence. Another intelligence. Not one of us, not anyone standing outside your office. Someone, or something, different from us. Different and powerful, terrible—"

"Arrant nonsense," snapped Astbury. "Really, girl, if you wish to be taken seriously, you'd do well to learn the difference between reality, perhaps strange but verifiable, and fantasy."

"Call me 'girl' again," Jess challenged in a dangerous voice. "I'm not some gullible fantasist. I thought you were smart enough to know that."

"And I thought you smart enough not to confuse gaps in our understanding with some ineffable agency." Astbury's tone was considerably cooler. "Don't fall prey to the same delusions that have ensnared better minds than yours. There is no evidence for what you claim—"

"So none of you felt it? Only D and me?" Jess's gaze swept the table, but the only person to meet it was Izzy.

"I did," she said, pale, black-lined eyes holding Jess's penetrating emerald ones. "And it wasn't the first time."

Astbury sniffed. "If you are referring to the individuals who assaulted you, who have incapacitated several of our agents, that is something else entirely. Thanks to those around this table, we are now very aware of the threat. Steps are being taken. Indeed, when Carson arrives I believe he wishes to discuss it with you at length."

"Good, great, awesome," Izzy said, flicking her hair over her shoulder and scowling at the older woman. "And about fucking time. It took you and the rest of the brass long enough to acknowledge what I and others kept telling you. But that's not what I'm talking about." She turned to Jess and her voice dropped, her usual brashness fading. "I've felt it too, sometimes. A looming threat, a predator circling the fringes of the campfire, a menace deep in the woods. It's different from the Scales agents, different from everything I know. I've felt it before, and I felt it again, upstairs."

"So did I."

Astbury, who had been shaking her head with increasing disgust, froze and looked at the speaker. Rosalind cradled her empty teacup as she went on. "I was skeptical too. But I cannot reject the evidence of my own senses, not after what happened at the Themis Center in Chicago. Whatever we encountered then was present this morning, albeit more distant. But no less alarming."

Astbury muttered something I couldn't catch. I surveyed the rest of the table. Charli had somehow turned paler and stole curious glances at Izzy when she thought the other woman wasn't looking. Kara rested their wrists on the table and stared without expression at some far off point in between.

Jamal, usually reserved to the point of emotionlessness, fidgeted and cleared his throat. "Perhaps I was preoccupied with the Intrusion, but I sensed nothing like that. However," he said more loudly, raising his hand to placate Izzy's indignation, "I can no longer ignore the assertions of four of the most powerful sensitives currently known to the HLF. Not when they echo assertions made by notable former members of the organization. Whatever this is, whether an... agency or something else we don't understand, we can't hide from it any longer. Not when those who originally advanced that belief are now directly attacking our own."

It was the closest he'd come to acknowledging our contention that some mysterious entity - what Jess and I called The Presence - had observed us while we tethered Intrusions. And, that night at the Themis Center, it had even communicated with us.

Perhaps I was too tired to think of anything better to say, but I found myself asking what I'd been pondering almost since I'd met her. "What happened to you, Izzy?"

She flinched, and her brashness returned. "What's it to you? You know nothing about me."

"No, and I don't need to. Not the details. But there's something in your past, some kind of secret or trauma. You don't have to tell me what it is. That's yours. But, I think it's why we can sense things, you, me, Jess, Rosalind. All of us, here in this building. We all have some trauma, something that triggered our ability. Am I right?"

Her expression turned shrewd. I didn't think she would answer at first, but then she nodded. "That's part of it. The Foundation thinks there's an 'activating event' - your 'trauma' - that allows people with the potential to sense and manipulate these phenomena. I was seventeen when it happened to me and I had no idea what was going on. I guess I'm lucky I survived until college. That's when the HLF recruited me."

I remembered how isolated and paranoid I'd felt in St. Louis, after I got out of prison and before I met Rosalind. I'd been twice Izzy's age and I couldn't imagine dealing with Imprints and Intrusions as a girl in high school. That rite of passage was tough on everyone, even without any of this nonsense.

Something else she'd said nagged at me. "You said 'people with the potential'. Doesn't everybody have it?"

She hesitated and stole half a glance towards the conference room doors. Someone would probably come looking for us soon. "You could've asked these questions in Chicago, you know."

"Maybe, but I'm asking them now. So?"

"Not everyone has the potential. Astbury, and those who came before her, think it's a genetic trait, passed down the generations like any other. They're tight lipped about how they know, but believe me when I tell you they know *everything* about you, and your family."

She left me then, disappearing after a few steps through the open doorway into the conference room. I followed, but only after I'd processed the implications of this latest revelation.

Chapter Four

SOME SORT OF TRIBUNAL

"All the way across to the other wing," said Astbury, disbelief pervading her strident tones. "That is remarkable. No wonder Izzy's shields were ineffective against the pair of you. It took a week before she could mount any resistance to another agent tethering the Intrusion over there."

"Did she get bored with seeing the same murder over and over again too?" I griped. I drained most of the tall glass of water I'd poured before our latest experiment, and sank into a leather armchair, which might have been the most comfortable piece of furniture on this whole damn island.

The bed I shared with Jess at our bland, conference center hotel was short, too firm, and dipped in the middle. Not that I objected to rolling towards Jess's near naked body during the night, but she was a furnace, and I struggled to sleep when I was hot enough to sweat. The HLF's lodging choice irritated me; I wished they'd placed us somewhere like the White Hart, where Charli had a room. Even if the bed was no better, I could at least enjoy the charm of the English countryside while I tossed and turned in the unseasonal September heat.

Astbury barked a laugh as she tapped on her phone. "Getting tired of Shotcombe House's resident ghosts, are you? Shame. I rather think it adds some color to the place."

"Watching one billowy-shirted brother kill another gets old after a while."

As I watched Astbury message one of her researchers, who sat with Jess and Izzy across the inner courtyard, I scratched the edge of the tape holding a sensor in place on my temple, wondering yet again what its readings told anyone. I swallowed more water and focused on recovering from mine and Jess's latest Level Three Tether attempt. We regained our strength faster each time, but the thirst never went away.

Jamal, observing me from an identical chair on the other side of the study, claimed we were building mental fortitude after so many Tethers in three days.

"It's something of an inside joke," he said, but his expression was as far from joviality as it was possible to be. His attempts to forge a connection with either Jess or Izzy had not been as successful, although Jess told me she could sense him, and he looked wearier than I felt. "The legend of the Bloody Brothers has captivated the area for over two centuries. Reviving the inciting incident, as part of field testing new techniques, appears to amuse our research team."

"Isn't it risky? I thought you told me once that destroying Tethers weakened the location's resistance to Intrusions? Shouldn't this place be riddled with them by now?"

"You're not destroying them," muttered Astbury, still absorbed with her phone.

"You're undoing and restoring the Tether almost immediately," clarified Jamal when no further explanation was forthcoming. "The energy associated with the Intrusion remains harnessed. However, new Intrusions have occurred, as we saw the day we arrived."

"Can you go again, D?" Astbury asked before I could revisit that topic. "With Izzy? Do you want to move closer?"

"Why can't we do this with Rosalind?" I countered. "Jess and I know her well, and if emotion plays a role in forging this connection, wouldn't she have a greater chance of success?"

Astbury pouted, as ever, at the mention of Rosalind. The two women hadn't avoided each other since we'd arrived, but neither had they sought each other out.

"Rosalind is busy elsewhere, exploring what she did to your so-called Presence in Chicago. And I'm not sure emotion is the driver for your connection with Jess. I believe it's something richer, empathy perhaps. Regardless, your attempts with Izzy have shown the most promise of today's combinations, so if you're up to the challenge, I want to try again."

I grimaced and fidgeted with my water glass. Izzy and I had connected our wills twice today, if only fleetingly and with barely enough strength to recognize its shape. What that implied, when neither Jess nor Jamal had done likewise, was not something I wanted to dwell on. Jess's flinty gaze as Astbury enthused over our "real progress" did not bode well for later.

A knock on the door saved me. Astbury clucked her tongue, then boomed "Open!"

Kara popped their head in and stared at me and Jamal. "They're ready for you now."

Jess and Izzy waited outside in the corridor, the latter with a sour expression. Jess slipped her hand into mine before Kara surprised me by ushering us all through a back door at the end of the hallway.

We stepped into a wide courtyard between the wings of the house. A break area, comprising mismatched wooden tables and chairs, yielded to a path of moss-infested flagstones between an untidy vegetable garden and what might charitably be described as storage. We followed it out of the shadows of the building into the grounds.

A dark, eight-foot-tall hedge loomed ahead of us. An impassive black-clad security guard stood by the single narrow opening. He acknowledged our passage with an almost imperceptible nod. Another hedge formed a path to the left and right, with further openings cut into it as if by a gigantic knife. We were in a maze, I realized, as Kara turned left, then right. It was both iconic and an apt metaphor for our attempts to understand what the hell was going on.

A few turns later, we emerged into a square opening about the size of mine and Jess's Chicago apartment. Raised flower beds formed an inner perimeter, within which four wooden benches surrounded an empty marble basin that might once have been a working fountain. Rosalind sat on one of the seats, hands in her lap. She nodded to us with an inscrutable expression, before turning her attention back to the two men standing to her right.

"And here are your companions," said the shorter and younger of the two, his accent the precise English of Jess's PBS dramas. A mop of curly brown hair surrounded a round, tanned face, darkened by a five o'clock shadow. His wool sweater and jeans gave him the air of a gentleman farmer, but while his handshake was friendly enough, I didn't miss the calculation in his brown eyes. "David Taylor, executive director of the Henry Lyons Foundation. I thought we might enjoy some fresh country air for this conversation, as long as the rain holds off."

I eyed the dark clouds gathering to the west. So far, England had defied its wet and dismal reputation by giving us warm, dry weather every day. The fall - sorry, autumn - colors, here and lining the roads on our journeys between the hotel and Shotcombe House, were even more breathtaking in the sunshine. I'd never lived outside a city as a free man, and how this environment relaxed me came as a surprise. I could handle a little rain, and if it broke up this long-dreaded meeting, so much the better.

"Carson Livingston," the taller man introduced himself. "I make sure you all get what you need to do your jobs." He didn't sound English, nor did his smile reach his pale eyes. Wrinkles outnumbered the wisps of snowy hair clinging to his scalp, and a thin white scar twisted the length of his left cheek down to the jawline. He wore a light blue dress shirt, charcoal suit pants, and black leather shoes, which combined were probably worth more than my entire wardrobe. This was what old money looked like. Were I not a couple inches taller, I'd have said he was looking down his nose at me, but there may have been more than snobbery in the intensity of his regard.

"Sit, please," said David, indicating the other benches. Jess and I sat opposite the two men, while Jamal and Izzy took the bench to our left. Kara hesitated before joining Rosalind, who ignored them completely. I started fidgeting. Was there some unwritten rule that wooden seating had to be so damn uncomfortable?

"First, my apologies for the delay," David continued, his voice and expression sober. "As you may have heard, someone compromised London airspace's air traffic control systems, so it is currently closed. One non-fatal collision at Gatwick, and two near misses at Heathrow in the space of a day. England's other airports are struggling to shoulder the burden. Carson and I only arrived back in the country last night."

"Do they know who compromised the systems?" asked Jess, leaning forward. Rosalind caught my eye and gave a subtle shake of her head. *Not yet.*

"I believe they suspect a Russian cybercriminal syndicate," said Carson. "Although the real answer is likely far more complicated."

"And a matter for law enforcement," David said. "I wanted to explain why we didn't have this conversation immediately upon your arrival. It was not my intent that you take part in further Foundation training, or other activities, until we addressed your actions in Chicago. All your actions," he added, glancing at Rosalind before looking over at Jamal and Izzy.

I noticed Izzy sported heavier than usual black eyeliner and had dressed for the occasion in a Green Day "American Idiot" T-shirt and almost shredded black jeans. Surprisingly, it was the usually taciturn Jamal who gave off the stronger vibe of defiance, bordering on contempt. His hands gripped the front of the bench on which he sat, and anger simmered in his wide eyes. This should be interesting.

"Do you think this is some sort of tribunal?" asked Rosalind, in the kind of dangerous voice that all but her dimmest students would take as a sign to stop talking.

"Well, let's see." Unruffled, and using the fingers of one hand as a checklist, the Henry Lyons Foundation's director recounted the events of late July, starting with the assault on Jess's boss at Paragon Insurance, Conor McKee, that left him in a coma. With unfailing accuracy, he described the trap we laid for his attackers, Jess's subsequent hospitalization, and our burglary of the Themis Center in a failed attempt to discover evidence about a terrorist attack on Chicago.

"I acknowledge that you, D, Jess, and Rosalind, have not 'signed anything'." He went on, turning to address Rosalind. "I also acknowledge that you were misguided by other HLF agents whose behavior was, to say the least, questionable. Nonetheless, you all accepted our guidance. We had a verbal contract, if nothing else, including standards and protocols we expected you to follow. Kara and I have spoken at length with Faustyn Lazarowski, your operations director in Chicago. Not only did you place yourselves in considerable peril, but you also put innocent bystanders at risk. Did you even stop to think there could be undocumented sensitives at the bar to which you lured your attackers? What might have happened to them, had things gone awry?"

"Scales of Equilibrium," I said. You could hear a pin drop. Even the birds stopped chirping. "I keep hearing you talk about the assholes who put Conor McKee and others into comas, who attacked us, who attacked Izzy, but I haven't heard you call them out for who they are. Marcus and his buddy, at least, were Scales of Equilibrium operatives, and I know you know who they are. Wasn't their head honcho one of yours once?"

"We know who the Scales of Equilibrium are," David replied coolly. Carson shifted in his seat, but his face remained expressionless. "And that made your actions in Chicago even more reckless. I suppose I should not place too much blame on you, D, or your friends. I can understand your fear and outrage. What I can neither understand nor condone is why those responsible for your training not only allowed you to proceed, but provided material support."

His head swiveled to where Jamal and Izzy sat fuming. "I don't care about your abilities or history with the organization. You are both HLF field agents and behaved recklessly. I expected better."

Izzy drew in a breath to deliver what I'm sure would have been an entertaining rebuke, but she never got the chance.

"With all due respect, David," Jamal said, his level voice oozing with contempt, "fuck you. This isn't prep school or the military. We're not children or raw recruits. We're all adults, trying to deal with phenomena beyond most people's comprehension in the best way we can. We make judgment calls every day, especially those of us *actually in the field*. How dare you and Carson and Kara sit behind your desks and judge me, or Izzy, or any of us? We've all lost more than you'll ever know. How dare you?"

Jess and I stared open-mouthed at each other. We'd never seen Jamal show this much passion. And the floodgates had only just opened.

"You sent me to St. Louis two years ago. Not only did I recruit two very capable field agents - one of whom was put in a coma by the Scales sympathizers who replaced me, by the way - but I discovered Rosalind and her protégé, D. I asked for permission to approach. Hell, Kara, I practically begged you! But you always told me to wait, for no good reason I could ever fathom. Who put the public at risk then? Watch and wait and hope they didn't harm themselves or others, or attract the unwanted attention of our business partner, Steven Rourke, that pillar of the St. Louis community. You let D and Jess move to Chicago, and sent me along too, to watch and wait some more. Jess, who was not only sensitive - and had forged a connection with D that allowed them to overcome Izzy's shields - but who had hacked into our communications, and discovered who knows how much information about the HLF. Jesus, David, I had to save D and Jess from a fate worse than death, before you even allowed me to talk to them! You accuse us of recklessness? How fucking reckless were you?"

Jamal perched on the edge of his seat, shaking, as if poised to leap across the empty stone pool and throttle the foundation director. Izzy laid a hand on his forearm, gazing at him with awe. David absorbed his vitriol in silence, and if not abashed, he did look thoughtful. Rosalind turned her distasteful stare on Kara, who cringed. They no doubt regretted even more having chosen that seat.

"You go, boy," murmured Jess.

"And you wonder why you struggle for respect within the organization," sneered Carson. Jamal froze, and the two men locked narrowed eyes. "That is exactly the reaction I would have expected from you."

"We don't all have the advantage of your privilege," Jamal stated, ice cold. Carson bared his teeth in a smile.

David looked like he was about to speak when Rosalind stood up.

"Have we concluded the official posturing and venting of grievances?" she asked. David blinked, opened his mouth, closed it again. "I'm sure you both felt the need, and I hope you've both got it out of your system. The Henry Lyons Foundation didn't need to fly us four thousand miles to the English countryside for that. D's right. The events that supposedly precipitated our summons were initiated by the Scales of Equilibrium, an organization in which my son is entangled. From what my husband tells me, the authorities increasingly suspect the Scales have a hand in, or are outright responsible for, many or most incidents of recent urban sabotage. We now know they attacked HLF field agents in Chicago and likely elsewhere. They also, if you hadn't heard, tried to kidnap me at O'Hare airport. That we were targeted, and the reasons for it, appear far more worthy topics of conversation to me. If you wish to continue the thumping of chests, perhaps we can adjourn until another time?"

The chastened silence lingered for several glorious heartbeats, before soft laughter broke it.

"Rosalind Hill," said Carson, shaking his head with a wry grin. "Your reputation does you no justice! Forgive us. You are quite right. There are much better reasons than censure for us to bring you all this way. You, D, and Jess have caused quite a stir. Perhaps my esteemed colleague wishes to exert more control over the message?"

David shot a look at Carson, then cleared his throat. "I meant what I said, whether you believe it was chest-thumping or not. But I have said it. My colleague is partially correct. For many reasons, the Henry Lyons Foundation is a decentralized organization. Nonetheless, rumors circulate: rumors of powerful new agents in America, agents who can somehow connect their wills and achieve exponentially more power. Power that can create stronger Tethers, say most of the rumors. Some claim the power has repelled psychic attacks by unknown adversaries."

Everyone turned to look at me, and I did my best to withstand the scrutiny without flinching. Rosalind sat down, but we all had to lean forward to hear what David said next. "A very few hint that the power was enough to fend off something else, to sever contact with an... Agency."

All heads swiveled to Rosalind, who appeared unperturbed by the attention. "That is why I'm here. The main reason, at least. You want me to replicate what I did at the Themis Center. And, if I understand the Scales motivations correctly, they wish to stop me from doing so."

"Did you have any more success today?" Jess asked. Unsurprisingly, she was most fascinated by what Rosalind had done that night, saving us from the scrutiny of The Presence.

Rosalind grimaced. "No. And I have thoughts on that. I'm not sure this divide-and-conquer approach you people seem to favor works very well. At best, it's inefficient. I haven't always agreed with Jamal, but I confess I share his frustration at the lack of support and outright impediments to our progress. We survived at the Themis Center in large part because of the training and guidance he and Izzy provided." Her eyes met Jamal's, and he nodded his gratitude.

"I never understood why you delayed our approach to D and Jess in Chicago," chimed in Izzy. "You knew they were as powerful as me by then. Why fight them instead of recruiting them? Not that it wasn't fun building all those shields for D to smash, along with my brain." She flashed me a look of mock indignance.

"I'd like an answer to that too," I said, turning to Kara. They'd kept their own counsel during the entire discussion, and it was time to put them on the spot. "I met Jamal several times in St. Louis, before I knew who he was, or anything about the HLF. Why forbid him from contacting me, or Jess, or Rosalind? Seems like we could all be at least six months further along, and better prepared for what we face."

Kara drew themselves up. "There were reasons," they said, affecting some of Rosalind's natural authority, but with far less conviction. "We're not obliged to share them all with you. I can say that, despite all the information Jamal provided, we weren't sure about you for a long time. Not every freelancer is worthy of recruitment."

I opened my mouth to reply, but Jess beat me to it. "You assholes thought we were Scales."

Her statement hung in the air, like a volatile explosive that could detonate at any moment. It had gotten dark all of a sudden. Gray clouds swarmed from the west, bringing a cool breeze that whispered of rain.

"We find ourselves in a tenuous position," David said at last. "As recently as a decade ago, we would have welcomed you with open arms. After... After Allen Weston's defection and his establishment of the Themis Institute, and more lately of the Scales of Equilibrium, we must exercise greater care. And that was before we learned of the Scales' direct attacks on our personnel. There has been no declaration of war, but there is no question in my mind that we're fighting one."

"And we don't want to bring in moles or even those sympathetic to the Scales," said Jamal, scratching his chin in thought. "But then why not share that with me, Kara? I knew who the Scales were, even then."

"Because I told them not to," said Carson, fixing Jamal with a steely glare. "There are already many rumors swirling about Agency Theory, and the extent of its lingering support within the HLF. Our field agents and researchers have enough to contend with, without seeing potential adversaries everywhere they go."

Jamal held Carson's gaze. "I don't think it's much of a stretch to imagine Agency Theory still has its adherents within the HLF. Not all may be sympathetic to the Scales, but I bet some are. For all I know, there could be some in this very garden.

"Are you accusing someone, Jamal?"

"Should I be, Carson?"

"Carson's right," declared David, leaning forward between the two bristling men. The first drops of rain splashed on my head. "At least in the sense that rumors of Scales activity within the HLF have already created chaos and strife. We do, of course, take that most seriously, especially now. And no one in this garden is under suspicion."

This last was directed at Jamal, who finally tore his eyes away from the Foundation's head of global operations. Carson merely sat back on his bench with a disgruntled air.

"We need unity, and we need purpose," David went on. "Having said what I said, I urge you, D, Jess, and Rosalind, to work with us, to share your new skills with our researchers and our agents. Jamal, Izzy, you have a rapport with them already. You will be instrumental in further unlocking their potential. Expand D and Jess's connection, learn how Rosalind severed the Intrusion. You all have the Foundation's blessing. You have my blessing. Whatever resources you need, they are yours. We are going into battle, and we need all the weaponry we can muster."

A steady, thumping rain greeted this pronouncement. Jess stood and clasped my hand. "To battle," she murmured.

Chapter Five
PROTECTION

For those of us whose knowledge of the British countryside came from travel shows and PBS crime dramas, the nearby village of Broadway was as iconic as you could get. They called it the "Jewel of the Cotswolds", which made more sense when Rosalind explained that the Cotswolds was the picture postcard region in which we found ourselves.

Glorious late fall sun illuminated the venerable, honey-colored stone buildings flanking High Street, sandwiching wide grass verges where streams had once flowed down from the hills. Shops, cafes and pubs, real estate agents and solicitors - the British term for attorneys, which I found hilarious - vied for the attention of locals and passers through. As the road began its steep climb up Fish Hill, a pub sign on the right recalled times in the mid-nineteenth century when Broadway was an important stagecoach stop on the London to Worcester route.

The village itself was much older, of course, almost impossibly old. Anglo-Saxon records of its importance dated to the tenth century. I was disappointed when Rosalind told me that the impressive tower on Broadway Hill, to the southeast, wasn't the remains of a medieval castle, or even medieval at all.

"It's a folly," she told me and Izzy, as we huddled over drinks at a corner table in the Crown and Trumpet. In contrast to its unassuming exterior, the inside of the pub was all black beams and whitewash, nooks and crannies, its tables, chairs and benches crammed in as best as the owners could devise. We'd secured a space in a bay window near an upright piano and a magnificent stone fireplace, adorned with equestrian paraphernalia. My eyes darted around the room in a frantic and futile attempt to absorb the details.

"A folly?" I wasn't familiar with the word, and sipped my cask ale while trying to decide if I could forgive its warmer than ice-cold temperature. I hadn't eaten breakfast earlier, and the beguiling aroma of offerings such as fish and chips or steak and kidney pie wafted from the rear kitchen, tugging at my appetite.

"Something built in modern times, often by someone with more money than sense, to look much older than it is."

"Oh. Define 'modern'."

"End of the eighteenth century, give or take a decade."

"Just the other day, then," Izzy said with a grin, sipping her tonic water.

"It does feel older, doesn't it?" Rosalind mused. She'd been in tour guide mode ever since we'd left Shotcombe House. We'd borrowed one of the HLF's fleet of tiny sedans for the length of our visit, and I was happy to let her drive. Did Ford know their cars were so ridiculously small in this country?

"Did you live here?" I asked her. "You know a lot about the place."

She shook her head. "No, I grew up in a village called Stow-on-the-Wold, about a dozen miles from here. My first boyfriend lived here though."

Her eyes grew sad and distant at that memory, and I exchanged an awkward glance with Izzy. Which was awkward in itself. I missed Jess, but she'd accompanied Charli and Jamal on a similar errand to Bristol. Izzy and I continued to make progress connecting our consciousnesses during Tether practice, and, surprisingly, so had Jess and Jamal. That made for interesting late night conversation.

"Is that when you knew Astbury?" Izzy asked. "I didn't get that wrong, did I? You recognized each other when we got here, and you've been avoiding each other ever since."

Rosalind pursed her lips. "Avoiding is a strong word. We do have history. Emma was my babysitter, and friend, once upon a time. Before... well, before a lot of things." She sighed. "Please understand, I have very mixed feelings about returning to this part of the world. It holds many memories, not all of them happy. I hadn't connected the name 'Astbury' to the woman I knew back then. It was quite a shock. But then, that seems to be standard operating procedure when working with the Henry Lyons Foundation. Ah, this looks like our woman."

I craned my neck around to see who she was talking about. Madam Sophia, renowned psychic of the area, was not what I expected. Her name had conjured visions of a wizened gypsy woman, huddled over a crystal ball in a dingy tent reeking of incense. Jess had corrected my use of the word 'gypsy' to 'Romani', but hadn't refuted the rest of the stereotype.

The woman who approached our table, having spied Rosalind's raised hand, was about her age and height, but her short dark hair held not a hint of gray. Wary, deep brown eyes peered at us through horn-rimmed eyeglasses, and with her fuzzy oatmeal-colored sweater and faded blue jeans, she gave off more of an art professor vibe.

"Mrs. Hill?" Her voice was deeper than her slight frame suggested, and held traces of an accent I associated with the eastern parts of Europe. It reminded me of friends from the Bosnian community I'd made growing up in St. Louis. "I am sorry to be late. I am not usually out this early."

"How do you do?" said Rosalind, rising to shake her hand and complete the introductions. Madam Sophia's grip was weak, almost as if my touch burned her, and her smile of greeting was tight. She didn't look like she wanted to be here.

I offered to buy her a drink, and she asked for a glass of white wine, "the sweetest they have." By the time I returned from the bar, she'd perched on the wooden chair nearest the door, hands folded over a slim, red leather purse in her lap. She listened with apparent skepticism to what Rosalind had to say. Izzy watched the newcomer with fascination.

"I have heard of Henry Lyons, of course," Madam Sophia said. She accepted the wine with a polite nod, inhaled its bouquet with eyes closed, and took the tiniest sip before setting the glass on the table. "We move in same circles, yes? You are competitors. Bad for business." She smiled, but it was anything but friendly.

Rosalind's lip curled before she forced her own, hardly more convincing smile. "As for that, I cannot say. Where I live, I'm not aware of anyone marketing your particular services, not with any decent reputation, at least. We're not here to discuss business arrangements. We're just looking for information."

Madam Sophia sat straighter and her eyes narrowed. "Not business? What do I get in return? More than just glass of wine, I hope?"

"We can pay you for your time, certainly," said Rosalind, her tone chilling by several degrees.

Madam Sophia licked her lips and glanced at me. "Perhaps something else. Protection."

"Protection?" I echoed, puzzled. "From what?"

"Threats. Vandals. More, perhaps." She lunged for her wine and gulped half of it. "Harassment. They want me to stop, to end my business."

I caught Rosalind's eye, sure she remembered the note Steven Rourke had slipped under my St. Louis apartment door early in my apprenticeship, a single printed word: "STOP". I doubted his reach, or his interest, extended to fortune tellers in the English Cotswolds, but the strong-arm tactics came from the same school of bullying and intimidation. "What kind of threats? Who's 'they'?"

"I don't know who," she said bitterly. "They leave notes, in door and on car. Spray paint. Threw rock through front window of my house. Left dead crow on doorstep." She shuddered, removing her glasses to wipe a tear from her eye.

"When did this start?" asked Rosalind, her tone far more sympathetic.

"A month, maybe two. I have not taken real job in two weeks. Real job, not entertainment. You know what I mean. I have to pay bills. But I don't want charity. My family, we come here when I was young woman, and I work every day. Every day! Always there are some who don't like us. They say 'lazy immigrants!'. I am not lazy! I love my new country! But now I am afraid."

"Have you gone to the police?" I bit my lip at Izzy's question. I bet I already knew the answer.

Madam Sophia shrugged. "Of course. Very young man. He said he would try to help. But I see nothing, no one, so what can he do? Much crime now. The police, they are busy."

I sipped my beer to forestall any unhelpful empathy.

Rosalind watched me with a thoughtful expression, then turned to Izzy. "I'm not sure I can speak for the Henry Lyons Foundation in terms of offering protection," she said. "Although I can certainly make a phone call to find out what our options may be."

"They've def beefed up security around HQ," murmured Izzy. "If they thought your information was valuable enough, they may devise something."

Right. "I could stay with you until they do," I said, drawing myself up. "Some people might think twice about bothering you if they saw me hanging around. Or I could at least check your place out," I added hurriedly, as Madam Sophia turned her wary, calculating gaze on me. "I don't want to impose."

"Would not be imposition," she said. "You are scarier than ex-husband." I wasn't quite sure how to take that.

Izzy frowned. "The brass won't like that. They want us to keep working on our connection, remember? We're making such great progress!"

"I believe that's D's point," said Rosalind, drawing attention away from my blush. "The HLF won't want to spare him for long, if at all. His chivalry, while also charming, will force their hand." She smiled, and I grinned back. *Give me a horse, a sword, and a suit of armor, and I can patrol the grounds. Sir D of St. Louis, at your service, my lady!*

"That's the hope," I said, turning back to Madam Sophia. "So, do we have a deal? What can you tell us about your 'real job'? What do you see? And what do you do about it?"

She nodded, then continued in a low voice. "I have always seen things. Ever since the fighting in Sarajevo. I thought it was effect of what I witnessed during the war. What is term they use? PTSD? We move from place to place, until we find home here, and I see things, sometimes terrible things. My husband, he get job as builder, he worked all the time. I stay home with our son and daughter, sometimes too afraid to leave, too afraid of what else I might see. Of what it might mean. But then I remember my grandmother, stories she told me, of her people and traditions, before she came to Sarajevo. Maybe these visions were not PTSD. Maybe I had been blessed with the Sight."

She paused as if to assess our reaction to her claim. Personally, I didn't care what she called it. We already had more names for the phenomena than we knew what to do with. It was natural that others would use terms that made sense to them, given their upbringing and culture.

No, what disturbed me was imagining what had caused her to flee her home in Sarajevo. As a small child in St. Louis, I'd been ignorant of the wars of the 1990s in the former Yugoslavia, but during high school, I'd hung out with some Bosnian refugees whose families were starting new lives in my city. Families that were often incomplete, often appallingly so. My friend Luka had told me stories of atrocities whose images would scar him for the rest of his days. If Madam Sophia had witnessed anything like that, no wonder any latent ability to sense Intrusions or Imprints had been unlocked.

She told us more, and I began to feel like a priest in a confessional. She unburdened herself of parts of her life she'd kept secret from everyone, including the husband who'd left her for another woman, and the children who, she told us with pride, were both studying at university. Starting with parents of her children's school friends, she'd dabbled in palm reading and the tarot, always 'for fun', as a way to entertain others, to make friends of her own. It wasn't long before one such friend told her about the ghost in one of her bedrooms, the room she couldn't bear to enter. Sure enough, Sophia had barely stepped through the door when the skin all over her body burned as if someone had set her aflame.

"I made myself look," she told us, the remembered horror written across her pale face. "I made myself see. It was a man, a man not much older than me. He tied rope to light in ceiling and hanged himself. I watched him die. And then I made it stop. I made room forget. Maybe I brought him peace, I do not know. But I made friend happy. And she tell other friends, and soon I am not Sophia anymore. I am Madam Sophia, seer and psychic. They call me from many places, many towns and villages. I am glad to help. But now, things have changed."

Rosalind leaned forward, eyes narrowed with intent. "Changed in what way?"

Madam Sophia licked her lips, then downed the rest of her wine. "I was at house in Evesham, just before Christmas. The young father of three boys, he had problem in older son's bedroom. The boy couldn't sleep. He and his brothers, and his mother, they weren't home. I could not know." The hackles rose on the back of my neck. "I saw the boy, in bed, sick. Very sick. His mother crying as she prayed next to bed. I make house forget, but I could not. I hear he is sick now. Cancer." I shuddered, and shared a mournful look with Rosalind.

"You saw the future?" said Izzy, all professional curiosity. "This was last Christmas? Did it happen again?"

"Two times," Madam Sophia replied. Her expression turned bleak as she looked at me. "And again, last week, in my own house. I saw it burning, and myself, trapped in the flames."

"Charli said they've been getting more and more reports of future intrusions from agents around the world," Izzy told us, while Madam Sophia visited the restroom. "They're much harder to tether, apparently. Lots of your Imprints kicking around. The brass are trying to keep it quiet until Astbury's team learns more."

"To what end?" Rosalind snapped. "Your Foundation do love their secrets, but keeping this quiet puts its own agents in danger."

Izzy scowled. "Yeah, it does. I'm tired of it. I've known too many people, good people, get hurt because they didn't know all the risks. You guys have woken me up, and maybe we can wake everyone else up. Even Charli's frustrated. She's brilliant, you know. She was the one who predicted the activity spike in Chicago when D and Jess moved there. She's fed the future Intrusion data into the model, but Astbury swore her to secrecy. I don't know if it's office politics or some other bullshit, but I'm sick of it."

"So we don't know what the model predicted from the future Intrusions?" I asked, careful to watch the corridor leading to the "Ladies Toilet".

"Nothing good." Izzy grimaced, but couldn't elaborate before Madam Sophia reappeared, and ushered me into her toy car.

The Mazda 2 was even more cramped than the Ford Puma we'd borrowed from Shotcombe House. To ensure I savored every last second of misery from the experience, Madam Sophia drove at a snail's pace, treating the winding, wooded country lanes with far more trepidation than they deserved.

I was still processing the implications of what she'd confided in us. The story of her sensitivity to Intrusions and Imprints rang true, and her reputation as a psychic gave her the perfect cover to investigate and deal with the phenomena. What had us reeling was that she'd seen no less than four future events, dating back almost a year, before Jess and I had moved to Chicago. Well, Rosalind and I were reeling; Izzy was grim but satisfied.

We drove in silence through the village of Chipping Camden, where the familiar brownstone buildings crowded the road much more closely than in Broadway. Out the other side - I had long since lost my sense of direction, and thick clouds obscured the sun - we took several turns through a neighborhood of increasingly modern and diverse construction. Either they'd run out of their iconic building material, or it was simply too expensive for the plainer and smaller houses at the edge of town.

I didn't expect Madam Sophia to live in an eccentric cottage in the forest, but I couldn't help but be disappointed when she parked, halfway over and almost completely blocking the sidewalk, in front of a modest two story villa. It was one half of a no-frills, white stucco building whose front garden was scarcely wider than her car. On closer inspection, the strip of grass in front of her bay window proved to be astroturf. I felt vaguely cheated.

The bay window itself was still partially boarded up, a sheet of plywood occupying the space where it projected from the house nearest the navy blue front door. Vandals had spray painted scarlet phallic symbols and a barely legible "THOU SHALL NOT SUFFER A WITCH TO LIVE" on the plywood, which was both immature and sinister. I felt an absurd urge to correct the spelling mistake.

"Have the police seen this?" I asked. She shook her head as she unlocked her door. I looked around, but saw no other pedestrians or faces in windows. "What do your neighbors think?"

Madam Sophia didn't reply until she'd closed the door behind us. The reek of sage almost overpowered me; I wasn't sure I could ever cook with it again. Taking shallow breaths, I followed her down a narrow hallway, past a straight flight of stairs leading upward, and into a modest kitchen. Everything was spotless, the faux-marble counters, the electric cooktop, the stainless steel sink and the two-person kitchen table. A large picture window overlooked a back garden scarcely bigger than the kitchen itself, but which thrived with as much plant variety as the grounds of Shotcombe House. She grew her own herbs, vegetables and what looked like gooseberries, decorating with tubs and beds of shrubs and flowers that must look spectacular in the spring.

"The neighbors, they are concerned," she said at last, filling an electric kettle with water from the sink. "Tea or coffee?"

I suspected the coffee choice was instant only. Time to give hot black tea another try.

"Some are concerned for me," she went on as we watched the water start to bubble through the clear glass of the kettle. "Some are concerned about me, and what trouble I bring to their neighborhood. What can I do? This is my home." She gestured at the walls. As with the hallway, framed photographs of all sizes hung in every free space, a crowd of memories competing for attention. Most were of her children, some of a black cat, very few included her, and none showed her ex-husband.

"I'm not sure what we can do," I told her. I guessed I was representing the Henry Lyons Foundation now. They'd better have my back. "I'm just visiting from the States."

"I've always wanted to go," she said, pouring boiling water into a red china teapot. "Tell me about it."

I gaped at her. Where should I start? What about my life in St. Louis or in Chicago could possibly interest a lonely, frightened woman, a refugee from the Balkan wars living in the heart of the English countryside? We had nothing in common, surely. Well, nothing except for Imprints and Erasures.

As I fumbled for words, we heard shouting from the street outside. Motioning for her to stay seated, I hurried down the hall and cracked the front door. A burly, middle-aged man wearing the plain shirt and pants of a construction worker stood next to Madam Sophia's Mazda, shaking his fist at someone to my right. "Leave her alone!" he bellowed. "I'm calling the police. And if I ever see you here again, I'm kicking your fucking arse, mate!"

I stepped through the door, and he flinched before wheeling on me. I held up my hands in appeasement. "I'm a friend. I'm here to help her. What happened?"

He squinted at me for a moment, then appeared satisfied. "I'm next door. Just got back from work to find some wanker in a hoody keying Sophia's car." He pointed at the hood. Most of a "W" had been scratched into the light blue paint. I turned and caught a glimpse of a tall figure in a black hoody and jeans, before they ducked down a side street. I could've sworn they looked right at me before they disappeared.

"Mickey, what... oh!" Madam Sophia appeared in the doorway, and her face crumpled at the sight of her car.

"We'll fix it, love." Mickey gave her a hug, then looked at me over her shoulder. "I'll stay with her if you want to go after him."

Did I? The last time I chased someone, the guy who'd stalked Jess on her way home from work in Chicago, it hadn't ended well. But hopefully I'd learned some valuable lessons since then. I nodded and took off at a cautious jog.

The neighborhood was a rabbit warren. Straight roads and the grid system must offend British sensibilities, since I had no sooner turned onto the side street before it curved and presented me with another intersection. I looked both ways, down narrow streets with cars hugging the low front walls of the houses on one side, barely allowing passage. The street to my right was a cul-de-sac, with nowhere to run. And at the end, in the middle of the turning circle, staring wildly around like a cornered beast, was my man.

I almost laughed. Had I no training at all, or had I lost my composure like I did that evening in Lincoln Park, I might've cornered my quarry and had a few words, at the least. But I knew he wasn't just a kid, one of a series of juvenile mischief-makers targeting Madam Sophia just because she was different. And I knew he wasn't alone. Sensei Ryuichi, from my Chicago dojo, had drilled this into me. The question was how many companions he had, and where they lurked. The white windowless van parked half way down the cul-de-sac was the most likely candidate. Did I gamble there wasn't a gang of Scales-tattooed thugs waiting to pour out of that van? Could I make the statement I wanted to?

The distant but rising wail of sirens cut the air, and I made my decision.

"What do you think you're doing, dude?" I called, striding with confidence down the middle of the road towards the guy in the hoody. "Keying a woman's car? That's not very nice." I edged towards the van as I drew level with it, weight on the front of my feet, arms loose at my side. "Did you break her window too? Paint penises and the slogan on the wood. You can't spell, you know—"

Hoody started walking quickly towards me as I caught movement in my peripheral vision. The driver side door of the van opened, and another black-clad figure climbed out, wielding something in their hand.

"Get in the van, bruv—"

The sole of my tennis shoe caught him squarely in the chest, the air in his lungs whooshing out as his body crumpled. I could never remember all the Japanese names of the moves we learned at the dojo, but Jess called this one the "mule kick". The force of it propelled him backwards, and his head smacked the road surface as he landed, whatever weapon he'd held skittering away under the van.

I took a moment to satisfy myself he was, at least for the moment, too stunned to be a threat, and that no one else was getting out of the vehicle. Then, I wheeled to confront Hoody, whose advance had faltered. Yeah, buddy, you bit off a bit more than you could chew, didn't you? I charged, and used the latest weapon in my arsenal, turning sideways as I leapt, and aimed a flying kick at his chest. He tried to duck and evade, which only made it worse as he took the blow above his ear instead. With a grunt of pain, he collapsed to the ground, and narrowly missed face planting the nearest parked car.

Move over, Bruce Lee!

My pulse raced as adrenaline surged through me, but I wasn't breathing hard at all. It was a far cry from my impulsive pursuit of Jess's stalker, or fifteen years ago, when I panicked after being jumped on a quiet street, and slit a man's throat. Now, I was in control, and stood over my groaning adversaries with confidence.

"You people are really shit at this," I taunted. The sirens were much louder now, maybe two blocks away. I had seconds. "Leave Madam Sophia alone. And if you want to talk to me and Rosalind, send us a fucking invitation."

Chapter Six
THE BLOODY BROTHERS

"What am I gonna do with you, you impulsive brute of a man?" Jess stepped out of our minutes-long embrace and punched me on the arm. The glint in her eye was still flirtatious, but she was annoyed too.

"I rather hoped the answer was obvious," I replied, gesturing to the double bed in our nondescript hotel room. It wasn't that comfortable for sleeping, but it served other purposes just fine. "And I don't mind 'brute', but I take offense at 'impulsive'. I thought I played that rather well."

Jess arched her eyebrow and planted hands on hips. "Do you now? What if you'd been wrong? What if the back of that van had been full of Scales thugs? What if they'd been hiding elsewhere? What if that gun had gone off—"

I took her hands in mine. "I know. It was a risk, but a calculated one. The police got there in time, and they're now taking Madam Sophia's harassment seriously. I think the HLF is too." I pressed her ring finger to my lips, marveling anew at the diamond in its midst. "But I know I'm risking more than just myself now. I'm sorry if I made you worry about me."

She maintained her steely gaze for another second or two, then sank against me once more, fingers clutching at my shirt. "What am I going to do with you?" she repeated, and then proceeded to answer her own question.

Afterwards, we lay naked and sweating on top of the disheveled sheets, staring up at the patchy ceiling paint job.

The single portable electric fan labored to give the illusion of air-conditioning, and while the mid-60s temperature was perfect for being outside, our hotel room was warm and stuffy. Jess's dragon-tattooed arm draped over my chest. I adored the way she'd sometimes doodle with her fingertips while she talked, or while deep in thought. I don't think she knew she did it, and it always gave me goosebumps.

"Did Madam Sophia tell you about all her future Imprints?" she murmured, breaking the contented silence.

It took a moment to drag my thoughts back to more mundane things. "At a high-level, yes. Why?"

"I'm looking for patterns, just like Charli and Astbury. Charli's already identified a couple, but she's leery of broadcasting them without Astbury's say so. The poor girl is super smart, but she doesn't have much self-confidence."

"To be fair, she's surrounded by a ton of strong personalities. Did she come out of her shell when you went to Bristol? You haven't said much about what you found there."

Jess sighed. "There isn't much to tell. We certainly didn't have the drama you did. I think the HLF is sending some poor bastard to monitor 'Doctor X', in case the Scales start harassing him."

"Doctor X?"

"Please don't make me say it again. Total douchebag. He's all show and bluster, and a bigot to boot. He clearly thought two chicks and a black guy unworthy of learning his 'secrets'. Jamal had to get quite persuasive. I'm warming up to him."

"That's saying a lot." Jess had never forgiven Jamal for concealing Conor McKee, her boss at Paragon Insurance in Chicago, was himself an HLF field agent. We'd only discovered this after Conor was attacked by Scales operatives, falling into a coma from which he had yet to recover. Already upset, Jess fumed over the implication she'd only been offered her first job as a software developer so Conor could watch over her, one of the two infamous freelancers who'd just moved to his town. Jamal insisted Jess earned the job on her own merit, and placing her on Conor's team was just a fortuitous opportunity for the HLF. She'd never quite believed him. We'd all been surprised when they began connecting their consciousnesses during Tether practice at Shotcombe House.

"But Charli was fine," Jess continued. "She lives in Bristol. She went to university there. It poured with rain, so we didn't see the city at its best, but she showed us the Clifton Suspension Bridge. It spans this really deep river gorge, all built up and everything. Super cool! Also a suicide hotspot, apparently. One of her friends threw himself off the bridge during final exams."

"Holy shit!"

"Yep. That's when she started seeing things, thought it was shock or depression or something. Then the HLF rolls up and offers her a job. Not as a field agent, but as an analyst. And she's killing it."

"She told you all that?"

"I might have paraphrased. I think she found me easy to talk to, while we waited for the insufferable Doctor. She teased Jamal about me hacking his emails. She thinks the HLF is too repressive, thinks they've never left the Victorian era. Which is funny, because ninety percent of their researchers are female. Other scientific institutions are probably more Victorian, and don't rate female scientists as highly."

I decided to leave that alone. "So did you get any details of future Imprints from Doctor X?"

"Some, yes. They fit Charli's patterns more or less. It sounds like some of them might have come to pass already, or are about to. But here's the question: how far in the future do you think they went?"

"Hard to say. I haven't heard anything too outlandish, flying cars or anything. A few years, maybe?"

"Well, that's just it. I didn't hear anything that couldn't happen tomorrow. Some of the memories we've witnessed are decades or centuries old. Why wouldn't we encounter others that are at least that far in the future?"

I frowned. "Maybe there's some sort of theoretical limit to future Intrusions. Or maybe the buildings in which they occur get torn down or something. I remember Jamal telling me once that Tethers relied on some form of man-made, physical structure to hold them, and that no one had ever encountered a free-standing Intrusion."

"Maybe," Jess murmured, drumming her fingers on my ribcage. "Or maybe we only have a few years left."

"That's a bit apocalyptic."

"You think that's far-fetched? Look at what's happening to the world, D. It's not just the Scales. They're not the only ones causing chaos and destruction. There's too many of us for the planet to sustain. Humanity marches across the globe at other species' expense, draining resources, fighting wars, creating famines, spreading disease. Shit, we only just made it out of one pandemic, and most of us are acting like it never happened, or couldn't happen again. What if it does? You think we're any more prepared? What if we don't see memories further in the future because there's nothing to remember?"

I drew her into my arms, stroking the warm skin of her back, and tracing the lines of her dragon tattoo. But while her tension melted away, mine simmered.

Her reasoning was bleak, and all too plausible. What disturbed me most was how it sounded an awful lot like the manifesto of Allen Weston in his book *The Gaia Contract*. The manifesto that drove The Scales of Equilibrium.

A thought occurred to me. "What if they never happen?"

Jess drew back to look me in the eye. "What do you mean?"

"I keep thinking about the Imprint in Shotcombe House, the day we arrived. It was a 'memory' of me in Kara LeVault's office. I've never been there. They forbade me from going, and I've no intention to go. What if I never do? What if we leave England tomorrow and never come back? What if Madam Sophia moves out of her house tomorrow and never goes back? How can a fire trap her there in a future that couldn't happen?"

"I don't know," Jess admitted, brow furrowed in thought. Then she yawned, disentangled herself, and burrowed into her thin pillows. "I don't think the future works like that, D."

And with that enigmatic statement, she closed her eyes. Within minutes, she slept, her breathing slow, steady, and untroubled. The night was old before I finally joined her.

Rosalind met us in the hotel lobby the next morning.

"I've had a word with Emma. We're going to try something different today."

"Which is?" I asked.

"I want to connect with both of you together. I have my own theory to test. I suggest you both prepare yourselves."

I craned around in my seat. Jess shook her head before closing her eyes and starting breathing exercises. Rosalind didn't seem in the mood for further conversation - perhaps she was preparing herself - so I didn't argue and followed suit.

We marched into the conference room at Shotcombe House to find Jamal and Izzy waiting for us, along with Astbury, Charli and another researcher, an older woman with curly gray hair: Jean? Jane? Rosalind and Astbury locked gazes while the rest of us said our hellos. Then Astbury gave a curt nod and backed her wheelchair away from the table.

"Come along, then," she said, in the manner of a parent humoring their demanding children. "Let's pay the Bloody Brothers another visit."

It occurred to me, as we followed her down the quiet corridors, that the sparsely furnished room to which everyone's favorite ghostly memory was tethered lay directly underneath Kara LeVault's office. Coincidence? And where was Kara? Not that we needed another spectator - more than one face gawped at our procession as we passed open doors on the way - but I hadn't seen them since our "coming to Jesus" meeting in the maze a few days before. Given how much they'd been around since we arrived, I was a little surprised they were missing that morning.

I set aside that distraction when we filed into the disused office. Only the very faintest waft of heat hinted that there was more to this room than met the eye. Shabby curtains leaked shafts of weak sunlight to explore a battered desk and chair, agitating a swarm of dust motes that swirled in anger at our entrance. Stacks of decrepit cardboard boxes lined one wall, whose ornate navy blue wallpaper peeled in several places. A forlorn stone fireplace squatted opposite, long past use. Even though the Intrusion had been repeatedly tethered, including by us, with barely a trace, no one wanted to work here. I couldn't blame them. The room's neglect and decay jarred with everything else I'd seen in Shotcombe House. It gave me the creeps.

"I want all three of you together, since it's your first time," declared Astbury.

Charli favored me with an encouraging smile as she taped sensors in place on both my temples. I still hadn't heard what conclusions, if any, had been drawn from whatever data these sensors gathered, but they no longer bothered me.

Astbury drummed fingers on her wheelchair's armrest. "We now know your connection requires at least one of you to sense an untethered Intrusion. We also know that the longer it remains untethered, the weaker our world's resistance to these phenomena becomes, and the greater your personal risk. Despite that, I'd like you to hold it open for as long as you can, so we can capture as much data as possible."

"We'll do our best," said Rosalind, resting one hand on the desk's discolored surface. She looked at me and Jess, standing together in the middle of the room. "D, can you lead us, please? Jess, I want you to pay close attention to what's happening outside the memory. Jamal, Izzy: You won't be part of the connection, but I'd like you both prepared to step in if necessary."

"Sure." Jamal drew out the word almost into a question. But I knew the answer, and so did Jess.

"You're trying to bait it," she stated. "You're trying to summon The Presence."

Astbury sniffed her disdain, and Rosalind chuckled without humor. "You do make it sound like we're conducting a seance! I suppose we are, in a way. The Presence only seems to manifest when the two of you are connected. The strongest such manifestation, by all accounts, was at the Themis Center, when I was, if not connected with the pair of you, then at least present in the room, and witness to the Intrusion's memory."

"But why?" I asked, gripped with sudden fear. "Why do you want to summon that thing?" We'd barely escaped the immensity of its regard last time. I had no desire to draw such attention again.

"Because she wants to prove it exists," snapped Astbury, as if impatient with my dimwittedness. "She wants to convince old skeptics like me, and others, if I'm not mistaken."

I glanced at Jamal, who looked both thoughtful and uncomfortable. Izzy, on the other hand, positively bounced on her toes.

"Partly," acknowledged Rosalind. "But I also want to understand what I did that night. Nothing we've tried since our arrival has allowed me to replicate what I did, how I excised that Intrusion entirely from the Themis Center. I suspect - I hope - that recreating those exact conditions will allow me to do so."

"And what if you can't?" I persisted. "What if we invite the murderer back to the scene of the crime, hoping to unmask them, only for them to kill us all?"

Rosalind grimaced, then gestured at the rest of our gathering. "A little prosaic, but a fair question. The three of us, connected, may wield sufficient power to recreate the Imprint, despite any interference by this Presence. If not, Jamal and Izzy are two of the most capable field agents in the HLF, with whom you two have already connected. Surely, the five of us working together should be able to do what's necessary."

I shook my head. "How can you assume that? We don't know what you did last time, at the Themis Center. You might just have gotten lucky, taken The Presence by surprise. We have no idea what it is, what its intentions are, or how much power it wields. For all we know, it could crush us all in the blink of an eye!"

"But that's why we have to do it, love." Jess took my hand and gave it what she likely thought was a reassuring squeeze. I realized how sweaty my palms were. She gazed up at me with earnest eyes. "Don't you see? If there's anyone else that knows anything about The Presence, they've likely aligned with our adversaries, the Scales. We need information, and we need it badly. David Taylor was right: the HLF *is* fighting a war, but it's sorely lacking in intelligence. It has weapons - it has us - that can contend with the ground troops, but that's just trench warfare. If The Presence is arrayed against us too, if it's their nuclear option, then we need our own Manhattan Project. We need to know what we're dealing with, and how Rosalind dealt with it before."

Everyone else waited as I considered Jess's appeal. Part of me saw the sense in her argument, but the frightened and, yes, petty side suspected she'd been the one planning this all along. She'd been first to really notice The Presence, and was vocal in her curiosity, as with all things. I wouldn't put it past her to manipulate Rosalind into proposing this, and maybe Astbury into agreeing to it. And Jess had the cheek to accuse *me* of rashness!

I disliked this side of myself. It represented the boy who'd withdrawn from his family, from a mother trying to do the right thing for her children from two different husbands. It represented a boy who'd wasted his opportunity at college because he'd translated the need to belong to providing drugs to friends, and friends of friends, associating with his mother's much-loathed cousin. That side of myself had blamed Steven Rourke for the events that led to spending over a decade in jail for killing a man. And it represented the man who, even after much self-reflection and rededication to making something of himself, hadn't had the courage to trust Jess when he'd begun this journey with Rosalind, hadn't been honest with her, or shown her the respect she deserved.

I trusted Jess now. I rejected that weaker side of myself. I may have misgivings over what we were about to attempt, but I knew she'd likely thought about it more than anyone. Knowing Jess, she'd agonized over it, worried about me, worried about Rosalind, before deciding it was still the right thing to do. I trusted her.

I took a deep breath. "Okay. Let's do this."

She smiled, a ray of sun bursting through the overcast, and kissed me. Her soft, cool lips soothed me more than any words ever could. "Let's do this," she echoed in a whisper.

I nodded at Rosalind before half-closing my eyes. The Catches were easy to find: I'd put them there myself two days before. The Two-Point Lock hadn't been perfect. I'd been distracted by my connection with Izzy, and I was still new to this more sophisticated form of Tether, necessitated by the strength of the Level Three Intrusion. This close, the hint of warmth I'd felt outside the room intensified into heat the old fireplace might once have put out.

I found the fusion points, and with the precise, delicate motion I'd learned, picked them open, one after the other. The memory unraveled like the growth of a sunflower sped up a thousand times.

I knew the scene well by now. Two ruddy-faced men in their early middle age, both steadily drinking away their family fortune as history remembered them, confronted each other in inebriated argument. Garish yellow lamp light illuminated rich furnishings and gilt framed paintings. A fire blazed in the hearth opposite a long wooden buffet. The older brother, George, extracted an almost empty glass decanter from a tumble of empty green bottles, and sloshed more brandy into his glass. After several minutes of, for me, silent argument about dalliances with his wife, he would club brother Edward's head with the decanter, smashing his eye socket and breaking his nose. Edward would die of his wounds the next day. I kept noticing different, inconsequential details about the scene. A vivid red scratch marred Edward's forearm, where he'd rolled up the cuff of his shirt, and I spared a second to wonder where that scratch had come from.

But only a second. As soon as I'd untethered the memory, I grew aware of Jess, of her familiar, intoxicating consciousness. I sensed it more keenly than her physical body alongside mine, and we connected effortlessly, intertwining until we were indistinguishable. Then we searched for Rosalind, not the woman standing across the room, but her essence, observing the memory with us. There were others there too - Izzy, sinuous and hungry; Jamal, potent but guarded - but Rosalind was easy to identify. Her spirit reminded me of a coiling dragon, imperious and powerful, fierce in attack or defense. She reached out, as if hesitant to disturb the D/Jess entity, but we accepted her. We absorbed her, remembering all our shared experiences and the depth of our friendship.

I gasped aloud. Everything took on a sharper focus, not just the visual details of the memory, but the heat from the fire, the scent of woodsmoke and body odor, the crackling of logs and the incoherent shouting of the Bloody Brothers. I'd thought Jess and I fit each other perfectly, yet Rosalind's consciousness infiltrated gaps we'd never imagined were there, and completed them. It was almost sensual. For a few moments, her thoughts remained distinct, and then they were ours. It was a high unlike any other.

This Intrusion is strong.

It gets stronger.

There are other Intrusions here.

Yes.

There are other minds here.

Yes!

We wait.

How long?

As long as we can.

As long as we must.

We—

:: YOU ::

Without warning, the implacable intelligence that was The Presence crowded out the memory, arriving with all the power and shock of an asteroid collision.

There was nothing to see just as, but for a few pinpricks of light, there's nothing to see in the vast darkness of space. The heat of the Imprint had long faded, the garbled yelling of the Bloody Brothers silenced, and all that remained was the menacing regard of an unfathomable mind. For the first time in my life, I truly contemplated the existence of God, or gods, because if this wasn't a god, what meaning did that term even have?

Terror overwhelmed my capacity to think, even to breathe. My eyes were still half-open, but I struggled to distinguish Rosalind or Jess or anyone else in the room with me, a room that blurred, softening at the edges.

And flickered.

I'm walking through a redwood grove...

No! I'm in England! I'm in Shotcombe House!

I descend into a dell, its red-brown earth scooped from the forest...

No! I'm right here, we're right here! Jess! Rosalind!

In the center of the dell is a door...

Where are you? Guys? Please!

:: D RODRIGUEZ ::

"No!" I screamed the word, louder than I'd ever screamed anything in my life, and my scream grew in power, reverberating not only through my skull, but also through the fabric of the universe. The image of the dell tossed and yawed, but instead of blinking back into darkness, I caught a glimpse of the disused room in Shotcombe House, where I'd stood all those millennia ago, before this, before The Presence. There were others in that room, other people I recognized, some sitting, some cowering on their hands and knees, some yet standing, braced as if on the deck of a storm-tossed ship. Someone clutched my hand in theirs (*Jess. Her name is Jess*), fingers interlocking with mine, warm, comforting, and alive, save for one band of cool metal that spoke of a future other than this torment. Across the room, a stooped, middle-aged woman clung to a wooden desk for support, agony etched on her face. Rosalind. As I thought her name, or maybe said it aloud, she raised her head and our eyes met. We remembered.

Power surged through the room in the space of a thought. The power of a blade, clean, straight, impossibly huge, its edge thinner than quarks. The blade sliced once, and the darkness fell away, cut adrift in the infinite void behind the universes.

Reality tumbled back in a riot of color, a hard wooden floor, a taste of blood oozing from my bitten lip, Jess's scent, and a clamor of groaning, gasping and retching. I convulsed, and lost most of the breakfast I'd unwisely consumed back at the hotel. Then I lay still, panting, my hand clutching Jess's, twitching feebly.

When I managed to raise my head, after I met Jess's eyes and assured myself she was really there, that she was really safe, I searched for Rosalind. She'd sunk trembling to her knees as Jamal, kneeling alongside, supported her shoulders. He wiped her lips and chin clean with a handkerchief, which was blotted with red.

"Thank you," she rasped, her eyes still unfocused.

Jamal nodded, but seemed at a loss for words. Then he turned to me, eyes wide in fear and awe. "That, I felt."

CHAPTER SEVEN
SACRIFICE THROW

"How is she?" I asked Kara as soon as they entered the meeting room. I was too tired to sit straighter in my chair. Besides, Jess refused to remove her head from the crook of my shoulder. "How's Rosalind?"

"She's awake and alert," they said, in as soft a voice as I'd ever heard them use. "She bit her tongue, which led to most of the blood. The med team is still running tests."

"Most of the blood?"

"Her nose started bleeding when we got her to the med suite. It stopped, but it was a concern."

"Is she gonna be okay? Shouldn't we take her to a hospital? Has anyone called Martin?"

I'd struggled upright as fear for Rosalind gripped me. What price had she paid for... whatever it was she did? Jess protested being dislodged, then fumbled for her half-empty tumbler of water on the table.

"I called her husband," Kara said, an edge creeping back into their tone. "He's on his way. I think it's time we brought him into the picture anyway. As for a hospital, our medical staff are more than capable. We should abide by their decision."

I glanced around the table. At one end, Astbury conferred with Charli and the other researcher in low, urgent voices as they examined their tablets. I was curious what their data revealed. How could mere numbers relate to what we all just experienced? I'd ripped off the sensors as soon as I'd had the strength, and they lay along with Jess's in a tangle of wires on the table.

Jamal and Izzy huddled at its other end, although both now sat in silence, alone with their thoughts. They hadn't been part of the connection that me, Jess, and Rosalind had forged, but they'd been keen observers of everything we'd sensed during the untethering, and subsequent excision of the Intrusion. Physically unharmed, but mentally shocked, they'd both corroborated the appearance of The Presence, and that the notorious Bloody Brothers Intrusion no longer existed, tethered or otherwise.

"I've never seen anything like it," Jamal murmured, looking up at Kara.

"It's truly gone?" They looked guarded, almost nervous. Or maybe I was seeing things. I felt a headache building, a steady, dull throb behind my temples, and floaters swam in my eyes.

Jamal nodded. "Without a trace."

"It was amazing!" Izzy said in wonder, as if talking to herself. "The power of their connection... and when it came... and what Rosalind did..."

Kara glanced at her sharply. "She replicated what they claimed she did in Chicago? The same technique?"

"As near as I can tell," confirmed Jamal, looking over at me and Jess. I shrugged.

"That's what I remember," said Jess. "It wasn't any sort of Lock, or channeling away of the memory like an Erasure. Rosalind just tore the Intrusion from the universe, like ripping a page from a book, and The Presence along with it."

"The Presence," Kara echoed, then simply raised their eyebrows at Jamal.

"Exists," he said. "Whatever it is. Or whatever it was. I've encountered nothing remotely similar in all my years as a Foundation agent. I'd be happy if I never did again. Whether that was the infamous Agency, I can't tell you. It never communicated to us."

"You didn't hear it?" I looked at Jamal, then Izzy, who both shook their heads. I turned to Jess and saw the question in her eyes before she asked it.

"You did? What did it say?"

I gaped at her. "But surely... we were connected! Didn't you hear it back in Chicago?"

She shrugged, then rubbed the bridge of her nose and winced. "I don't know. Nothing clear. I couldn't really hear or sense anything. The Presence drowned out everything."

I tried to remember discussing the words I'd heard, or had drilled into my brain, after the Themis Center escapade. I'd assumed we had, but had we? Damn, it was getting hard to think.

"Here, love." Jess slid a couple of painkillers across the table, and I swallowed them with the last of my water.

Kara collected a glass pitcher from the buffet and refilled our tumblers. They hovered over my shoulder. "It spoke to you?"

I realized Astbury and the others were also watching and listening now. Astbury's arms were folded in challenge.

I licked my lips. "It knew my name," I said at last, surprised by the horror dripping from my voice. "How did it know my name?"

Jess took my hand. "We don't know what it is, or what it's capable of. We perceived each other's consciousnesses, why couldn't it? What couldn't it discover about us—"

"That's enough," snapped Astbury. She unfolded her arms, and her hands gripped those of her wheelchair. "I concede there may be something else out there, some form of intelligence we don't yet understand. But don't throw away the respect I've developed for you by invoking omnipotence. Appealing to Agency goes against everything the Henry Lyons Foundation has worked towards in almost two centuries. It's simply deus ex machina."

"Deus who?" I said, mostly to interrupt Jess. Headache or otherwise, I recognized the signs of a pending eruption.

"God from the machine. When no scientific explanations suffice, humanity often invokes the god of the gaps, some arbitrarily powerful prime mover capable of anything. It's intellectual laziness."

Jess took a deep, audible breath, and when she spoke again, her words were slow and deliberate. "That's not what we're saying here. The Presence is another part of the picture, another aspect of the phenomena. A powerful one, no doubt. But we're not claiming it's the reason the phenomena exist. And we're not claiming it isn't, either. We need more data. And maybe this is how we get it."

Astbury stared at her for a long second, then relaxed her grip on her wheelchair and smiled in satisfaction. "Well done, g... well done, Jess. I agree. The existence of such an entity disrupts our entire predictive model. We need more data, and we need it quickly. And for that, we need more Intrusions. Kara, can you please draw up a list—"

I coughed, and all heads swiveled towards me. "I am *not* doing that again."

Astbury frowned. "Don't be absurd. That's why you're here."

"You don't know how close we came," I hissed. "Or what would've happened had Rosalind not done what she did. Which, by the way, I still don't understand. Does anyone? Didn't think so. Before we go putting ourselves in harm's way again for your little experiments, perhaps we should check in on the health of the only person we know who can protect us from it!"

My voice rose, my temper fraying at the edges, and I couldn't do anything to control it. My head pounded, the pain worsening with each passing second, the pills ineffective. Gray swirls obstructed half the vision in my right eye. I remembered Fiona, my half sister, describing the migraines she used to get as a teenager, and it sounded a lot like this.

"Are you alright, D?" Jamal leaned forward in concern.

Was I? Suddenly, I didn't feel well at all. Something splashed on my hand as it rested on the table. I glanced down, struggling to focus. Red drops. Red meant something bad, didn't it?

"Help him!" was the last thing I remembered before the roaring in my ears swallowed me whole.

I awoke into murk, unable to pinpoint the source of dim yellow light. I lay, fully clothed, on what felt like a hospital bed, my torso raised at a forty-five degree angle. An IV drip stood next to me, its thin plastic tube conveying colorless liquid to the needle in my right forearm. Wires taped to my forehead dangled towards a mysterious metal device the size of a shoe box, suspended from another stand on the other side of the bed. My left hand rested in my lap, a heart rate monitor clipped to my index finger.

I took a deep breath and began a damage assessment. Nothing hurt. I could move both my arms and legs without pain, but not without effort. My headache had gone, although someone must have stuffed my skull with cotton wool. Was I just exhausted, or was I on painkillers? I scrutinized the IV as I raised a cautious hand to my nose. The skin of my nostrils felt tender, but no fresh blood stained my fingers when I inspected them.

Where was I? The small room's white walls were featureless, uninterrupted by windows, picture frames, or anything suggestive of my location. On closer inspection, I realized that the "wall" to my right was a free-standing screen, and more light leaked through the gap between it and the ceiling. A spark of panic kindled within my sluggishness. Had I been kidnapped? Had the Scales got to me after all?

"Hello?" I croaked and instantly fell into a coughing fit. That hurt alright. My mouth was so dry. I heard the scrape of a chair from the other side of the divider, and a muffled grunt of pain.

I licked my chapped lips and tried again, in something like a sepulchral whisper. "Hello? Is someone there? Can I get a drink of water?"

"You'd think water would be standard issue around here." The screen turned and Rosalind stepped into view.

"Oh thank God," I murmured, closing my eyes for a second in relief. When I reopened them, I noticed Rosalind clutched her own IV stand in one hand, and dark smudges on her forehead suggested she'd been wired up too.

"How do you feel?" she asked, studying me with concern.

"Beat. Like I've just done a day's backbreaking labor. And I'm so thirsty."

"I am too. I just sent the medic to fetch more water."

"A medic? Are we in hospital?"

"No, we're still at Shotcombe House. Give me a minute." She wrestled one handed with the screen, turning it so I could see another bed like mine on the other side. That half of the room was no more inspiring in decor, but a closed door pierced the far wall.

"That's better," she said, climbing awkwardly back onto the bed. She perched on the edge, instead of laying down. "Much though it galls me to admit, I'm still weak. Not getting any younger, you know." She smiled without humor.

"How long have we been here?"

"A couple of hours, in your case. Longer for me." She grimaced, shifting in a fruitless search for comfort. "Long enough for the pokers and the prodders to poke and prod. They assure me, of course, that everything is fine. 'Symptoms akin to a significant concussion', I believe was the expression. Does that sound 'fine' to you?"

I tried to rub my eyes without poking them with the heart rate monitor. "They didn't say anything about me, did they?"

"Not within my earshot, and I'll give them credit for that." She coughed and winced. "Where is that water?"

We sat in silence for a minute or so, both staring at the door that refused to open.

"At least the HLF admits The Presence is a thing now," I murmured, mostly to myself. "Or at least, those who were there with us do. Jamal did, even Astbury did. I think they have Kara convinced too."

"I'm sure Emma didn't concede that willingly, and I'm sure she'll want more data."

"She said as much."

Rosalind fixed her gaze on me. "I'm not doing that again, D."

"I said as much."

"Did you? Good. How is Jess?"

"Okay, last I saw." Where was she? Why wasn't she at my bedside? Not that there was much room for her. "Hopefully, she's fighting the good fight on our behalf," I added hopefully.

Rosalind smiled. "That she can do, our Jess. I don't think she holds up Emma on a pedestal anymore. That will be good for both of them."

I pondered my next question, but I figured that if anyone had a right to ask it, I did. "What did you do, Rosalind? How did you - what's the term you used? - excise the Intrusion, and The Presence along with it? You said you weren't sure, back in Chicago, at the Themis Center. Do you know now?"

Her smile thinned, but she nodded as if she'd expected the question. "I have some idea, although I doubt I can express it in suitably scientific terms. It's not good. On both occasions, it was a purely visceral reaction, but I don't doubt my decades of martial arts training played their part. Do you remember our encounter with Donovan Brooks at Chouteau Village?"

"When he and Lana were imprinting a new memory after we'd just erased six of the damn things?"

"Precisely. Before we could stop or deal with the Imprint, we had to prevent them from interfering. You're big and fit and physically intimidating, and Jess is no slouch, but Donovan was a second-degree black belt. The responsibility, as I saw it, was mine. Yet, even with more credentials to my name, he was larger and more powerful than I. Understanding one's opponent, what may work and what certainly won't work, is key. My best option was the sacrifice throw, to use his own size and strength against him, while taking damage to myself."

"It was awesome!" I said, grinning. "Even if he did break your nose."

She sniffed, then returned my grin before it faded abruptly. "My instincts guided me to do the same thing against The Presence. I absorbed some of that entity's power, then threw it away from me, which was a far more savage act than channeling away a memory during an Erasure. And it took a piece of me with it."

"What do you mean, a piece of you?"

She squirmed in her seat, and glanced at the door, which remained stubbornly closed. "A piece of my soul, or my psyche if you prefer. I don't know what their test data shows, but I can feel an absence, a part of my brain that no longer functions. That's not sustainable, D."

I stared at her in horror. The term "sacrifice throw" had never sounded so sinister. And I wasn't only horrified on her behalf. We'd been connected, me, Rosalind and Jess. Had pieces of our souls been sacrificed too?

"So how do we beat it? How do we beat an opponent like The Presence?"

Her baleful expression was my only answer.

The head medic, an earnest young man with a pencil-thin mustache, and what Rosalind told me later was a Glaswegian accent, kept us another hour for observation. I heard him mutter a word that could have been "anomalies" as he peered at his laptop, before he released us with a strong recommendation to rest. I could tell Kara and Astbury were frustrated, eager to make the most of the time we had left, but by their accounts and her own, Jess had successfully kept them at bay.

"I told them I'm as curious as anyone," she said, as we drove back to our hotel. "And we only have two more days until our flight home. But that was a legit battle, and we all need to nurse our wounds." For her part, she claimed the pain meds had worked. Her nose hadn't bled, at any rate.

Martin arrived mid-afternoon, with an axe to grind. I remembered how furious he'd been a year ago, after Rosalind suffered her broken nose. He'd lashed out at me, and I couldn't blame him.

"I'm sick and tired of you people putting my wife in harm's way, while you hide behind your desks!" he raged, mostly at Kara and Jamal, who stoically absorbed his anger.

Rosalind allowed him to vent, then gently took him by the arm and steered him back to our car. Tense silence accompanied us back to the hotel. Jess and I waved off his muttered apology before the couples parted in the lobby. He had a point, and Rosalind knew it too.

The next morning, I went for a run. Partly, I wanted the exercise. Rosalind had led us in some light training during our visit, but I'd warmed to some British food, especially their meat pies, sausage rolls, and Cornish pasties, and I needed exercise to compensate. But I also wanted to savor my environment.

Shotcombe House's grounds included a perimeter footpath, and I'd seen others running on it. Jess said Charli had offered to show her the basics of how Astbury's model worked, but that she'd join me the next day. I was grateful for the solitude, for a chance to clear my head, and neither the cool breeze nor fitful drizzle deterred me.

I had a lot to think about, but as I jogged along the packed dirt and occasional gravel of the footpath, I allowed my brain to wander. We'd learned a lot. Intrusions sometimes revealed glimpses of the future. The connection Jess and I established by instinct during Erasures and Tethers could extend over distance, and to other empathetic sensitives.

But, of course, many questions remained unanswered. How deep did sympathy or support for the Scales of Equilibrium run within the Henry Lyons Foundation? What exactly was The Presence, and how would the HLF acknowledge its existence going forward?

There were also new questions. One, perhaps less momentous in the grand scheme of things - but which had gnawed at me since Izzy's comment on the day we arrived, was: how much did the HLF really know about my family?

This collision of thoughts almost prevented me noticing the man sitting on a bench next to the path. I'd been climbing a gentle incline directly behind the house, winding through a stand of dense oaks and chestnut trees. My chest felt it, and my stride grew dogged as the slope flattened out into a brief open space. I raised my head and almost stumbled when I recognized him. Carson Livingston, the HLF's head of operations, who I hadn't seen since the meeting in the maze over a week before.

He wore a RedSox baseball cap, navy blue windbreaker, and canvas pants, and watched my approach without expression. I was tempted to offer a token greeting and run on, but I couldn't shake the suspicion he'd been waiting for me.

"I will say the Brits have a fantastic climate for outdoor exercise," he said, cracking a friendly smile as I slowed to a halt, placing my hands atop my head. "If you don't mind a little rain, that is."

I eyed his hiking boots, which looked fresh out of the box. "Not the best footwear for running."

"Oh no, I've never been much of a runner. My doctor tells me walking is an underrated form of exercise, and perfectly adequate for someone my age. I still have to do it, of course." His smile turned self-deprecating, but I couldn't miss the glint of curiosity in his eyes.

A shaft of early-morning sunlight fought through the clouds, and I turned to look through the trees. From this vantage point, I could see over the maze almost directly between the two rear wings of Shotcombe House. The former stately home lured me into its embrace, hinting at history and secrets. Well, one less secret now. The surrounding grounds were still so green, and all I could hear over my heavy breathing was birdsong. Some calls sounded familiar, others were strange to me. I'd been an avid birder as a boy, and could still recognize most native Missouri species by sight and sound. I wished I had the opportunity to learn about the birds I could hear on this run.

"It's beautiful here," I found myself murmuring.

"It is," Carson agreed, and a wistful tone entered his voice. "I think many of us yearn for the promise of such an environment, a quieter, less frenetic life than the one we have. I always have that yearning when I come here, and it speaks to your character that you do too. But, of course, you are soon to return to the hustle and bustle of the big city. Have you found what you came here looking for?"

"Yes, and no," I answered, both truthful and vague.

He chuckled. "Fair enough. Do you think we learned everything we wanted from you?"

I turned back towards him. His manner was relaxed, but I sensed this wasn't a casual conversation - more an exit interview. "You'd have to ask Astbury," I said. "Or maybe Kara. Although, I assume you've already done that."

"Indeed. You've done what very few people have ever done, D. You've rattled them. They're fascinated by you, and by Jess and Rosalind. They're desperate to learn what your abilities are, and how you use them, but they are also, candidly, terrified of you. And perhaps they should be."

I licked my lips and wondered if now was a good time to resume my run. Carson unsettled me, and I couldn't explain why. "You use the word 'they' a lot. Aren't you one of them too?"

"Of course," he said, but his expression darkened, not helped by the scar on his cheek. "We're all part of the same organization. But, as I suspect you've both heard and seen, we're not all in perfect alignment. Outside of agreeing that there are real phenomena worthy of study, there is much diversity of opinion in what the Foundation should or should not do about them."

"And what's your opinion?"

"Me? I think we spend an inordinate amount of time worrying about how to best confine or eliminate the phenomena. Are they truly such a bad thing? Henry Lyons didn't think so. Worthy of study and understanding, certainly. Humanity studies natural phenomena such as hurricanes and tornadoes, not so we can prevent or eliminate them - because we can't - but to increase our chances of surviving them. Are Intrusions really that different?"

"Clearly they hurt people," I countered, recalling the beds full of coma patients I'd seen in Chicago. "And they make life hell for others. Perhaps they're more like allergens. You want to learn how to live with them, but also find ways to reduce them too."

Carson inclined his head. "An interesting analogy. Do you know why so many people struggle with pollen allergies these days, especially in the cities? Because there's so much more pollen than there used to be. City planners in the mid-twentieth century decided to solve the 'problem' of seeds and fruits clogging their newly laid out residential streets by planting only male trees. But male trees do what males of any species want to do: procreate. Now, there's nowhere for all that pollen to go, and surprise, we humans can't adapt to it fast enough. In solving one problem, we created another, arguably a worse one. Sometimes, it's best to leave well enough alone."

I pondered this, as I pondered him. Carson hadn't spoken much at our "tribunal" in the center of the maze, other than to spar with Jamal. He was the first person I'd met in the Foundation who was less than gung ho about tethering Intrusions, although I remembered Rosalind's handlers who'd taken over from Jamal in St. Louis. They'd turned out to be Scales operatives, attacking Donovan Brooks and putting him in a coma. I wondered where they were now.

Wasn't Carson supposed to discuss these attacks with us? I wanted to ask, but decided on a subtle approach. "Do you think we humans are screwing up the environment, Carson?"

He raised his eyebrows. "Do you disagree?"

"No. But I think there are better and worse ways to handle that situation, just like there are better and worse ways to handle Imprints and Intrusions."

"Are you suggesting I'm a Scales of Equilibrium sympathizer?"

So much for subtlety. His tone was mild, but he stared me down with a flinty gaze.

"Are you?"

"Just because someone doesn't agree that the proactive tethering of Intrusions should be our only strategy, doesn't mean they support or sympathize with Allen Weston and his band of fanatics. There are more than two paths, you know."

"Perhaps. Did you know him well?"

"Weston? Not particularly. He was as driven as Astbury, although he didn't have the same scientific mind. Few do, to be fair. He's a fabulous orator, or rabble rouser if you prefer. I can easily imagine how he could build himself a following. A born cult leader. Have you ever met him?"

"Not exactly. I've heard him speak though."

"So you know. You'd be prepared, if you were ever to seek him out."

"Why would I seek him out?"

Carson paused, as if he'd said something he hadn't meant to. "The man has a lot of theories," he continued, speaking slower and more quietly, as if there were spies in the trees. "Some of them are wild, but not all. No-one attracts a following without kernels of truth. You, your fiancée, and your friend, have recently encountered an entity, something powerful that none of us understand. Weston encountered it first. He called it the Agency before he started prattling on about Gaia. Amidst all his new age, superstitious hocus pocus, he likely knows more about that entity than any other person alive. If you're looking for answers, he might have them."

My Fitbit vibrated, apparently under the impression I'd finished my day's exercise. I needed to get back to the house. This conversation had unnerved me and given me even more to think about. But I had one more question.

"Have you ever encountered that entity yourself?"

Carson shook his head, but not before I noticed a flash of anger twist his face. "No. I've never been sensitive myself. That was always my daughter. She was quite the rising star in the Foundation, not unlike yourself. Bought into the entire tethering philosophy. You and Jess aren't the first to form some kind of psychic connection, you know. She and another did, a decade ago. But we never got a chance to study it, like we have with you."

"Why not?"

All emotion drained from his face. "Because she died, D."

Chapter Eight
A Conduit

The early morning drizzle accelerated into a full-blown down-pour by the time I completed my run. I'd brought a towel and a change of shirt with me, but our car was locked and Rosalind had the key. The guards rewarded me with strange looks as I passed through front-door security, which I took as silent comment on my soaked clothes and dripping hair. I offered them a sheepish smile in return and hurried down to the restroom in a mostly futile attempt to tidy myself up.

Entering the meeting room, I was surprised to find everyone glued to the TV screens, which were on for the first time. Within seconds, I understood why.

A young British news anchor spoke in solemn tones alongside a live aerial shot of the North Point nuclear power station. The cooling towers and brutalist rectangular blocks of the plant squatted by the shore of Lake Michigan, just south of the Illinois border with Wisconsin, about fifty miles north of mine and Jess's Lincoln Park apartment. Plumes of white smoke billowed from the towers as a news helicopter circled at a distance. The lurid red banner at the bottom of the screen read "NORTH POINT DISASTER: CHICAGO EVACUATION PANIC".

"What happened?" I demanded, standing frozen in place behind my chair.

Jess reached up from her seat to take my hand, her face fearful. "They're not saying much yet, just that there've been 'multiple incidents' with the reactors. Everyone's guessing at least one meltdown, if not two. All we know for sure is that emergency services are evacuating everyone within a twenty-mile radius. The entire metro area is panicking, and they've deployed the national guard to maintain order. Good luck with that, as you can imagine."

I glanced at Jamal and Izzy, who both lived on Chicago's North Shore, not that far from us. Jamal watched the news coverage stony-faced, texting rapidly on his phone. Streaks of smudged black eyeliner trailed down Izzy's face, horror in her eyes. Charli sat next to her, looking unsettled, as if she wanted to give more comfort, but feared the consequences.

Rosalind, holding Martin's hand atop the table, turned away from the broadcast with a grim expression. As she met my eyes, I guessed what she was thinking. Was this the attack on Chicago their son, Daniel, had warned us about three months ago? Was he still there, amid the growing panic? What role had he played, if any?

I dared not ask any of those questions aloud, not here.

"Have you heard from your grandpa?" I asked Jess instead, and she shook her head.

"Dad's been trying to reach him, but without success, last I heard. Grandpa could just be out walking his dogs. He never takes his cellphone with him. My work chat is blowing up though. It's chaos there. All the highways are gridlocked already, and there are reports of looting. Half my coworkers are trying to get away as soon as they can, the others are trying to shelter in place. I tried messaging the Millers too, to check on our apartment building, but no reply yet."

"Communications are spotty," Jamal interjected, not looking up from his phone. "The cell network is close to overwhelmed. This is going to get much worse before it gets any better."

I tried calling Luca Capelli, my boss, but got no answer. He refused to text, claiming it was too impersonal, so I didn't bother trying. I had better luck with his niece, Alaska, who'd taken over my vegetables station and occasionally hit me up with questions. *Restaurant's closed. Trying to make uncle leave, at least for a few days. Stay in England if you can.*

My half-sisters, Fiona and Mary, sent me a flurry of messages, expressing concern and urging me and Jess to return to St. Louis, at least until more was known about the Chicago situation. I still wasn't used to their concern, especially Mary, with whom I'd shared mutual loathing until very recently, after our mom died. Mary had thawed considerably, especially after Jess and I announced our engagement. But I wasn't sure I was ready to live with either of them, even temporarily.

I sank into the chair beside Jess and wrapped my arm around her shoulder. She burrowed into my embrace, and for a while we just sat there, listening to, but not watching, the news broadcast. It was too awful.

"Let's review your options," David announced, muting the news feed. The Henry Lyons Foundation director had entered the meeting room a few hours after I arrived, stopping to grasp hands and shoulders in the manner of someone comforting a grieving relative.

The mood was somber. For collective stunned dismay, sitting in my high school classroom after the 9/11 attacks was its sole rival. Only Astbury had ventured to suggest we pursue further research, to "take our minds off what you cannot control", and had slunk away in frustration, taking Charli with her.

"No one wants to work today, David," Jamal said mildly.

"I completely understand. No one expects you to. Well, almost no one. But I was thinking longer term. I believe you're all scheduled to fly back to America on Saturday, the day after tomorrow, correct? Has anyone contacted your airline? You may find your flight has already been canceled, and rescheduling to be more difficult than you think."

"It has been canceled," Martin confirmed, waving his phone in resignation. "All flights to Chicago have been canceled until further notice, and the airline's booking website is offline."

David nodded. "The shockwave of the North Point power plant attack is only on its first circuit around the country, if not the world. This will magnify all real and imagined border crises. Faith in law enforcement and the security of critical infrastructure, already eroding, will diminish further. There are already calls to shut down, at least temporarily, all other nuclear reactors in America, but there isn't enough power generation capacity from other sources to compensate. You can expect brownouts, especially in the major cities, where civil unrest is already brewing."

"Are you telling us we shouldn't go home?" Jess demanded, with more than a hint of defiance.

"Not at all. Simply that, given the prevailing expert opinions I just summarized, returning to the day-to-day lives you enjoyed before your visit is impossible, at least in the short term. Even those of you not living in Chicago," he continued, looking aside at Rosalind and Martin, who gazed back at him impassively. "The Foundation is in a position to help, and I would like to do so. I want to put you all on the payroll."

I glanced at Jess and saw my surprise echoed in her expression.

"What does that mean, precisely?" asked Rosalind.

"A limited-term contract, for now, to be 'consultants' with the Foundation. I'm sure we can devise convincing roles that best utilize your individual skills. There will be a stipend for those whose paychecks may be interrupted," he said, looking directly at me, "and to provide for temporary housing if necessary. We also have some influence with UK Visas and Immigration, so if you choose to remain here longer term, we can grease those wheels."

"And what if we want to go back to the States?" I said. "No offense, and we're grateful for the offer and your hospitality and all, but our lives are there. In Chicago, especially."

David shrugged, equal parts sympathy and helplessness. "I understand. In your shoes, I'd want the same thing. But it's unclear when, or even if, you can return to your apartment, much less to your jobs and daily lives. We'll know more in the coming hours and days. Would it be so bad to wait it out here, away from the chaos?"

I caught Jess's eye. We'd had time to explore all kinds of possibilities in hushed conversation, as the North Point disaster unfolded on TV screens. She looked as frightened as I felt, but also determined. We couldn't just sit still and "wait it out", trapped in a foreign country.

"What if we wanted to go back, but not to Chicago?" I asked him. "Or St. Louis either. What if we went back to look for something?"

"To look for what?"

Jess took over. "Have you heard about our latest misadventure with The Presence? Everyone accepts the damn thing exists now, and that it's powerful. But no one can agree on much else, because we simply don't have the information. Not here. There's one person, however, who may have the answers we need."

"No." David shook his head emphatically. To his left, Izzy sat bolt upright in her chair and stared at Jess with her familiar, hungry expression. Jamal looked both worried and thoughtful.

"No?" Jess stood up and planted her hands on her hips. I scooted my chair back a pace or two.

"If you're talking about tracking down Allen Weston, then no. The Foundation broke off all contact from that lunatic years ago. He is both unhinged and dangerous, especially with the rabble with which he's surrounded himself. If you seek more information about his 'Agency' - your 'Presence' - the HLF has some of the finest analytical minds in the world at its disposal. With more research—"

"We're not doing more research," Jess snapped. "Not about that, not in that way. We don't know what long-term damage

D and Rosalind suffered from our last experiment, maybe me too. We're not so desperate that we're ready to risk everything, not yet. And we're not naive. We have as much, if not more, first-hand experience with the Scales of Equilibrium, Weston's 'rabble', as anyone here. We even have FBI contacts who might help."

Martin shifted in his chair, but kept his own counsel.

David frowned at Jess, raking his hair. "Even if you found Weston, do you think he'd simply tell you what you want to know?"

"Depends on how we find him," I said quietly. "But I think we need to try. Too much rides on the answers."

We argued for another ten or fifteen minutes. Izzy threw in vocal support for our plan, and even Jamal, while expressing reservations about our safety, thought it had merit.

Rosalind was strangely quiet, following the conversation but brooding, as if unwilling to share what opinions or ideas she had. She finally spoke up as David protested, for the third time, that the HLF was unwilling to fund a manhunt for Allen Weston. "And if we choose to do so on our 'own dime', as they say in America?"

He blinked, almost as if he'd forgotten she was there. "What do you mean?"

"We aren't without funds," Rosalind said impatiently. "Martin and I have more than enough put aside to help our friends through troubling times. If the HLF's assistance comes with such unreasonable strings attached, if our cooperation and effort and the risks we've taken on your behalf mean so little to you, then we will go our own way and solve the problem ourselves."

Martin's phone chose that moment to start vibrating. Rosalind spared it a look of immense irritation before her husband scooped it off the table with an apology, and stepped out of the room to answer.

"Even if it risks handing your unique abilities directly to him? To the man who's used his notion of an Agency to drive all this?" David waved his hand at the talking heads debating in silence on the screen behind him. "Even if it risks more carnage?"

"What do you think we're going to do?" I said. "Join Weston's band of merry maniacs, and help unleash The Presence on humanity? After what we've seen? We're just after information. We can take care of ourselves."

I hoped that was true.

David stared at me, then at the rest of us, one by one. "You're all resolved on this? I see. Very well. Let me see what I can do about your flights. In return, please work with Astbury as much as you can. Your contributions to our understanding of the Intrusion phenomena have already been significant, and not unappreciated."

One of North Point power station's reactors had partially melted down, much like at Three Mile Island back in 1979. The other had been "scrammed" before it sustained any significant damage. This was explained, over and over again, as the emergency insertion of all reactor control rods into the core, stopping potentially explosive nuclear reactions in their tracks. Each repetition of this explanation somehow reassured me less.

Despite increasingly wild speculation on social media, the official stance was careful to avoid calling it an attack. But they weren't calling it an accident either: "incident" appeared to be the preferred term. No-one was buying it, certainly not me, Jess and Rosalind.

Was this what the Scales of Equilibrium had planned at the Themis Center? Was Daniel involved? It would scarcely be credible for a fringe, supposedly pro-environment terrorist group, were they not causing increasing havoc worldwide. The public were finally taking notice, and American cities weren't the only ones simmering with anxiety and unrest.

Illinois state police established a quarantine zone around the North Point plant. Although the reactor operator and Nuclear Regulatory Commission assured the public that radiation release had been minimal, that didn't stem the exodus from the Chicago metro area. It looked like our prospects for returning home, while not without risk, might be possible one day, but not soon. Whether there would be jobs and a life waiting for us was an open question.

Jess and I were deeply grateful to Rosalind for her offer of support, should we need it. She waved it off, as though we'd been foolish to believe anything else. "Besides," she said with disdain, as we drove back to our hotels that afternoon, "for all David Taylor's bluster, I'd be surprised if the HLF doesn't provide some sort of assistance. Whether you want to get on the payroll is your decision."

While we fretted about all this and awaited news of our return flights, we used our last official day at Shotcombe House to help Astbury with one more experiment. The brusque lead researcher made an effort to show sympathy and concern about the North Point disaster and our plight, but she tightened her lips when one of her technicians asked us if we were really going to hunt down Allen Weston.

"Enough idle chatter," she barked. "I need everyone to focus if we're going to achieve anything today."

She split us into two groups, and we drove to the outskirts of Worcester, a town whose name I stumbled over repeatedly, much to Jess's amusement. "WUSS-tuh," she said slowly for the tenth time, as if speaking to a child. Only her impish grin saved her from my recriminations.

Jess and Jamal rode with Rosalind. Martin went with them, determined not to leave his wife alone with anyone from the HLF. Izzy and I accompanied Astbury to a nondescript, modern-looking row house on a quiet residential street. Its only remarkable feature was the cold that prickled my skin upon entry. Team Jess had invaded an antique store in the high street, whose owner had closed for the day.

"You're almost a quarter mile apart," Astbury announced, phone in hand. "D, I want you and Izzy to connect and re-tether this Imprint. Jess or Rosalind will try to connect with Jamal and do the same. I want to see if you can perceive each other."

The word jarred memories of The Presence, and I caught Izzy's eye as I struggled for the inner calm necessary to focus on handling an Imprint. For the first time I could remember, her eye makeup included a color other than black: half moons of bright pink mirrored the same color on her eyelids. The effect was disconcerting. More so was the quiet broodiness that had replaced her typical snark and arrogance. I wondered if she had family and friends in Chicago, and if they were in danger. I knew little about her background; she had deflected any conversation in that direction.

She cocked her head, appearing to come to life. "You ready for this, D? I'll handle the Tether if you want to focus on the connection."

I still felt a pang of guilt as my awareness reached for and combined with Izzy's. In some ways, it was a more intimate act than a physical embrace. Where Jess was all beguiling warm caress, Izzy's sinuous consciousness concealed jagged edges at her core. She clung to me all the same, and I forced myself to ignore her very real and attractive body little more than an arm's reach away.

I suppressed the sudden taste of blood and the screams of rage, as she picked the Imprint's Single Point Lock, and looked beyond the young couple whose violent argument had scarred their home for all to see who could. Cautiously, alert for any sign of The Presence, I probed outside the memory, not really understanding what that meant in terms of real space. I tried not to think, just to open myself up, to search for the familiar signatures of Jess's or Rosalind's spirits. I sensed urgency from

Izzy, and then I felt it too: a vast power in the far distance, like the cloud front of a hurricane barreling across hundreds of miles of ocean. But, at the same moment, I found her, an emerald glittering in the void. Jess. And she wasn't alone. Our consciousnesses touched - *It's you! It's really you!* - and we shared one magical moment of sheer exhilaration, before I was yanked away.

Frustration yielded to panic, but before I could figure out where The Presence was, Izzy folded up the memory with incredible speed and precision, locking it in place.

"Holy shit!" she gasped, clutching at my arms, her alarming eyes wide as they bored into mine. We both trembled as we supported each other, and I couldn't think of anything to say. *Holy shit* pretty much summed it up.

"That was... remarkable," breathed Astbury. She cupped her hand over her phone as she talked low and rapidly into it.

Jess all but launched herself into my embrace when we regrouped back at Shotcombe House. There were no words; we both still reeled at the implications of what we'd done. I watched over her shoulder as Charli approached Astbury, head cocked in question.

Astbury nodded. "You were right, Charli. Good instincts. Intrusions can act as a conduit, at least over short distances. This is revolutionary."

She rotated her wheelchair in search of Rosalind, who stood with a fresh cup of tea in hand next to an impassive Martin. The corner of Astbury's mouth quirked upwards. "My, Rosalind. When you lot do head back across The Pond, I hope I can rely on you to help nurture these new abilities."

"That depends on how and when we return," Rosalind replied.

"Yes. Well, we still have the pub booked tonight for your farewell dinner. Be a shame not to share a table again, properly this time." Astbury glanced at Martin, then smiled, for the first time, with what appeared to be genuine warmth. "Your husband is striking, isn't he? Quite the catch for the young rebel from Stow."

Rosalind laughed and diffused all the tension in the room. Even Martin smiled sheepishly. "Oh, I'm not sure who caught who."

"Then you'll each have to tell me your side of the story over dinner, and I'll decide."

"I'd like that. It would be good to finally catch up properly."

I felt a tap on my arm and turned to see Charli had sidled up alongside me. Her expression was serious, uninfected by others' good cheer. "Something happened while you were in Worcester. Something you should know about."

I tensed. Already on edge, despite Astbury and Rosalind's conviviality, I raised my eyebrows. "What happened?"

"You remember Madam Sophia? The psychic you lot met in Chipping Camden? Her house burned down this morning."

"What the fuck?" I snarled, and she shrank back in alarm. Jess gripped my arm, but I shook her off, suddenly furious. "The HLF was supposed to protect her. *I* was supposed to protect her! I gave her my word!"

"We tried! But we don't have the resources to watch over someone twenty-four seven. I'm sorry, D."

"It's not your fault, Charli," Jess told her in a fierce voice, scowling at me. "Is Madam Sophia safe? Was she hurt?"

Charli shook her head. "I don't know, sorry. Kara said we were going to take care of her, but wouldn't say any more."

"We'll fucking see about that." Before Jess could protest, I stormed up the staircase and along the corridor to Kara's office. One Scales attack had displaced untold thousands of my fellow Chicagoans, preventing us from returning to life in our new home city, but I wasn't responsible for that. I *was* responsible, as I saw it, for Madam Sophia. The fact that she'd foreseen her home's destruction in a recent Imprint filled me with a creeping dread.

I rapped on Kara's office door, but didn't wait for a reply before thrusting it open. They looked up at me in alarm and rose from the seat behind their desk.

"D! What's the meaning—"

"Madam Sophia," I growled. "Charli just told me the news. Is she hurt? Where is she?"

Their eyes flared before darting to the open office door. "I can't tell you. It's—"

I slammed my fist down on their desk, dislodging a pile of papers that half-collapsed onto the floor. I was losing my temper and powerless to stop it. "Don't give me that secretive bullshit, Kara! She asked for our help. She asked for *my* help! Where is she?!"

"She's unhurt," Kara gasped, raising their palms as if to ward me off. "We got to her in time, but I can't tell you where she is, for her own safety."

They talked rapidly, stepping backwards as I rounded the desk. One of my flailing hands collided with a monitor, and it crashed to the floor.

I paused, breathing hard, and stared at the broken glass around my feet. When I raised my head again, I met the fear in their eyes with horror in my own.

"Shit. It really happened." I sagged, then stumbled backward until I could slump into a chair. I forced myself to breathe, to slow my racing heart. I was appalled, both at my abrupt loss of control and at unintentionally fulfilling a predicted event. I'd watched this exact argument play out the day I arrived at Shotcombe House, in an Imprint.

I'd become the unwitting subject of the very phenomenon that now plagued my life.

The clink of a glass on the desktop roused me. I looked up to see Kara pouring a finger's width of some golden brown liquid into it, then again into their own glass.

"Twelve-year-old Glenmorangie," they murmured, taking their own seat once more. "Best I have on hand."

"Sorry," I mumbled. "I... I don't know what came over me, why I was so angry. I'll pay for the monitor."

They shook their head and took a deep breath of their own. "Don't worry about it. You're under a lot of stress. I'm not always the best with words. Sorry. It was close, but Madam Sophia escaped her home and any serious injury. The fire brigade got there in time to save neighboring homes, but hers is too damaged for her to return. We've offered to put her up in a bed-and-breakfast until it can be repaired, and she will be protected full time. But we're restricting that information, and I think it's best that you don't know the details."

They locked eyes with me as my defiance battled my shame. For the first time, I noticed that one iris was a distinctly lighter shade than the other, more hazel than brown.

"Fine," I said at last. "As long as she's safe. Sorry, again. There's no excuse for losing my temper like that, with you or Charli."

They nodded their acknowledgement, then bit their lip. "Is it still your intent to search for Allen Weston?"

"It's on our list," I said warily. I hadn't decided if I could trust Kara, especially after the stunt I'd just pulled.

"You don't have to give me details," they said, as if reading my thoughts. They pulled a folded piece of notepaper out of their desk drawer and offered it to me. "But unless you already have leads, I may be able to help. This is the address and phone number of the location where Marcus Kunstler and Adam Zimmerman are enjoying Foundation hospitality. The Scales operatives who attacked you and Jess in Chicago."

"Yeah, I know who they are." I took the paper and read the address. Looked like we were headed back to Illinois. "You won't tell me where Sophia is, but you're giving me this?"

They grimaced. "I'm more concerned about her safety than theirs. But D?"

I raised my eyes to meet Kara's earnest, mismatching ones. "Yeah?"

"Please don't mention this to anyone else. Let's just keep it between us."

I held their gaze for several heartbeats, then stuffed the paper in my jeans pocket. "Sure. Can we go to dinner now?"

Chapter Nine
SAFE TRAVELS

It was an odd farewell dinner, because when we all sat down at the ten-person table in a cozy private room at The Plough, no one knew when those of us from the United States would be leaving.

"We're working on it," David apologized, after ordering half a dozen bottles of red wine. "Carson's pulling some strings, but there's only so much he can do."

"Maybe we can go see some sights after all," said Jess, tackling her Beef Wellington with relish. The taste she allowed me was better than my insipid chicken pub curry, but my dessert of Eton Mess saved the meal.

Astbury and the Hills huddled at one end of the table like old friends. Charli had accepted my shamefaced apology for belligerence, but spent the meal absorbed in quiet conversation with Izzy. Jamal tapped on his phone under the table, while Kara and I shared an awkward silence. David held forth, reeling off one anecdote after another, then plied us with increasingly improbable travel advice. "Hire a boat and sail around the Scottish Isles," he suggested, wine sloshing in his glass, but never spilling. Jess got the giggles and finally excused herself to "powder my nose".

Uncertainty over our immediate plans aside, a lavish meal in an English country pub was a pleasant end to the day. I relaxed as we drove back to our hotel, nestled in the backseat with an equally drowsy Jess. We'd worry about tomorrow when it arrived. We tumbled into bed, but it was a long time before we thought about sleep.

My phone buzzed me awake in the murky pre-dawn, the promise of daylight infiltrating the edges of the curtains. I cursed and rolled over, careful not to disturb a softly snoring Jess. Her phone vibrated too, from somewhere on the floor it sounded like. I cursed, wondering if I should find it for her. When mine buzzed again, twice in quick succession, I sighed and heaved myself up to sit on the edge of the bed, rubbing too little sleep from my eyes. I read the three texts, all from Rosalind, then shook Jess awake.

"Daniel's been arrested," I told her.

We threw clothes on and met Rosalind in the breakfast room. I wasn't hungry, but grabbed coffees before joining the ladies in the corner. However tired I felt was nothing compared to how exhausted Rosalind looked, as if she hadn't slept all night.

"We got the call just after returning to our room," she said, voice muted and lifeless. "Well, Martin did, from Special Agent Jones. I suppose I should thank her this time. She's claimed jurisdiction over the case, and has Daniel in her custody." Jess reached out and took Rosalind's shaking hand in hers.

"Where?" I asked. "How?"

"She wouldn't tell us much over the phone. Martin got the impression Danny turned himself in, but... I don't know. I don't know anything anymore."

Rosalind hung her head, as vulnerable and desolate as I'd ever seen her. I didn't like it, and neither did Jess.

"Where's Martin?" she demanded. "Why leave you alone to explain this?"

"Oh." Rosalind looked up, emotion kindling in her eyes. "He'll be down in a minute. He's packing. That's the other thing I had to tell you. The FBI are sending a plane to fly us back to the States, all of us. You need to be packed and ready to go by noon."

We gaped at her.

"Of course," said Jess, digesting this news along with her coffee. "Any idea where we're going? Have you told the HLF? What about Izzy and Jamal?"

Rosalind smiled with something like her usual demeanor. "Always the barrage of questions, Jess. No, I don't know where they're holding Daniel. I sent a message to Emma before you joined me, but haven't heard back. I suggest you reach out to the others. I believe the offer of transportation, at least, is extended to them. And don't sign anything if you don't want to. I meant what I said about taking care of our friends the other day."

"Let's go," I told Jess. We passed Martin on our way to the stairs, and my companionable handshake morphed into a hug.

"Daniel's safe?" I murmured.

He gave me a wintry smile. "For now. Rosalind's filled you in?"

"We're off to pack now."

That didn't take long, but we both jumped into the shower, despite its daily struggle with water pressure and heat. We had no idea when or where we'd next have the chance. Then I called Jamal and explained the situation, leaving Izzy to Jess.

"I heard," he said. "Astbury called me ten minutes ago. I assume you're not stopping by Shotcombe House first?"

"Do we need to?"

"That depends on if you're taking David up on his offer. Sign up as consultants, and earn the full weight of Foundation support behind you."

I glanced at Jess, sitting cross-legged in the middle of the bed. We'd discussed this.

"I'm not convinced the full weight of the Foundation is what we need right now. Not if it comes with strings attached. What do you think?"

"Me?" Jamal paused, and the line bumped and crackled as if he was changing his grip on his phone. "I'm the last person to advocate for the fidelity of the Henry Lyons Foundation. I recruited you in good faith, because you needed the training, and, if I'm honest, because I hoped you'd shake things up. Which you did. But if you have means to do what you want to do, to hunt down Allen Weston, then do it. Just be careful."

"Thank you. We will. Are you traveling back to the States with us?"

"No. There are reasons for me to stay here another day or two. Have a safe trip and keep in touch. Even if you stay off the HLF payroll, I still consider you my students!"

Two unmarked white sedans drew up in front of the hotel entrance promptly at noon. The English weather had conjured persistent, soaking rain to see us off, but the stocky, gray-haired man who stepped out of the first car appeared unhurried as he entered the lobby to greet us.

"Detective Inspector Andrew McCoist, Scotland Yard," he said, introducing himself and shaking each of our hands in turn. Deep lines scoured his clean-shaven face, but piercing blue eyes projected vigor and intelligence. "It's just the four of you, aye?"

I blinked. The variety of accents in this country continued to amaze me, and everyone acted like they understood each other perfectly. I guessed he hailed from somewhere in Scotland. I resisted leaning forward to distinguish one word from the next.

"Yes, I believe so," said Martin. Izzy had also declined the offer of a flight back to the States. Although, according to Jess, who'd spoken with her, she hadn't been happy about it. The HLF probably didn't want her getting mixed up in our pursuit of Allen Weston.

McCoist cracked a broad smile, as if ferrying stranded tourists from their hotel to the airport was a highlight of his job. "All fine. We've time to wait out this wee rain shower, or we can be on our way. You're ready to go? That's the spirit! Two of youse ride with me, and the others with DS Nasar." He gestured toward a younger, solemn woman, standing just inside the entrance door, holding a black golfing umbrella above her perfectly manicured head. "You'll be safe with both of us, but I have the better jokes!"

I wasn't sorry when Rosalind and Martin elected to join McCoist. As pleasant and disarming as he was, I wasn't sure I could endure his endless torrent of affable good humor.

"Where are we going?" I asked DS Nasar, once Jess and I had stowed our luggage in "the boot", and buckled our seatbelts. "Heathrow's still closed, isn't it?"

"Mostly, yes," she said, turning around in her front passenger seat. I still thought of it as the driver's seat and suppressed a moment of panic that she'd taken her eyes off the road. "We're flying you out of Manchester."

"How far is that?"

"A couple of hours, depending on Birmingham traffic."

She was cordial enough, but refrained from speaking unless we asked questions. I guessed she was the perfect foil for the garrulous DI McCoist. After establishing they worked together on a task force investigating terrorist financing, and often liaised with the FBI and Special Agent Jones, we lapsed into brooding silence. I gazed at the scenery through heavily tinted windows, wondering if I'd ever return to enjoy it without other obligations.

Scotland Yard's finest ushered us through security at the smaller Manchester Airport and directly to our gate. Smaller than Heathrow perhaps, but still larger and far busier than Lambert Field in St. Louis. We were glad to have the escort. The main passenger concourse seethed with worried, frustrated, and short-tempered passengers, victims of long-delayed or canceled flights. They spilled out of restaurants and retail stores, entire families sprawling on the floor amidst the debris of their luggage. Tension simmered, threatening to boil over at any moment. For the first time in my life, I took comfort in the company of law enforcement.

At the gate, we descended stairs and emerged onto the tarmac. I felt like I was in a spy movie, hurrying through persistent rain towards a sleek Gulfstream jet painted white with blue and red trim. Special Agent Jones huddled under an umbrella at the bottom of the steps leading up to the plane. A taller white guy with a buzz cut stood alongside her, also dressed in a black suit. Jones looked exasperated, whether at the rain or waiting for us, or both.

"Carmella, good to see you again, lass!" McCoist beamed as he reached out to shake her hand, but his charming Scottish brogue elicited no more than a tight smile.

"Traffic bad, Andrew? We could've used a private airfield."

McCoist shook his head, expression sobering. "Not anymore. They've locked down UK airspace. Manchester was as close as we could get at short notice." He withdrew a large brown envelope from under his rain jacket, and passed it to Jones, who exchanged it for a smaller one. He cocked his head and favored us with one last crooked grin. "Alright, you lot. Safe travels. Be a pal, and help this lovely lady out."

Jones snorted and started up the steps. We mumbled our thanks and followed.

The inside of the jet was utilitarian rather than luxurious, more minibus than limousine. I wasn't complaining. For one thing, I could stretch out my legs without jamming them under a row of seats. Rosalind, facing me and buckling her seatbelt, chuckled as I sighed in contentment. "This will ruin Economy class for D forever."

"I could get used to it," I confessed, then looked up as Jones and the other agent took the two seats across the aisle. He said nothing at all, merely scrutinized us with vaguely distrustful curiosity.

"Comfortable, are we?" Jones said, wrestling her seatbelt around her. "Good. We have much to discuss." Then she closed her eyes, and appeared to doze while the plane taxied, then took off, scything through the clouds as it left England in its wake. I suppressed a sigh of regret. It really would be nice to visit when we could just enjoy the sights.

Jones stirred as a musical chime announced the lifting of seatbelt restrictions, which she took immediate advantage of. "Right then. You've all been busy since our last meeting. I want to hear all about the Henry Lyons Foundation and their connections to The Scales of Equilibrium. But, as a courtesy to you, Martin, since you've provided invaluable assistance to our ongoing investigations, let's discuss your son first."

Rosalind left her seatbelt fastened, but leaned toward the agents. The one who'd finally introduced himself as Drake Levitz propped open a laptop, so she addressed Jones directly.

"Where are we going? Where is Daniel?"

"Denver. We're hoping to land at a military base outside the city, and avoid the headaches of the main airport." She grimaced. "Commercial US airspace has its own challenges, not least of which is the loss of the Chicago airports, and a significant chunk of air corridor above them. We're holding Daniel in a secure location in the area."

"A secure location?" Martin peered around his wife, frowning. "A police station holding cell?"

"No. He was arrested under a federal warrant, and he's in our custody. I can't tell you exactly where, because I won't know myself until we land. It's for his own protection. He's safe, for now."

Neither Martin nor Rosalind appeared reassured. "What do you mean 'his own protection'?" Rosalind demanded. "Protection from whom?"

Jones met her challenging gaze levelly, but there was a hint of sympathy in her eyes. "I've been trying to understand your son's involvement with the Scales of Equilibrium since our first meeting. Before he arrived at the Themis Center, he'd already spent six months in Chicago after being discharged from a similar facility in Denver. He contacted you in July, allegedly warning you about an imminent attack on Chicago, which may or may not have anything to do with the North Point disaster. Not long before, he emphatically rebuffed you when he met D and Jess on the walking trail. Why the change of heart? If it was a change of heart."

"If? It was the first direct contact we've had from him in years!"

"Indeed. But he never mentioned an attack, or that anything bad was going to happen to your friends. Just that he wanted them out of town. Perhaps you read something into his messages that wasn't there."

"I may not have seen Daniel in years," Rosalind said coldly. "But I think I understand him better than you do."

"Perhaps," Jones said, with an unapologetic shrug. "Nothing happened on the date he gave you. Only he can tell us for certain, and since he refuses to speak to anyone but D, we'll all have to wait a little longer to find out."

It took a moment for everyone, including me, to register what she'd said. All heads swiveled in my direction. Rosalind gave me a grim smile, while Martin looked like I'd sprouted an extra head.

"Why me?" I asked, as much to myself as anyone else. "That one time I met Daniel, he basically told me to back off." I didn't mention his staged threat of implicating me in the death of a fellow ex-con. Rosalind was upset enough.

"It must be your magnetic personality, love," quipped Jess, but the frown creasing her forehead suggested she imagined other reasons.

Jones shook her head. "He didn't explain. He hasn't said much of anything since walking into a suburban Denver police station yesterday morning."

"So it's true? He turned himself in?" Martin sounded horrified. Rosalind closed her eyes and shuddered.

Jones turned to her colleague. "What were his exact words to the desk officer?"

"Let's see here," Agent Levitz murmured, fingers dancing over his laptop trackpad. He cleared his throat. "'My name is Daniel Hill. I'm with the Scales of Equilibrium, and I've just come from Chicago and the North Point power station. Tell the FBI I want to talk to D Rodriguez.'"

"The Bureau's agents in Denver were on the scene in minutes, and I heard within the hour," Jones continued. "Daniel refuses to say anything more, other than to repeat D's name. I had him moved immediately by people I trust to protect a potential witness and asset. Protection from whom? If his overture is genuine, I doubt the Scales of Equilibrium are happy with him at all."

Chapter Ten
GAIA DESERVES BETTER

I never expected an FBI safe house to be so frumpy.

Nestled halfway along a quiet, semi-circular street on the edge of the Denver suburbs, with the white-capped Rockies marching along the horizon in the background, the interior of the modest two story home was as floral as its exquisite front yard. Curtains, cushions, blankets, and tablecloths vied with the wallpaper to bring the garden inside, a riot of color accented by carpets and cluttered furniture.

The home was clean, immaculate, and incredibly claustrophobic. I kept waiting in vain for someone's grandma to totter in from the kitchen, carrying a plate of chocolate chip cookies.

In an effort to be inconspicuous, Agent Levitz and I posed as electricians, rolling up in a standard issue white transit van with the words "THOMSON ELECTRIC" painted on each side. Both of us dressed in jeans, work boots, and navy blue work shirts with the company logo on our chests. I'd been surprised and impressed that the gear all fit so well. Someone had done their homework on me, but as Jess said, my shoe and pants sizes were the least of what the FBI likely knew about me. Lots of people knew more about me than I was comfortable with.

The twenty-something redheaded agent, who didn't introduce herself after letting us inside, led us through the botanical overload of the living room into a plainer kitchen. Daniel sat at a four-seater kitchen table, which might have been hewn from a single slice of California Redwood. He looked terrible.

Scraggly, unwashed hair framed his gaunt face, whose patchy stubble appeared undecided about how to form a proper beard. Scotch tape held together the two halves of his eyeglasses, from which bloodshot eyes peered at me. The hands cupping a sunflower-themed coffee mug trembled, and I doubted it was from fear. Or, at least, I hoped it wasn't.

With as much calm as I could muster, I set down my red steel tool chest, drew out one of the ladder-back kitchen chairs, and sat. Daniel watched me warily, but didn't say anything until Agent Levitz extracted the laptop from his tool chest and propped it open on the table.

"I only want to talk to D," Daniel said in a lifeless monotone. This was a far cry from the brash, confident Scales of Equilibrium devotee who'd accosted me and Jess in Chicago four months before.

Levitz paused, then glanced at me. I shrugged. He was the FBI agent, the one who was supposed to know what he was doing. He frowned, then his lips tightened, and he packed up again. "We'll be in the living room," he told us, and followed the redhead out, sliding a pocket door to close off the space behind him.

Daniel and I stared at each other for long moments. Special Agent Jones had spent a good two hours drilling me about how to handle this conversation, how to ask the kinds of questions to learn what we wanted from Rosalind and Martin's son. But now that I sat here, in a suburban Denver kitchen, alone with the man who'd been an accessory to the murder of my ex-prison buddy, Train, in Chicago, I couldn't remember half of it.

"How much trouble are you in, Daniel?"

He grimaced, the first real sign of emotion I'd seen. "Quite a lot, I imagine."

There was a pitcher of water at one end of the table, surrounded by glass tumblers painted with daffodils. I poured myself a glass and sipped as I tried to organize my thoughts. "I'm trying to imagine the possible reasons why you would have strolled into a random Denver police station and demanded to speak to me," I said.

"What makes you think it was random? Nothing I do is random. Not anymore."

My skin prickled, and I gripped my tumbler so hard I was lucky it didn't shatter. "Why me? Why not your parents? Why not just tell the FBI what you have to say?"

"Because you're the only one who'd understand, and because you're needed here."

"Needed how? By whom? The Scales? They've already tried to kidnap me once, over in England."

Daniel blinked, and either his confusion was genuine, or he'd acquired some mad acting skills. Then his eyes smoldered with indignant rage. "Fuck the Scales of Equilibrium! This isn't what Gaia wanted! How can we save the planet by destroying it? It doesn't make sense. It just doesn't make sense anymore. I thought I was part of something, part of something noble and... and *right*. But it turns out they've turned me into just another terrorist. Gaia deserves better!" His shoulders slumped, and he stared in dejection at the table surface.

Gaia. Was he still a true believer then, a heretic shunning his former cult? I couldn't grapple with that yet, though it intrigued me. "You warned us, earlier this summer, to leave Chicago by August 1st. Was this why? Is that all me and Jess and your mother were able to do that night in the Themis Center, delay you by two months?"

He flinched at my reference to Rosalind, but raised his head. He spoke barely above a whisper. "We needed Lyall. He had the contacts at North Point. I just helped smuggle the equipment into them and got them out again afterwards. That part was supposed to be bloodless."

"You think bloodless killing is any better than slicing someone's throat open with a knife? Yeah, I know what you did. Lyall held the knife, but you did your part. Train wasn't my friend, but no one deserves to go out like that. And whoever died, or will die, or gets sick from the North Point disaster doesn't deserve it either. Are we all complicit in the slow death of our planet? You could look at it that way, especially if those you venerate direct you to. But most of us are just trying to get by, to hold on to our own place in the world, to keep our head above water. We'd happily do so without burning forests or dumping plastic in the oceans, but we don't have that power. Don't blame us for that, and for God's sake don't kill us for it!"

I don't know who was more surprised by my outburst, him or me. Certainly, the thoughts had been kicking around my brain for long enough, nurtured by the more articulate and passionate of Jess's opinions on the topic. I'd always had respect for Greenpeace protesters and the Greta Thunbergs of the world, even as I distanced myself from the idea of acting on that respect. But I didn't understand how the Scales could justify perverting that pro-environment cause, regardless of what their founder believed he'd discovered with his Agency Theory.

As if reading my thoughts, Daniel cracked a wry smile. "You'd enjoy a conversation with Allen Weston. You know who he is, don't you?"

"Oh yeah. He's the leader of your little cult, mixing the Kool-Aid for you all to drink. Be careful of that stuff, Daniel. It can kill you."

For a moment, the mocking arrogance of the man I'd met on the walking trail reappeared. His bloodshot eyes blazed, and he straightened up in his chair, as if about to do battle, or at least arm wrestle. Then the moment passed, the fire dwindled, and he hunched over his coffee mug again with a doleful expression.

"I understand how you'd see it that way," he said, now sounding tired and defeated. "Those who bring a powerful message, one that resonates with people, often attract fanatics, those who want to be part of something so bad, to do something positive with their pitiful lives. We see that in religion and in politics too, don't we? There's a reason the Scales of Equilibrium owns and recruits from rehab clinics and homeless shelters.

I was lost too. I... I don't know how much of my story Mom and Dad have shared with you, but I was angry and lost and scared for so many years. Allen and the Burned Man were the first ones to make a difference, the first ones to understand. Don't confuse the followers with the one they follow. Allen is a good man. He understands Gaia."

There were so many questions I wanted to ask, but I latched on to what intrigued me most. "What does he understand about Gaia? What do *you* understand about Gaia?"

Daniel held my gaze and licked his upper lip as if savoring some remembered pain. "You know, D Rodriguez. I know you do."

My blood turned cold, and my arms erupted in gooseflesh. Something in the way he said it took me back to that terrifying moment at Shotcombe House when The Presence had spoken my name. Spoken without anyone else hearing. Spoken by drilling the words mercilessly into my brain.

"Yes, you've perceived Gaia. Now you know. I'm just a messenger, and a poor one at that. Allen is a better one. Together, we hoped to bring Gaia's message to everyone before it's too late. You could've helped us, you and Jess too. Even Mom. But they've poisoned your minds against us, haven't they? The Henry Lyons Foundation. They want to keep Gaia, the soul of our planet, wrapped in chains while humanity destroys its body. And they're training you to do the same. Is that what you really want?"

"How can you know what The Presence, what Gaia, wants?" I whispered. I wasn't concerned about Levitz and the other FBI agent overhearing - I assumed the kitchen was bugged, and they were listening to every word - but I could scarcely believe I was having this conversation with, of all people, Rosalind and Martin's estranged son. "All I've ever sensed is vast intelligence and power. So much power. How can you tell if it's good or evil, or if those labels even mean anything to something like that? What experience did you have?"

He shuddered and finally took a drink from his mug, which shook slightly. "I didn't understand either, at first," he said, his voice as sepulchral as mine. "I was scared too. Shit, I was terrified! He found me. He explained it to me. Gaia is crying out for help. We must listen. Don't you see? We have a responsibility. Those who can hear must take the message to those who cannot."

Back when I'd been a guest of the State of Missouri, doing twelve years for voluntary manslaughter after a street fight gone wrong, I'd kept to myself as much as possible. It was as if by keeping myself apart from other prisoners, I could convince myself I wasn't like them - I wasn't really a criminal. Others banded together and tried to lure me in. The gangs were one, either those of the petty downstate gambling bosses or, perhaps seeing in my complexion a kindred spirit, those connected to the Mexican cartels running drugs through the gateway city of St. Louis. I spurned them all, and although they left me alone, I earned their contempt. Not so those of my fellow inmates who had turned to religion to atone for their sins. Their fervor and persistence grew stronger with each one of my rejections, each one less polite than the last. Daniel's earnest sincerity reminded me of those righteous zealots, and it was all I could do not to recoil in my chair.

But, I had a job to do. I wasn't here to be his counselor, and I struggled to find much sympathy for a man who'd willingly participated in, at least, the sabotage of a nuclear power plant, no matter who his parents were.

"If 'taking the message' involves blowing up nuclear reactors, gassing bank buildings, or poisoning water supplies, you can count me out," I snarled. Daniel flinched. "Is that what Weston says Gaia wants? If that were true, I'd fight against your Gaia until my last breath. You're no better than the mobs that have followed righteous causes down the ages, burning witches, willing to kill and destroy to prove your point. I don't know what mental gymnastics you perform to help you sleep at night, but I want none of it."

"But I'm not sleeping at night," he muttered. "Not anymore. Not since... You're right, of course. It was supposed to be a bloodless revolution. That's what they told me. I know I sound like a religious fanatic, someone who wants to go around knocking on doors and asking people if they've been saved. It wasn't like that at all. We were supposed to appeal to reason, to use science and evidence to back up Gaia. No one listened. He said we had to make a point, to show how serious we were. And then we had to make another. Gaia didn't lose its way. We did."

I sat back in my chair and forced myself to take a drink of water. Part of me wanted to hear more about his interactions with "Gaia" or The Presence, but I wasn't sure he was ready or even capable of telling me. "What are you doing here, Daniel?" I asked at last. "Why did you turn yourself in and risk the ire of Allen Weston and the rest of the Scales? What are you hoping to achieve?"

"To talk to you," he replied immediately. "To someone who knows, or at least has an idea of what I experienced. But also," and now he straightened, as if bracing himself for an unpleasant but necessary task, "to atone for my mistakes, and face up to my responsibilities. I wasn't strong enough to leave when I should, before North Point. I... I wanted to warn you, and... I want to make things right with Mom and Dad. Before I pay for what I did." His expression was bleak and determined, and I hoped for his sake he was sincere. I was only the first of many who'd want to talk to him.

"Fair enough. I hope you do. Make things right, I mean, with your parents. They haven't shared much of what happened between you, and quite right too. That's private. But trust me, don't leave it too late to repair old wounds with family."

He nodded, but doubt and despair haunted his eyes. "I think perhaps we have more in common than I thought. Perhaps that's why Gaia chose you."

A chill ran down my spine. "What do you mean?"

"I've played my part. Now it's time for you to play yours. I don't know what that is. Only you and Gaia do."

I licked my lips. I wanted to refute him, tell him I wanted nothing to do with Gaia or the Scales' crazy schemes. But personal experience told me he was fragile, and I dared not imperil his reconciliation with Rosalind and Martin. Besides, I still needed something from him.

"If I wanted to talk to Allen Weston, on my own terms without getting kidnapped by his thugs, how would I do that? Where would I go?"

He grimaced. "Allen's hard to find these days. He can't exactly go on another book tour."

"So you can't tell me?"

"I don't know. Honest. All I can tell you is where I was going before I had my change of heart. There's a compound in Montana, just off Interstate 90 west of Bozeman. It looks like one of those militia camps. We were told to make for that after we fled Chicago."

"And you think Weston will be there?"

"I suppose there's a chance. But even if not, someone might be there who knows where he is. Just be careful, D."

I grinned. "Me? I'm always careful."

CHAPTER ELEVEN
YOU AND YOUR FAMILY

"Absolutely not."

Special Agent Jones stood at one end of the glass conference table, spreading her hands on its surface and leaning forward for emphasis as she glared at us. Behind her, visible through the floor to ceiling windows of the modest skyscraper hosting the FBI office, swirling gray cloud swallowed the sprawling Denver cityscape in slow motion. The Rockies had long since disappeared from view.

Agent Levitz glanced up from his ubiquitous laptop, fingertips poised over its keyboard. On the projection screen behind his boss, the mouse cursor paused in its frenetic juggling of a half-dozen screencast application windows.

"Why not?" Jess snapped, her right hand playing with one of the black leather drink coasters like it was a fidget spinner. Some of Rosalind's disdain for Agent Jones had rubbed off on her. Daniel's parents were currently back at the safe house, posing as the visiting relatives they actually were. I could only imagine how difficult their reconciliation with Daniel would be.

"Because you're private citizens, not law enforcement agents," said Jones, attempting to stare Jess down. She didn't know my fiancée very well.

"And? We'll be surrounded by a mob of you guys. We came here to look for Weston. We need to talk to him, before you do whatever Feds do to megalomaniacs!"

"You can talk to Weston *after* we've secured him, *if* I say you can. He's one of the most wanted individuals in the world. The FBI, Interpol, and the security services of dozens of countries are looking for him, to disrupt, if not end, the chaos his organization is causing. I've spent months of my life on the road, and I haven't seen my partner since I met you in Chicago. We're doing this properly, and that does *not* include special treatment for random civilians who want to ask him about weird supernatural shit!"

"That 'weird supernatural shit' is what's driving all this, though," I said, marveling that mine was the calmest voice in the room. D Rodriguez, the voice of reason! "I don't think apprehending Allen Weston alone will stop the Scales of Equilibrium. I think we need to understand *why* he and his followers are doing what they're doing, not just how, or when and where. Me and Jess are your best bets for understanding why, but we can't do that if he's locked away somewhere."

Agent Jones speared me with her irritated gaze, then let out a dramatic sigh.

"Bring up the satellite view," she told Levitz, waving her hand at the projection screen. Levitz duly located the relevant window and maximized it. A large flat gray square sat top center, surrounded by a chaotic cluster of smaller rectangles. A single road wound past treeless hills, skirting a small lake, before disappearing at the bottom left of the screen.

"This is a death trap," Jones proclaimed. "I do not command unlimited resources. Every man and woman who participates in this raid does so at significant risk. They know and accept this. They are trained for it. Their jobs become ten times harder if this turns into a hostage situation. And if I let you two wander in there by yourselves first, I can almost guarantee that will happen. So, absolutely not."

"But you owe us!" Jess cried, tossing away the coaster and thudding her fist down on the table. "You wouldn't even know about this compound if it hadn't been for D!"

"I owe you?" Agent Jones raised an incredulous eyebrow. "I just flew you and your friends all the way back from England. I don't owe you a damn thing. But, I am grateful to you, D. Because of that, I'm willing to take you both along as remote observers, and to give you your interview opportunity. But, give me any more grief, and you can stay here, or walk back to Chicago for all I care."

In the end, it didn't matter. Weston wasn't there.

"Two adult men and a woman surrendered without a fight," Jones told us, two nights later. Jess and I had been going out of our minds, skulking in a rundown chain motel room west of Bozeman, while the FBI marshaled their forces and raided the compound. The Wi-Fi was spotty, and the TV offered only a dozen channels, catering mostly to kids or right-wing conspiracy theorists. Less than twenty miles away, our quarry potentially lurked, and we were staring at the walls.

I'd been in prison in 2014, during the Bundy Standoff over cattle grazing rights on federal land. To some of my fellow inmates, Cliven Bundy, his family, and their supporters had been heroes. I remembered the raucous cheering when the Bureau of Land Management forces backed down. Despite my own incarceration and distrust of the St. Louis City police, I hadn't joined in. I was very conscious that a bunch of armed white guys had prevailed against law enforcement, while those of darker complexion, such as myself, had not. My cellmate at the time, an older black guy who generally kept to himself, broke silence to declare: "Those were brothers, Feds gone mowed 'em down like dogs."

Yet this raid outside Bozeman had ended with a whimper, not a bang.

Levitz showed us three photographs on his laptop. "Recognize any of them?"

Jess shrugged and shook her head after only a few seconds, but I took my time. I have a terrible memory for names, but faces are something else entirely. I was fairly sure I hadn't seen the younger of the two men before, a terrified, scrawny white guy. The handsome black man with an insolent expression, however, looked familiar, but I couldn't place him.

"I recognize her," I said at last, pointing at an older, curly-haired woman, lips curled in a sneer. "She was one of the cleaners at the airport last month, at O'Hare." I turned to Jess, who frowned at the picture. "She stayed at the gate while you followed the ones who tried to kidnap Rosalind. She and the others must have escaped before airport security could find them."

"Tiffany Morelle," said Jones, reading from her phone. "Three parking tickets and two DUIs. Illinois license, currently revoked. Nothing else."

"And involvement in an attempted kidnapping," I prompted. "What are you gonna do with them?"

Jones shrugged. "We'll hold 'em for now. Find out what they've done, what they know. We did find something else."

She extracted an envelope from her inside jacket pocket and handed it to me. My name was scrawled on the front.

"I do so love getting mail," I grumbled. Jess peered over my shoulder as I extracted the single sheet of notepaper within.

"What does it say?" Jones asked, patience fraying as I read and reread the simple message. "Who's it from?"

"A guy called Lyall Morrison."

"The guy who slipped away from Chicago police custody after we captured him at the Themis Center?"

"Yeah." I licked my lips, suddenly chilled to the bone. "It says: 'Go fuck yourself. I'll be seeing you and your family.'"

Jess disliked talking on the phone. She claimed she struggled to read people by voice alone, that she needed visual cues to inform the meaning of what the other person said. Texts and Snapchats were different, apparently, because they were short snippets of content to be read or seen at the discretion of the receiver. Video calls were tolerable, but the voice-only kind were reserved for only the most dire of needs.

I had no such reservations. I'd gone too long without hearing a friendly voice through much of my adult life. Rosalind and I spoke regularly, especially after Jess and I moved to Chicago. I'd just finished catching up with her, as she and Martin prepared to catch a flight home to St. Louis, when I got a *'Free now'* text from Fiona, my half-sister. Jess lay on our motel bed, coiled around a book she'd borrowed in desperation from Agent Levitz, so I placed the call.

"Hey Fi, glad you could make time. How are things?"

"Tolerable, if these damn kids would stop bickering," she grumbled, to a backdrop of what sounded like typical pre-school drama. "Guys, I'm on the phone! Eric, can you...? Thanks, hon. Sorry about that."

"No worries," I said, as cheerfully as I could. I still couldn't imagine myself as a father, especially of young children. The mere thought terrified me. "Another day in the circus, huh?"

She paused before replying. "I'd like to think so. But, the truth is, we're all on edge. Brady and Maeve are too young to understand the details, but they're more sensitive than you'd think. They pick up on things. They know me and Eric are worried about events in the news, about the nuclear disaster in Chicago, the protests downtown here on Market Street. They know I'm worried about you. Did you hear about that plane crash in Rome? I'm not sure I could ever fly again. I'm so glad you made it back from England!"

"Fi. Take a breath."

"Who has time for that?" She gave a shaky laugh, then I heard her slow exhale. "Sorry, I'm really struggling here. We all are. But we have each other, so we'll muddle through. How are you? Where are you?"

"Somewhere in the middle of Montana. I don't even know the name of the nearest town."

"What the hell are you doing in Montana? I thought you flew back to Denver?"

"We did. We took a detour, but it's kinda hard to explain. The FBI are involved."

Fiona gasped. "The FBI? Oh D, are you in trouble?" She stopped herself before saying "again", but I heard it anyway. I tried not to let it bother me.

"Nope, not guilty," I said lightly. I weighed what I could tell her without revealing more than I should. I hated lying to anyone, so less was better than more. "Not that kind, anyway. Martin's been helping the FBI track down the finances of the group they think is behind all this urban sabotage. Jess and I crossed paths with some of them in Chicago before the North Point attack. The Feds asked us to come up here and identify some suspects they captured. Now we're trying to get home, or somewhere to call home for a while. It doesn't sound like we can return to Chicago anytime soon."

"I'm sorry," she said. "I know you and Jess were really proud of your new lives up there. How's she holding up?"

I glanced at Jess, who gave no sign that she was paying attention, although I knew she listened to every word. "Frustrated at the Feds. Worried about her grandpa, who still won't leave his house in Evanston because of his dogs. Maybe a little crabbier than usual." That earned a reaction of the single finger kind. I grinned and turned away. "We're thinking about coming back to St. Louis for a while once we can figure out how to get there."

"Oh! Good! Do you need a place to stay? We don't have a lot of space, but I could make Eric clean out the spare room, finally."

"Thanks, Fi, but don't trouble yourself. Or Eric. We're gonna stay with the Hills, at least to start off with. They managed to get a commercial flight back this morning."

"Rather them than me. You know, I've only ever met them that once, when they stopped by at the end of Mom's wake. I'm still unclear how you guys know each other."

I bit my lip. "The short version is that it's kind of a work thing. I'll save the longer version for when you have a glass of wine in your hand."

"Oh, it's like that, is it?" She laughed. "If they're friends of yours, they're friends of ours. You can never have too many people looking out for you."

"Agreed. That's kind of the reason I'm calling. Have you noticed anything or anyone strange recently? Maybe someone hanging around your neighborhood you haven't seen before? Any weird messages or voicemails?"

There was a pause, and then the uncertain, worried Fiona returned. "No? Apart from the usual relentless political campaign barrage. I'll ask Eric, but I'm sure he would've said something. Is there a reason we might have?"

"I hope not, and I don't want to worry you more than you already are. Someone I ran into this summer, up in Chicago. Well, let's just say we're not on the best of terms. His name is Lyall, and he's bad news, threatened me and my family. The Feds promised to pass it on to St. Louis City PD, but all law enforcement is stretched pretty thin these days. Just keep an eye out and take extra care. And tell Mary and Patrick too."

"I will. I'd ask you what this is about, but I'm not sure you want to tell me."

"Not over the phone. When I'm back, maybe. You deserve the truth. Maybe it's time to tell you a lot of things."

"I look forward to it." A piercing shriek in the background preceded a child's sobbing, then Eric yelling. "Jesus Christ," muttered Fiona. "Sorry, D. Gotta go. Take care of yourself and your lovely fiancée."

"Will do."

I weighed my phone in my hand after the call disconnected. My lovely fiancée remained engrossed in her book, while my troubled thoughts lingered with my dysfunctional family. They weren't mixed up with the Feds, the Scales of Equilibrium, the Henry Lyons Foundation, or with Imprints, Erasures, Tethers, and Intrusions. They hadn't encountered a mysterious and terrifying Presence in their waking world. But, if Fiona was anything to go by, they still keenly felt the troubles of the world, brought on by all the above.

I'd been the black sheep of the family for so long, I wasn't used to dealing with this protective instinct. I wasn't used to caring so much. But what could I do? I was over a thousand miles away, still waiting for Agent Jones to come through with a ride home. Even if they felt disposed to do so, the St. Louis City police department didn't have the manpower to provide protective details for Fiona's family, Mary's family, and my stepfather too. Or any of them, really.

If only I knew someone with an ear to the ground in St. Louis's criminal underworld, who commanded sufficient resources both legal and illegal, who understood at least some of the tensions between two secret societies, and the paranormal phenomena they feuded over.

My thumb hovered above my phone screen, then I swiped the contact card away before stuffing the device back in my jeans pocket. I wasn't ready for that conversation. Not yet.

CHAPTER TWELVE
FOOLISHNESS

Jess and I huddled together for warmth near the open doors of an aircraft hangar at Malmstrom Air Force Base. As civilians, we were not at liberty to wander from our designated spot, which provided minimal shelter from the biting wind and driving rain that delayed our departure. I couldn't wait to leave, even as unwanted baggage on a military flight.

"You have my number," Special Agent Jones reminded me for at least the third time. "If you hear anything about the Scales, especially about where Allen Weston may be, call me. Day or night, it doesn't matter. Call me, and don't do anything foolish."

"And if you find him, you'll call us, right?" Jess replied, but her heart wasn't in it.

Jones gave her a thin-lipped smile. "Your number won't be near the top of my list, but I promise I'll get to you eventually."

And we'd just have to be satisfied with that. The FBI owed us nothing more, especially after doing us this final "favor" of flying us through chaotic domestic airspace to St. Louis, or close to it.

Scott Air Force Base lay on the Illinois side of the Mississippi, roughly twenty miles from where the Gateway Arch heralded the city sprawl on the western bank. A messy patchwork of Metro East suburbs staggered between them, threaded by Interstate 55 on its way north to Chicago, and the light rail of the MetroLink. No one was picking us up, partly because military bases didn't have a passenger pickup area, but mostly because we didn't know when we would arrive. So much for "military precision".

"We can call you a cab, or take you to the MetroLink station," offered the young NCO, who greeted us as we deplaned, into much the same conditions as we'd left behind in Montana. It was the first time anyone had spoken to us, since we'd secured ourselves in jump seats that, leg room aside, had me longing for economy class.

"Can you take us somewhere we can rent a car?" I countered. He said he could, and we followed him through fitful rain to a waiting unmarked sedan.

"That's a bit extravagant," said Jess, adjusting her backpack. She stopped short of asking for an explanation, waiting for privacy. We didn't get any until the NCO dropped us off at the nearby MidAmerica airport. I'd forgotten that St. Louis sported a second commercial airport in its eastern suburbs, tiny though it was, hosting just one budget airline.

"We're not gonna find out where Weston is by skulking around St. Louis," I told her, while we stood in line at the terminal's single car rental counter. Our drop-off had coincided with the arrival of a flight from Florida. "The Feds won't tell us anything, unless there's something in it for them too. Rosalind said Daniel doesn't know more than he told me, or isn't telling if he does. I'm thinking about the tip Kara gave me the night before we left England."

A fire smoldered in Jess's emerald eyes. "You want to go see Marcus?"

"It's the only other lead we have. And I don't think they'd've given it to me unless they thought we'd need it."

"Oh, I'm in. Let's go see that asshole!"

It was a two-hour drive to Bloomington-Normal, a college town roughly halfway between St. Louis and Chicago. I spent the first half of that drive, most of the way to the state capital of Springfield, attempting to dissuade Jess from her more murderous inclinations towards her former co-worker.

She'd never liked Marcus much. No one had. Apparently, he'd cultivated a distant, lone wolf personality. However, she'd respected him as a coder. She'd also fretted for weeks after he'd warned her in a parting email not to trust Conor, their boss, who'd turned out to be a Henry Lyons Foundation agent. Any shred of respect had vanished once she discovered Marcus was one of the two Scales of Equilibrium devotees who we'd lured into attacking us, after they put Conor in a coma. She'd wanted to hunt Marcus down immediately, but Jamal claimed not to know where the HLF was holding him.

"We don't even know what condition he's in, if he's even conscious or lucid," I reasoned, not without a twinge of guilt. Connected with Jess, I'd lashed out at their attempt to trap us in a psychic cocoon, rendering them unconscious at the very least. My own righteous anger at what they'd done to Conor, and had tried to do to us, dissipated as I worried how badly I'd hurt them. I didn't want to kill anyone, not again. Even if no court-admissible evidence could pin the blame on me, I'd still know.

"He's gonna get a piece of my mind, whether he can understand it or not." She looked askance at me, not quite taking her eye off the road. "You trust me, right?"

I suppressed my sigh and covered her hand with mine. "Of course. I do. I just want to get whatever useful information we can from him, before you tear him a new one."

She grinned, before shaking me off the steering wheel. She'd claimed driving privileges on the basis that she'd miraculously managed to sleep during the flight from Montana. Her expression sobered. "And you're still not gonna tell Rosalind where we're going?"

"No. I don't want to risk the Feds intercepting any such message. Pretty sure this falls under what Agent Jones would call 'foolishness'." I squirmed in my seat, pretty sure Rosalind would find it foolish too, and would try to talk me out of it. "I told her we were back in the area, but had an errand to run, and we'd see them later tonight. Reckon we can make that if we don't get delayed."

Jess muttered something that might have been "It's your funeral", then we lapsed into silence and listened to her Spotify playlist until we reached Bloomington. Or Normal. I'd only ever stopped there once before, last winter, when Jess and I towed a U-Haul trailer with all our worldly belongings toward Chicago. That time, we'd simply ducked off I-55 for gas and fast food, eschewing the fabulous brew hall Martin had raved about for something more budget-conscious.

This time, my phone's navigation app took us through blocks of hotels, gas stations, and restaurants clustering the Interstate. We drove past big box stores and strip malls of smaller retail, before veering off the business loop and into the heart of a middle-class residential area. These houses were small, densely packed, but well-maintained. Most yards were free of the red and brown leaves still falling from the mature trees flanking the roadway.

"This can't be right," I said, as we made our final turn onto another such street. Jess squeezed the Toyota Camry into a free spot. I'd expected some sort of clinic, if not a hospital, something obviously medical.

The address Kara had given me was a brick bungalow, not unlike the one in which I'd grown up back in South St. Louis. A single empty wicker chair occupied the concrete porch, and two empty plant pots hung above the faded black iron railing. The blinds were drawn on the front picture window, although I thought I spotted them twitch as I heaved myself out of the car, stepping around a deep rain puddle. I was too far away to detect any Imprints, but a sense of unease nagged at me.

"Looks like the HLF has safe houses too," said Jess, shrugging as she joined me on the sidewalk. "Now what?"

It had been almost three months since our confrontation with Marcus, likely long enough for him and his buddy to recover from any physical or psychological trauma we'd inflicted. For that matter, Jess had been back up and at it mere days after she caught the blowback. The two men were likely just "guests" of the HLF.

"I guess we knock on the door," I replied. "It's either that or turn around and drive back to St. Louis."

Jess snorted and walked up the steps onto the front porch. "Coming?"

I rang the doorbell and scanned the porch more carefully as its dull chimes faded. Two home security cameras watched us from either end of the overhang. I assumed there were others around the building. How much deterrent would they be if the Scales came to reclaim their own? Or would they bother?

I heard the metallic thump of a deadbolt and turned as a middle-aged white man opened the front door. A round cheerful face peered at us through the screen, but it wasn't until Jess pulled that back too that I saw his graying buzz cut. A University of Illinois sweatshirt couldn't disguise his paunch, but something about his poise suggested he could handle himself.

"Can I help you?" His voice was deep and devoid of accent, at least to another Midwesterner.

"My name's D, and this is Jess," I said, smiling in what I hoped was sincerity. "We'd like to have a word with Marcus Kunstler. Kara LeVault sent us."

He looked confused for a moment, then returned my smile and offered his hand to shake. "Of course. I'm Bob. Come in. We'll see if Marcus is awake."

Whoever had decorated the interior must have visited the FBI safe house in Denver and sworn off anything vaguely bright and botanical. "Neutral" was the most charitable term I could think of, with "austere" and "depressing" waiting in the wings. Dim lighting, dark greens and browns, conspired with sparse furnishings to deter guests from overlong visits.

A short woman sporting a long, braided ponytail rose from an armchair as we entered the living room, setting the book she was reading face down on an end table. Bob introduced her as his wife, Alice. Something tickled the edges of my memory.

"Kara sent them," he told her. "They're here to see Marcus."

Alice's forehead wrinkled as she inspected us, but I guessed she was a decade younger than Bob. "Are you now? How do you know Kara?"

"We just met them, actually," I said. "We were with the Henry Lyons Foundation in England until three days ago."

"Then you must be used to this rain. I think Kara's defected. The dismal weather better suits her disposition."

"*They* seemed perfectly comfortable in all the sunshine we had," countered Jess, bristling. "But we didn't come all this way to talk about the weather. We want to see Marcus. Are you guys his keepers? Do we have to fill out a form?"

Alice's thin smile of welcome faded entirely. "We're his protectors. And as far as protocol goes, a phone call in advance would have been more courteous than showing up on our doorstep unannounced. What do you want with Marcus?"

"To ask him questions about the Scales of Equilibrium," I interjected, before Jess responded with a more confrontational version. "I assume you know who they are."

Alice shared her look of mutual dislike with Jess for another moment, then wrenched her eyes away to address me. "Of course. But the Foundation has already interviewed him, and Adam too. What more do you two want?"

"It's them, Alice," Bob whispered. "I recognize their names now. You were the agents in Chicago that day, the ones who fought off Adam and Marcus, who stopped them putting more of our people into comas."

He gave me a quick military salute. Embarrassed, I started to respond in kind, but seized control of my hand at the last moment. Instead, I tugged at my ponytail.

"You're not going to attack him, are you?" Alice said, eyes narrowed. She didn't seem nearly as impressed with us as her husband. I convinced myself that was the reason for my instinctive dislike.

"We just want to ask him a few questions," I confirmed. "Alone, preferably. Ten, maybe fifteen minutes, then we'll be on our way."

The couple conferred in silence, then Alice shrugged. "Fine. I'll go rouse him and bring him downstairs."

"Can I get you anything?" Bob offered after she left the room. "Water? Iced tea?"

"We're fine, thank you," I said.

"Your wife doesn't like me much," Jess observed with a sardonic smile. Our eyes met briefly, and hers flared in alarm, or warning. I was missing something.

Bob grimaced and lowered his voice. "She chafes at this assignment. We've been here almost a month, and she thinks we have better things to do than be 'glorified nursemaids'. Personally, I'm grateful for some peace and quiet."

"What's the deal, exactly?" I asked, mirroring his volume. "I thought they'd be in some medical clinic."

"They were at first, but too many questions were asked. Our superiors moved them here, and we're the second pair of agents tasked with 'monitoring' them. They're not handcuffed to their beds or anything like that." His lip curled in distaste. "Although, they are medicated to suppress their mental activity, so I don't know how alert Marcus will be."

Despite my antipathy towards the man, part of me was outraged on his behalf. He may not be in physical shackles or behind literal bars, but drugged and housebound was no better a prison sentence than mine had been.

Jess's look of revulsion suggested she agreed with me. "How long does the HLF intend to keep them here?"

Bob shrugged. "By all means, ask Kara that very question. Perhaps you'll have a better chance of getting answers."

She opened her mouth to reply, then flinched and covered her mouth as if assailed by an overpowering stench. Simultaneously, my ears popped and the room temperature plummeted, a slab of cold air settling over me like a wet blanket. Bob's eyes shot upwards, wide with panic.

"Alice!" he gasped, and made for the stairs, but not before Jess. I stood, almost literally frozen, while they bounded upwards, then cursed and set off in pursuit.

An invisible blizzard tore down the staircase, and I ducked as I climbed. I was halfway up when I heard Jess cry out, and I fumbled for her spirit, the shape of her projected consciousness. We'd had no time to prepare and carefully establish our connection. I reached for her as I would for a fellow passenger on a sinking ship during a storm, to clutch her to me as we jumped for a lifeboat. I found her almost immediately, but that wasn't all I found. Other shapes were there, other consciousnesses, and as we connected, sharing our alarm, panic, and rage, they coalesced. And they attacked.

Fucking Marcus! Jess blazed, and I didn't understand, but that was for later. In a past time, the 1970s or 1980s I guessed from the garish wallpaper, the bedroom at the top of the stairs had played host to a tragedy. A young mother lay dying, with her husband and young sons at her bedside. Their sorrow was palpable, every bit as heavy and immobilizing as the frigid air of the Imprint.

Yet I could only spare it a fraction of my attention. Arrayed against us were at least four hostile wills, connected more tenuously than me and Jess, but working in unison nonetheless. They built a wall around us, a mental cocoon to trap us in this terrible memory, perhaps forever.

I was so stupid. In Chicago, we'd set a trap for the Scales of Equilibrium, with ourselves as bait. Now, they'd returned the favor, and we'd walked heedlessly into its jaws.

We rallied. We dug deep into our reserves, probing for weaknesses in the construct, a place where we could shatter their confinement and break free.

And what then? Jess wondered. *Remember what Jamal told us. This memory, it's a Level Five, the most powerful there is, and the hardest to tether. We've never taken on more than a Level Three.*

So we release it. Fuck the HLF. Who cares if the Intrusion comes back, or more than one? We just need to survive.

We fought back. I'd been told I possessed the most raw strength of any sensitive the HLF had discovered for years, and Jess was no slouch. Against two assailants, maybe even three, we might've stood a chance. But four proved too much to counter, and slowly, brick by invisible brick, they built an impenetrable prison around us. I was reluctant to gather all our mental strength and fling it at the barrier, the brute force approach that usually worked for me. Last time, Jess was hospitalized overnight with a concussion none of us could convincingly explain. But we were fast running out of options.

Who's there? The thought seeped through our connection as we fought to hold back our confinement. I couldn't see what it meant at first, but then, through a gap in the almost completed wall, I detected other consciousnesses, other sensitives, not assailants. We concentrated on the gap, wedging our collective will like a foot in a door, and reached through, a desperate plea for help. And recognized their shapes.

That's Izzy.

And Jamal!

Belatedly grateful for Astbury's experiments back at Shotcombe House, and quelling the unhelpful surprise and demand to know how they were there, now, when we needed them the most, we drew them towards us and connected. We morphed to align ourselves into one unit, and although I detected Izzy's righteous fury and Jamal's calm determination, I couldn't say which of the four of us directed our actions. We had the same goal, which was to resist and then undermine the wall that Marcus and the others were a handful of bricks away from completing.

Instead of lashing out, we concentrated on widening the gap through which we'd discovered each other. A tremor reverberated around the edifice, then what I thought of as bricks dislodged, widening the gap. We redoubled our efforts and the wall fragmented until, with the suddenness and devastation of an earthquake, it collapsed, taking our awareness of our assailants with it. Exultant, we were left alone with the poignant memory of a young family's last minutes together.

Until, swooping in like a tsunami on fast forward, The Presence arrived to blot out everything else.

Elation turned to dread, our waning strength incapable of anything but registering the sheer magnificence and monstrosity of the thing. No, there had to be more than that. We must have at least a shred of defiance left in us—

:: YOUR POWER GROWS ::

Really? It didn't feel like it, or at least we'd spent most of it repelling our attackers. Even at our best, though, we couldn't take on The Presence. Our opponent was too strong.

But it wasn't invulnerable. Dammit, Rosalind had beaten it twice! How had she done it?

A flicker.

I'm walking through a redwood grove...

No. Not again.

I seized control of my connection with Jess, Jamal, and Izzy. No one resisted. No one else had a plan. It was this or nothing.

No guts, no glory.

I poured everything we had into The Presence, embracing it, grasping at surfaces that were freezing cold and burning hot, soft as feather and hard as diamond. I focused just a tiny fraction of our consciousness on the memory, the manifestation of the Intrusion. Then I *ripped*. With one savage cut, I flung us away from the Intrusion, from The Presence - or it away from us

- tearing fragments of our souls along with it, trailing blazes of incoherent light like blood spatter against the psyche of the universe.

And then the darkness devoured me.

CHAPTER THIRTEEN
STEM THE BLEEDING

Someone was knocking, no, *pounding*, on the door.

What door? Who? Where the hell was I?

Damn, my head hurt.

"D?"

I groaned and tried to separate my glued together eyelids. A chink of dim light made it through, just enough to detect motion, another face hovering near mine. Jess.

"Stay there," she whispered, then eased past me and down the stairs.

What the hell was I doing sprawled on a staircase? Despite what she said, I tried to move. All I could do was flex my hands and shuffle into a slightly less uncomfortable position as Jess answered the door.

"Who's there?"

"Jess? It's us, Jamal and Izzy. Help is on the way. Can you let us in?"

"Umm, oh, there's a deadbolt. There you go. Alice must've locked the door before going upstairs."

Jamal, Izzy, Alice. The names quested through my brain, looking for something to connect to. Panic. Sorrow. Fear and rage. A man in a sweatshirt. A father and his children huddled around a bed. A wall and—

A hand gripped my shoulder, and I flinched, which at least jarred my eyes wider open. I recognized the face: dark skin, mostly bald scalp, circular rimless eyeglasses propped up by a wide nose. Was that a smudge of blood on his upper lip?

"Jamal?" I croaked.

He smiled with what looked like relief. "We've got to stop meeting like this, D. Here." He offered me a piece of white cloth. I stared at it in confusion. "It's perfectly clean, I promise you. It'll help stem the bleeding until our medic arrives."

Bleeding? He pressed the handkerchief into my hand and guided my hand to my face. The instant it made contact, I felt the stickiness of blood on my cheek, still seeping from my right nostril. No wonder I was light-headed.

"Hold it there," he told me, climbing to his feet. "Jess, can you fetch him some water? Izzy, let's make sure we secure this lot until Faustyn gets here."

I struggled to sit up, and at least be less in the way, as Izzy ascended the stairs. Her eyeliner was smeared, and a red stain splashed the iconic design on the front of her T-shirt. I recognized the album cover of Joy Division's Unknown Pleasures album. That had been one of Mom's favorite shirts. I could still see her wearing it, at an age not much older than Izzy, although Mom's hair was flaming Irish red instead of bubblegum pink.

Izzy paused, her expression inscrutable. "Who needs crisp lines when we've got you?"

We stared at each other, then I nodded and so did she.

"Izzy!" Jamal's voice was urgent. "They're waking up!"

"Gotta go," she murmured, and flashed her familiar cocky grin before bounding up the last few steps.

Jess arrived moments later, a big bottle of spring water in each hand. I accepted one and took a long, slow drink before inspecting the handkerchief clutched in my other hand. Shit, had I lost that much blood?

"I think the bleeding's stopped," she said, lifting my chin and examining my nose. "But you should probably take it easy. We all should."

I took her hand in mine and searched her beautiful face for injury. "How are you?" I managed.

She rubbed her nose self-consciously and glanced at her fingers before replying. "I just washed up. Looks like we all got nosebleeds from what you did, but none as severe as you." She took my hand back and squeezed. "How did you do that? It's what Rosalind did back in England, and that night at the Themis Center, wasn't it?"

"Sacrifice throw," I muttered, then closed my eyes as a wave of weariness washed over me.

When I came to, I found myself sitting in an armchair in the living room. A tired-looking bald guy, dark smudges blossoming over the pale skin under his bright blue eyes, held my hand.

I flinched before realizing he was taking my pulse. He wore burgundy-colored scrubs with what looked like the insignia of a local hospital emblazoned on his chest, but my vision was too blurry to read it.

"Pulse and blood pressure are normal," he declared, rising from a crouch and picking up an olde-timey kit bag. "Hydrate, and avoid anything too strenuous for a day or so. Anyone else?"

This last was directed at the man hovering, arms folded across his chest, next to the disused fireplace. His beard was a little longer and untidier than when I'd last seen him, but I remembered that exasperated expression all too well.

"I think that's everyone," replied Faustyn Lazarowski, in his scratchy voice. I cleared my throat on his behalf. "Thank you. I'll take it from here."

The paramedic nodded and headed for the front door. I straightened up, and noticed Jess occupying the armchair next to mine, legs gathered beneath her and arms draped over its back. She glared at Faustyn with open dislike, while Jamal and Izzy tapped away on their phones at either end of the couch.

"You appear destined to wreak havoc wherever I go," Faustyn said at last. He addressed me, but stole occasional glances towards Jess's unfriendly eyes. "Although I understand you aren't entirely to blame for this latest episode."

"What are you doing here?" I rasped. I looked around for my water and discovered it on the adjacent end table.

"Many of our Chicago agents took refuge here, those who didn't have a place to go, or could easily reach. I'm still responsible for them. We haven't abandoned operations just because of our temporary displacement. The nature of the work has changed, that's all."

I was curious what he meant, but another, more important question drove that away. "Where's Marcus and the others? Are they still upstairs? Bob and Alice, they were in on it too, weren't they? They had to be!"

Faustyn raised his hands to slow my flood of questions. "They're safe and harmless for now. I'm taking care of it. Properly this time."

"How?"

"I'm not going to tell you. The less you all know about their whereabouts, the better."

"But we came here to ask them a question," Jess interrupted. "An important question. That's why Kara sent us here. Can't we have five minutes with Marcus before you spirit him away?

Faustyn pursed his lips and then sighed. "Give me a moment, and I'll see what I can do." He turned to Jamal as if to say something more, but Jamal raised an eyebrow and he thought better of it. Faustyn dug out a phone from the inside pocket of his charcoal suit jacket and stepped out the front door.

"Pompous ass," muttered Izzy, tossing her phone onto the couch cushion. "How are you feeling, D? Everyone's worried about you, even the suit."

"I'm fine," I said automatically, "or at least as fine as I ever am after dealing with an Imprint. I'm more aggravated with myself for leading Jess into an ambush."

"We should've known," said Jess, a bitter note in her voice. "Bob and Alice. Robert and Alice Harrington, perhaps?"

I gaped at her. "The couple who were supposed to be training Rosalind in St. Louis? I thought they'd been 'recalled' by the HLF after putting Donovan Brooks in a coma? What were they doing guarding Scales guys who'd done the same thing?"

"Great question. Kara's got some explaining to do." Jess glanced over at Jamal, who waved his phone in the air with a grim smile.

"I'm trying to reach them. It's late in the UK, but I just heard back. They're gonna call in a couple of minutes."

"Tell me something, before they do," I said. "What are you both doing here? Jess and I would've been lost without you." More accurately, we would likely both be in comas. I shivered anew at our narrow escape.

"Kara sent us here," Izzy explained. "Said they'd given you the tip, but thought you might need backup. Didn't say why, or at least not to me." She looked at Jamal, who shook his head. "We flew into Indianapolis yesterday and drove into town this morning. Security cameras alerted us at lunch, and Jamal burned rubber to get here. We sensed what was going on as soon as we got out of the car. You're welcome."

She grinned, but with more respect than cockiness. I stared back at her, and at Jamal.

"Thank you," I said at last. "Your timing couldn't have been better."

Jamal's phone rang. "Hello Kara," he answered. "I'm putting you on speakerphone. D, Jess, and Izzy are here with me. We've got a few minutes alone, and a lot of questions."

"I have no doubt." Kara's voice was tinny and muffled by the transatlantic connection. "Before you do, any updates beyond what you've sent me?"

"Faustyn's outside making arrangements for Marcus, Adam, and the Harringtons. But I assume you know more about that than I do."

"More than I would like. I'm taking on a larger operations role for the time being. And, no offense to anyone present, but the details are strictly need-to-know. It's for your own protection."

"We want to talk to Marcus," Jess said firmly. "Or this Adam guy, I guess. That's why you sent me and D here, wasn't it?"

There was a pause, then a muttered exclamation. "Sorry, the cat almost knocked over my wine glass. The short answer to your question is 'yes', although technically I only gave the information to D. I apologize for putting you in harm's way, and I'm glad you emerged relatively unscathed. I was just the messenger, you see. The suggestion came from Carson."

Jamal's forehead furrowed as he caught my eye. "That's interesting."

"Carson told me I might get answers from Allen Weston," I said slowly. "That morning I met him on my run around Shotcombe House. He basically planted the idea, although I thought it was an offhand comment at the time."

"Carson rarely makes offhand comments," Jamal said, lip curling. "Answers about what, may I ask?"

"The Presence. It's too much of a taboo subject within the Henry Lyons Foundation. If anyone knows anything useful, they've had plenty of time to share, and chosen not to. And, as we just saw, we need answers soon."

Jamal nodded slowly. "I can't argue with that. So, Kara, why send Izzy and I here? Was it really just on the off chance D and Jess could use our help?"

"I rarely do things on the off chance, Jamal," Kara replied, with a hint of amusement in their voice. "I was... uncomfortable with Carson's request."

"Uncomfortable how?" demanded Izzy, glancing at the front door.

"Let's just say it wasn't the first time he's asked for specific resource allocations that, coincidentally or perhaps not, resulted in damages to our assets—"

"Gods, can you sound any more like HR?" muttered Jess.

"—and, frankly, D and Jess are two of the most valuable assets we have. Especially... well, I don't want to get into that over the phone. Suffice to say that once you have your answers, we'd prefer to have you back here, somewhere we know we can protect you."

"We just got here, Kara," Jamal pointed out, for the first time sounding both tired and irritated. "And I'm no longer sure I would trust any of Carson's connections."

"You shouldn't, and you likely won't have to. Carson's AWOL."

I leaned forward, carefully, and lowered my voice, conscious of the ticking seconds. "What does that mean?"

"I mean, he's not responding to anything or anyone, as of yesterday morning. David's alarmed; Carson rarely goes dark entirely, even on his rare vacations, and certainly not when everything is blowing up, metaphorically speaking."

I caught Jess's eye. "Has something happened to him? Is he sick? Or..."

"Do you think he's Scales?" she finished.

"I don't know. Not for sure, not yet. Look, I've told Faustyn to give you a few minutes with Marcus - under Jamal's super-vision. Keep it brief. I can't help you much over there, and Faustyn's dealing with the Chicago situation. Don't trust any-one you don't have to, and, I hate to say this, that includes law enforcement. All I'll say is that we may need your particular expertise, and that of Rosalind sooner than later. Think about it and let Jamal know when and if you're ready."

The call disconnected abruptly, leaving a stunned silence in its wake.

"Shit," whispered Izzy. "Do you think he—"

The opening front door interrupted whatever she'd been about to ask, and Faustyn stalked into the living room, looking harassed.

"D and Jess, five minutes. He's upstairs. Jamal, go with them please. Keep things civil."

Jess sprang to her feet and helped me climb out of my chair. "Come on, old man," she teased. I stuck my tongue out. How was that for civility? We followed Jamal upstairs, and, unnoticed or disregarded by Faustyn, Izzy trailed behind.

Jamal led us into a tiny back bedroom, just large enough for the unmade twin bed and the large, olive green rucksack, whose contents spilled haphazardly over the threadbare carpet. The unmistakable sour tang of stale sweat assailed us even before we crossed the threshold, and it had nothing to do with an Imprint.

I barely recognized the man who lay propped up on a pair of pillows. Gone was the long ZZ Top beard I remembered from our only meeting at a work party at Conor's house early that summer. Patchy stubble vied with chapped red skin, and Marcus appeared thinner and weaker to me, but I recognized his supercilious look of contempt, albeit through bloodshot, semi-focused eyes.

"Can you give us a moment?" Jamal asked the short, dark-skinned man who stood with arms-crossed next to the head of the bed. He wore a plaid shirt and jeans, and peered up at me and Jess with frank curiosity as he stepped into the upstairs hallway.

"Five minutes, amigo," he told us. "Leave the door open."

So much for secrets. But I wasn't sure I could breathe properly with four other people in such a confined space already reeking of body odor. Jamal wrinkled his nose and stayed on the threshold, whereas Izzy made a show of gagging and stood as far back as she could while remaining in earshot. Jess, however, acknowledged the stink with only a passing flare of her nostrils as she stepped inside, stopping just beyond arm's reach of her former colleague. I stood at her shoulder and gave her the floor.

"Hello, Marcus," she said, her voice much calmer than I'd expected. She scanned the room, dwelling on the tattered blinds and dark stains on the oatmeal-colored carpet. "I expected better digs for a sociopathic incel. Been donating all your income to conspiracy theorists and lunatic politicians, have we?"

"Fuck you, Jess," he rasped, although a smirk tugged the corners of his chapped lips.

"Not in a million years. Especially now you've taken up with these Scales losers. Is there a sex aspect to this cult of yours, or are you still having to do it all yourself? Smells like the latter."

Jamal shifted in my peripheral vision, likely as fascinated by Jess's interrogation technique as I was.

"I'll say this for you," Marcus intoned after a long pause. "You and your boyfriend deserve your reputation. Yes, you had help, but you fought off four of us for far longer than you should've been able to. Shame you're fighting on the wrong side. Remember my last email to you?"

Jess narrowed her eyes into mere glints of emerald. "I remember. 'Don't trust Conor'. Not long before he was attacked, and fell into a coma. Was that you?"

Marcus shook his head, then winced. "Not guilty. Not directly. But I'm not sorry either. I reject everything he stood for, publicly and privately." He gestured weakly in Jamal's direction. "These Henry Lyons assholes are ruining the world, and I'm only sorry I didn't try harder to help you see it."

"Last I checked," said Jess, fuming around the edges of her self-control, "the HLF weren't the ones sabotaging nuclear reactors or poisoning water supplies. You and your fellow cultists are killing people and damaging the very planet you claim you want to save."

He shrugged. "People will die. Sacrifices must be made. I don't expect you to understand."

"Condescending, arrogant, and sociopathic," Jess bristled. "Yes, Marcus, you may be in a cult."

Jamal cleared his throat and held up his hand with two fingers raised.

"Did you feel it too?" I asked quietly, while Jess was distracted.

Marcus turned his unsettling, wavering gaze on me and paused before answering. "Are you a religious man, D? Have you ever met God? No? If you were, if you had, I could accuse you of being in a cult too. That's all organized religion is, when you strip it down: a bunch of people believing without question someone else's interpretation of the word of the god they think they know. Except most of them have never met one. I hadn't either, until Gaia, or whatever Weston calls it. You call the Scales of Equilibrium a cult? I call it an army."

"And if we wanted to meet the general of your army for a parley, how would we do that? Where might we go?"

He chuckled, and I resisted the urge to punch him in the face. Outside, Jamal whispered pleas for a few more seconds.

"Why, you two don't have to go anywhere," Marcus said at last, recovering something of the sneering disdain he'd had at Conor's party. "If Allen Weston knows you want to see him, he'll come find you."

CHAPTER FOURTEEN

MEET US AT THE EYEBALL

Dismal weather persisted throughout the week leading up to Halloween. Far from menacing or playful, the decorations in Rosalind and Martin's Webster Groves neighborhood looked sullen, even after sunset, when candlelit carved pumpkins battled the persistent miasma of freezing drizzle. It was a far cry from the previous year's joyful celebration, of costumes and trick-or-treaters, of apple bobbing and mulled wine.

Of course, last year, fire had destroyed Hickory's kitchen and much of the dining room overnight, taking my cooking career in St. Louis along with it. Trick or treat indeed.

The Hills' guest room was cozy and clean, and a welcome refuge from the increasingly dire series of hotels and motels we'd lived in most of the month. Our stay at a budget "motor court" just east of Bloomington had been the worst. Neither Jess nor I had been up for the drive back to St. Louis after our run-in with the Scales and The Presence. Due to the thousands of refugees flooding south from Chicago, every hotel, motel, or bed-and-breakfast in the town was either booked solid or outrageously overpriced. We finally found and squeezed into a tiny room with a leaky sink and a single double bed. Jamal and I ceded the bed to the ladies, but neither of us could bring ourselves to lie down on the stained, threadbare carpet. We'd sat with our backs propped up against the thin, cold walls and I hadn't slept a wink.

I almost cried when Rosalind ushered us into their guest room early the following afternoon. I inhaled the clean fragrance from a vase of fresh-cut flowers on the dresser, then collapsed onto the queen-sized bed. It swallowed me whole. I lay down for a nap and had to reheat my portion of Martin's Shepherd's Pie when I woke up after dinner.

The Hills were gracious hosts, genuinely glad to see us back, more or less safe and sound from our travels. Rosalind fussed over my lingering symptoms from the excision of the Bloomington Intrusion.

"I'm both impressed and heartsick that you succeeded in doing what I did," she told me three days later. She'd returned home from teaching at Gold Cross to find me sprawled on their living room couch, almost comatose from a pounding headache. "Especially after fending off four attackers seeking to imprison you in your own mind. My symptoms were mild that first time, up in Chicago, but I struggled with several days of headaches and nausea after the incident at Shotcombe House. I'm more forgetful than before. Martin's noticed it. That's one of the reasons he's so angry at the HLF. I wonder if being connected with others exacerbates the effects, or if it's some sort of progressive brain injury?"

I found myself unable to care for those first few days. Jess bounced back immediately, and even returned to work, albeit with an old laptop she borrowed from Martin. The corporate slog hadn't stopped in our absence, although Paragon Insurance reeled from the aftermath of the North Point disaster.

"Turns out we carried a number of policies for North Point, as well as lots of other city businesses," she told me during a mid-morning break to sneak some Halloween candy from Rosalind's pantry. "It's been a financial gut punch. Many projects are on hold, and we're all worried about layoffs."

"Are you gonna be okay?" I asked, gently recovering two of the four mini Snickers bars from her hand. I replaced them in the large Tupperware bowl our hosts had prepared for the evening.

She pouted, grinned, then lapsed into a troubled expression. "I'm one of the newest hires, so if it's last in, first out, I'm screwed. All I can do is pad my resume and be ready to hit the job market running. I could end up working for the Henry Lyons Foundation, after all."

"Maybe we'll both be on their payroll then," I said gloomily.

I'd finally received a phone call from Chef Luca. He told me Trattoria Capelli was on indefinite hiatus. "The experts think there's been little if any radioactive contamination beyond the vicinity of the plant. But they're still testing. Those with any choice are staying away for as long as they can, just to be sure. Most stores are closed, hotels shuttered. It's worse than COVID. By all accounts, the Loop is a dangerous ghost town, and River North's not much better. Even if I could lure you and my other staff back, I doubt we'd have customers. I'll let you know if things change. Sorry, D."

I was sorry too. As grateful as I was for the Hills' hospitality, I was determined not to sponge off them once my minimal savings ran out. But my options were limited. St. Louis had yet to suffer a major act of urban sabotage, but the city was on edge. You could feel it any time you braved the miserable weather. Grocery store shelves emptied of necessities, gas prices spiked. People were turning inward, protecting their own. It wasn't happening suddenly, as in the first onslaught of the pandemic, but like a reverse of our slow emergence from lockdown.

I called Mike Szemis, my old boss at Hickory, not because I hoped he'd give me a job - that was an impossibility, given the conditions of the loan he'd received from Steven Rourke - but to see if he knew of anyone who might be hiring, even a line cook.

"Sorry, D," he'd said, echoing Chef Luca. "Everyone I know is just trying to hold on to what they've got. Some aren't going to make it. I'm honestly not sure Hickory's gonna make it. I'm taking it week by week."

We chatted for a while, but my heart wasn't in it. My cooking career prospects looked bleak.

"Why don't we all get out of the house for a while?" Rosalind suggested one Saturday morning, her tone as bright as the almost-forgotten sunlight. Martin had just left for his weekly round of golf. We had dinner plans at Jess's parents' house in the evening, but the two of us jumped at the chance to enjoy what might be some of the last pleasant weather of the year.

Jamal texted as we were walking out the door, asking if we could meet and catch up. We'd all gotten gun-shy about saying too much over message or voice calls, no matter how secure the service claimed to be.

"Nothing is totally secure," claimed Jess, and no one argued.

Rosalind took it in stride. "Have him join us as at Laumeier if he's free. Meet us at the eyeball."

I'd heard of Laumeier Sculpture Park, in the nearby suburb of Sunset Hills, but had never visited. Rosalind summarized its history as we wandered around. The original owners of the hundred plus acres of land, including an expansive estate house built in 1917, had given it to the St. Louis County Parks system in 1975. The following year, local sculptor Ernest Trova donated forty pieces of his work, and other renowned artists soon began contributing further outdoor sculptures, many of them decidedly odd.

"Modernist," insisted Rosalind, as I stood scratching my head at a jumble of huge, red-painted steel tanks. The park was now a bona fide tourist attraction and a center for the arts. Couples and family groups vied with us for space on the wooded walking trail, and crowded around one curious display after another.

"I love this place!" enthused Jess, as we explored the wooden pavilion next to an enormous abandoned concrete swimming pool, which the surrounding woods were slowly reclaiming. "We should get married here."

"I'm not sure this structure is safe for a wedding party," I said. Rosalind found something interesting at the top of another staircase. Jess and I had agreed not to plan a wedding until we knew how things stood with the Henry Lyons Foundation, and the Scales of Equilibrium for that matter. Too much turbulence. But we couldn't ignore it either. I couldn't, since I was the one who'd gone down on one knee two months earlier.

She laughed and gave my arm a playful punch. This was the Jess I loved. "Not right here, goofball. But I bet there's an event space we can rent, and we def need to say our vows in front of that steel tank sculpture you loved so much!"

"Save me," I grumbled.

"That's the idea," she murmured, melting into my embrace.

I held her in silence for a couple of minutes, heedless of the flood of small children scampering around us, and a father's frustrated appeal for them to slow down and be careful.

"If that's what you want, we'll make it happen," I said at last. "We'll find a way out of this. Whatever hole we've dug for ourselves, I promise we'll make it back out together and be stronger for it."

She squeezed my back. "I think we have to stop digging first, but maybe that's what we have to do to find our way back out." Her face lit up with another grin. "I can't claim life with you is boring, D. You sure know how to show a girl a good time!"

I wasn't quite sure what to do with that, and was spared by the buzzing phone in my pocket. "Jamal's here. Let's find Rosalind and see what fresh horrors he brings."

Jamal stood some yards distant from a massive eyeball about twice as tall as he was. I didn't recognize him at first, but the burly man wearing a dark green jacket, sunglasses, and a University of Wisconsin baseball cap looked up from his phone and waved as we approached.

"Let's walk," he suggested, leading us away from the crowd around the, frankly, creepy sculpture. Once alone, surrounded by yards of open lawn, he stopped and removed his sunglasses. The eyes he rubbed looked tired. "How are you all holding up?"

"Scraping by," I said, when neither of the women ventured an answer. "How about you? How long have you been in St. Louis?"

"Since Thursday. Izzy's coming down too, tomorrow or Monday. She's trying to get back into her apartment in Old Town, but of course Chicago's still a mess. Any word on your place?"

"We finally heard back from our neighbors," Jess confirmed. "The house is still standing and secure, or at least was when they evacuated a week ago. What does Izzy want so much to take the risk?"

Jamal shrugged. "It's her home. She's Chicago, born and bred."

"Then why come here?" Rosalind interjected. "Not to disparage the city I've called home for almost thirty years, but St. Louis doesn't seem her speed."

"Oh, I'm sure there'll be whining," he said, lips twitching into a wry grin. "But she's coming because the HLF asked her to, just like they asked me."

"And why would they do that?" I said, although I suspected I knew the answer.

"I think it's fair to say the organization is in turmoil, possibly at an inflection point. Not only has Carson vanished, but several other field agents have disappeared or stopped reporting in. A couple of Astbury's researchers too. There's no specific evidence to connect them, whether they're the victims of foul play, or if they've quit, or even defected. But, in the context of everything else, it's troubling."

"I can't speak for any of the others, but I believe I know where Carson's loyalties lie," said Rosalind quietly. "Daniel still won't say much about his life after he ran away from home, and particularly not about his time with the Scales of Equilibrium. But he did tell us how he ended up in Chicago, and at the

Themis Center rehab clinic. He'd been given a job as an orderly in a hospital close to downtown, what he'd hoped would be a fresh start. But his 'visions' - which he refused to describe in any detail - followed him there, and soon he was using again. Sure enough, he was fired and forced into rehab once more, but this time, he received a visitor when he arrived. An old man with a burn scar down the length of one cheek, who showed interest in his visions, and told him he was important to 'addressing the imbalance'."

Jess gaped at her, likely mirroring my own expression.

Jamal was more intent. "How confident are you that this 'old man' was Carson?"

"It would be a stretch to say I was confident," Rosalind replied with a thin smile. "I only met the man once. Daniel's description could apply to any number of old white men with such scars, who ask probing questions about 'visions', and who use terms like 'balance'."

Jamal looked like someone had just force fed him a spoonful of foul-tasting medicine.

"There's something between you and Carson, isn't there?" I said, remembering their confrontation in the grounds of Shotcombe House. Jamal had stopped short of calling Carson a Scales sympathizer back then. "You don't like each other much."

"We don't always like the people we work with," he muttered, then coughed and drew himself up. "But finally having evidence that they're likely working against you, after everything... well, it might help clarify things for the Foundation, at least. And, believe me, any clarity we can get right now, we'll take."

"Because?" prompted Jess, likely chafing at how long it was taking him to answer my question.

"Intrusions are surging," he said. I had to lean forward to hear him. "Based on reports from the field, they're appearing at almost double the rate predicted by Astbury's latest model. Sometimes, we get spikes in certain cities, such as the one Charli predicted in Chicago when D and Jess moved there in January. But this latest surge is across the board. St. Louis might typically expect one or two new Intrusions per month. The latest prediction is four. And Maria tells me she and her team have tethered seven in the month since we left for England.

"There are other human costs too. Untrained sensitives, unable to handle what they encounter, are falling into comas or other forms of mental distress at an alarming rate. Scales of Equilibrium attacks on our own agents, as well as freelancers such as Madam Sophia, have been reported worldwide. Information is patchy because communication is patchy. Rumors of hostile infiltrators and powerful rogue agents have compounded a very real fear of the compromised security of our comms. You gave our IT security team a scare last year, Jess. Now, they're terrified."

"This is what I've been telling everyone," huffed Jess, for all the world like me and Rosalind hadn't believed her. "Some things need to be said, but we all need to be careful what we say and how we say it."

"I appear destined to live in some sort of dystopian spy thriller," said Rosalind, pursing her lips. "I had hoped for better from my golden years."

"Oh, come on," I chided, feeling compelled to try to lighten the mood. "There's tons of life left in you yet, Rosalind. In the world too."

"There's more," said Jamal, determined to rain on my parade. "A significant percentage of these new Intrusions present memories of near-future events. The information is anecdotal, and Astbury balks at drawing premature conclusions, but some memories appear to directly contradict others."

I frowned. "What does that mean? Are they fake, or just hints of things that could happen?"

"It could be a manifestation of the many worlds theory," Jess suggested. "Each action we take, each decision we make, creates a fork in the universe. Both possibilities are true somewhere.

There could be an infinite number of universes out there, and these new Intrusions allow us to glimpse some of them." She looked awestruck by the idea.

I shivered, and Jamal also failed to share her enthusiasm. "As Astbury said, let's not jump to any conclusions. We need much more data."

"Do you pay attention to social media?" Jess challenged him. "I've noticed a recent uptick in posts about hauntings and ghosts in general. I figured everyone's just more on edge because of all the urban terrorism, but maybe there's more to it. Maybe these are the accounts of your 'untrained sensitives' and a surge of Intrusions and Imprints. The mainstream media aren't paying attention, not yet, but some independent and fringe services are starting to take notice."

"We have limited control of the media," Jamal said, lips set in a line of distaste. "Although the noise does have its uses."

"So what else does Emma have to say?" demanded Rosalind. "I don't imagine such aberrant behavior flying in the face of her beloved model sits well with her."

"It does not. But, of course, the beauty of such a model is that it learns from new data. They're running new projections daily, from what I hear. And what I hear is concerning." His voice dropped still lower. "My degree was in geology. Volcanoes have fascinated me ever since a family vacation to Hawaii as a child. I retained that fascination into adulthood, and although I couldn't break into the field as a professional, I follow as much of the research as I can. Predicting major eruptions is incredibly difficult, but there are signs, indicators of increased potential for such a cataclysm. One of those signs is a marked increase in the frequency of minor earthquakes detected in and around the volcano, sometimes resulting in a crescendo of power just before the eruption itself."

"And you think that's what's happening with the Intrusions?" I asked, echoing his sepulchral tones. "What does that eruption look like?"

He shook his head. "I don't want to guess."

"I think we can," said Rosalind. She exchanged a glum look with me and Jess, then I tore my eyes away back to Jamal.

"So," I said, "back to Izzy. Why is the HLF sending her here to join you?"

Jamal met my eyes, calm and cool. I thought I detected a hint of compassion in him before he answered. "So we can do whatever it takes to persuade you to join the Foundation. The three of you are the only known sensitives to have defeated the Agency. You may be our only hope of preventing the eruption."

Chapter Fifteen
OUR OWN RESOURCES

After a weekend of family dinners and ominous conversations in public parks, I was ready to scuttle back to the Hills' house and hide for a few days. Not that Jess would allow me to be so dramatic, of course, not without good-natured but relentless mockery. Yet it had not been so long ago that I shunned all but a very few people. By those standards, I'd been a social butterfly for the last couple of months.

Jess's parents had welcomed Rosalind and Martin into their home with customary good grace. As soon as Calvin Evans discovered a fellow avid golfer in Martin, the two of them huddled in enthusiastic and perplexing conversation about courses they'd played, equipment they used, and famous professional players, past and present. They lost me within minutes. I'd never understood the game's attraction, having only once whacked a series of ill-fated golf balls around a local par-3 course.

Rosalind and Zawida held court at the other end of the table. After a cautious initial discussion centered on the traditional Kenyan dishes Jess's mother had prepared, they launched into a wide-ranging exploration of each other's backgrounds. Jess hovered on the edges, contributing now and then, but content to listen, ready to forestall any of her mother's attempts to pin us down to a wedding date.

I allowed both conversations to wash over me while I gnawed at Jamal's revelations earlier that day.

I dragged Jess along to Sunday lunch at Fiona's house, a much louder and chaotic affair. Mary's three kids were older than Fiona's, and more prone to whining than outright screaming. Both mothers became increasingly snappish throughout the family-style meal of roast beef and potatoes, green beans, and carrots. Eric, Fiona's husband, carried the conversation with unexpected and impressive stoicism, asking me and Jess a series of polite, benign questions about our life in Chicago, and recent English "vacation".

Nevertheless, I detected an undercurrent of unease.

"We're being careful," Fiona quietly assured me, as I helped her carry dirty dishes into their kitchen. She refused point blank to let me load the dishwasher, and I could respect that. We all had our own system, and this was her territory. "Eric's taken your warning seriously. We haven't seen anyone watching our house, or the daycare, and we don't go out and about any more than we have to with these toddler terrorists. Mary and Dad say no one's bothered them either."

Mary chose that moment to enter the kitchen, clutching serving bowls in her hands. She and I had been on amicable, speaking terms for all of four months, following our unexpected reconciliation after Mom's death. Most of that had been in our family's Snapchat group, however. We hadn't seen each other face to face since the funeral. Given the chaos at the lunch table, we'd only managed a few cautious words to each other.

"What's this about, D?" she asked. I took the bowls from her and set them on the counter above the dishwasher. Fiona ignored them. I could only imagine what Mary thought, based on my life up to this point. I didn't know what Fiona had told her, and I hadn't told Fiona much.

"It's not exactly what you think," I said at last. "I'm not in trouble with the law. If anything, they're on my side this time. But I am caught up in something, something that might be hard for you to believe. It's almost impossible to explain."

Jess glided in and offered to take dessert - apple pie and ice cream - into the dining room. "Try," she told me, hefting dish and tub for balance. "They deserve to know. Eric and I have got the kids."

And so I tried. As the dishwasher purred in the background, I told my sisters about the strange sensations that had plagued me for years, especially since returning to St. Louis after prison. I explained how a chance meeting with a woman called Rosalind Hill had turned into an apprenticeship, and given me the ability to dispel the phenomena, for me and for others. I summarized the actions and motivations of two mysterious secret societies with which Jess and I had become entangled: the Henry Lyons Foundation and the Scales of Equilibrium. And, while I omitted many details, for reasons of time and information overload, I hinted at some unknown, powerful entity haunting these imprinted memories.

After I finished, surprised to be uninterrupted by screaming or wailing children, I braced myself for their inevitable accusations of insanity.

"You know," Mary began slowly, "there's that spot in my guest bedroom, right by the window. I get the shivers every time I go in there. Could that be one of these Imprints?"

I goggled at her. "That's possible. I... We can take a look at it, if you like."

She nodded, several emotions warring over her face. Skepticism, of course, and fascination, plus a healthy dose of lingering sibling dislike for all that we'd begun mending fences. But what I saw that really slew me was hope, and a kernel of admiration. Big brother was more than just a junkie and a murderer after all.

"I must say," said Fiona, brow furrowed as she ran one hand through today's turquoise-highlighted hair, "that's not what I expected to hear. Jess can see these things too? Now I really want to meet your friend Rosalind."

"Give her and Martin a few days to recover from meeting Jess's family, and I'll set it up."

She chuckled, then sobered immediately. Jess returned, carrying a stack of dessert bowls, and raised an eyebrow in my direction. I shrugged and gave her a tight smile.

"But that still doesn't explain why you think we're in danger," Fiona persisted. "It sounds like this group, the Scales of Equilibrium, are the bad guys - especially if they're behind all these attacks - and you've all had a couple run-ins with them. But what does that have to do with us?"

"I'm not sure it's a Scales thing, exactly. There's one person, a big bald white guy called Lyall, who's taken a particular dislike to me."

"Yeah, 'cos you snapped the asshole's arm in two," Jess said with a satisfied grin.

"In self defense," I hurried to clarify, before the startled looks on my sisters' faces undid months of progress. "He threatened us with a gun. And he's killed before, in cold blood. We've seen it."

The doubt didn't entirely fade from Mary's eyes, but Fiona calmly appraised me. "Sounds like a nasty piece of work. We'll continue our vigilance, as long as you think we need to. But we're not without our own resources." She held my gaze until she was sure I knew exactly what she meant.

"No," I admitted with a long sigh. "We're not. And it's time we used them."

Jamal parallel parked his white Toyota RAV4 rental with practiced ease, on a side street closer to Benton Park than Cherokee Street. We'd arrived in the latter stages of dusk. One by one, sullen yellow street lamps replaced the last fitful embers of late fall sunlight. A chill breeze assaulted me the moment I stepped onto the cracked, uneven sidewalk. With my leather jacket zipped up to my chin, I stuffed my bare hands into its front pockets; wearing gloves in November was out, on general principle.

I knew this street. I knew all these streets for blocks around. They were old acquaintances, the kind you nod at and greet politely at high school reunions, if you're into that kind of thing. For over a year, I'd walked my commute between Hickory and my apartment near Tower Grove Park. I got bored sticking to the major roads, to Cherokee and Arsenal Streets, to Jefferson Avenue and Grand Boulevard. I'd mix it up from day to day, zigzagging through the imperfect rectangle they bounded, a neighborhood as quirky as it was diverse. It had been as much a home to me as my mother and stepfather's bungalow in South City.

The Lincoln Park streets didn't feel the same, not yet at least. Who knew if they'd have a second chance to become so?

"Ready, D?" Jamal waited for me a few steps down the sidewalk. He wore the exact same clothes as at Laumeier Park, but his baseball cap was a nondescript black.

"Yes, sorry. I'm woolgathering. This area brings back a lot of memories, most of them good, and none related to Imprints."

He nodded. "I understand. I expect he does too."

"Count on it." I was delaying, and I knew it. *Come on D, you've faced down the Scales of Equilibrium twice, and gone toe to toe with The Presence. You've got this.* "Come on, then."

I struggled to recognize Hickory when I entered the dining room. If I half-closed my eyes, I could still see the chipped chocolate brown paint on walls cluttered with framed photographs of yesteryear St. Louis. I could remember the layout of the booths, wrapped in split and faded vinyl, and the square aluminum tables that packed the black-and-white checkered floor between them.

Then, when I opened my eyes fully, this vision of the past faded into urban chic, bright whites and charcoal furnishings, reclaimed wood tables and laminate panel floors. The bar and two of the original four wall-mounted TVs were the only continuity. Except for its owner, my former boss, and as much of a friend as one could call a boss: Mike Szemis.

"D! It's genuinely good to see you!" he said, pumping my hand in an enthusiastic handshake. More silver had crept into his hair since the summer, and perhaps an extra line or two wrinkled the skin around his one good eye, the other hidden under its ever-present patch.

"Good to be back," I replied, a statement that didn't have as much truth in it as I would like. "I like the new vibe. Did you upgrade the kitchen too?"

"Thanks! Yeah, we had to replace most of the equipment and..." He tailed off and a shadow passed over his face. He continued in a low murmur. "The stuff got upgraded, the people not so much. I miss having you back there."

It had been a year since the fire. I thought I'd reconciled myself to losing my job, to moving on. Mike and the rest of the staff at Hickory had been my family when most of my actual family disowned me. Part of me longed to return to simpler times. But just as Hickory's updated dining room was barely recognizable, so was my life. Simplicity wasn't an option.

"I miss it too," I admitted, "and I'm looking forward to being just a customer. Thank you for setting this up."

Mike's good eye flashed towards the back corner booth, and he couldn't suppress a grimace. "I hope you know what you're doing."

"Me too. We'll seat ourselves."

So, unable to delay any further, I led Jamal over towards that corner booth. Our dinner companions didn't rise, but Steven Rourke extended his ring-studded hand for us each to shake.

"I'm sure that was a pleasant reunion, if a little awkward," he said. His smile was ironic, and his tone laced with faux-British pomposity. So I was getting *that* Steven Rourke. "I'm pleased to see you again, Jamal. It's been, as they say, a minute."

"Good evening, Steven," Jamal said, sliding into the booth next to me.

I thought I detected a flicker of unease in Rourke's eyes as he did so, before his amicable insouciance returned. "You remember Emi, I'm sure."

The young Japanese woman next to him continued to watch us with a bland expression, without acknowledging her name. I gave her a small nod as Jamal politely greeted her, neither of which elicited any reaction at all.

"Emi doesn't waste much time on socialization, I'm afraid," said Rourke. "I'm surprised Jess isn't joining us. I have yet to properly meet your fiancée."

"News travels fast," I said. "Sorry, Jess is otherwise occupied tonight."

Actually, Jess was furious. She'd been itching to get a crack at my mother's infamous cousin for months, and was unimpressed when I asked her to stay behind. "I thought we were in this together," she'd raged. "You have my back and I have yours."

"It's not that I don't want you there, love," I'd soothed, with only limited effect. "But if we bring too many of us, this won't work. Steven doesn't react well to being outnumbered. If he doesn't believe he has control of the situation, he'll shut down, or just leave. We want something from him, and his past business relationship with Jamal gives us the best chance I can think of to get it."

"Fine," she'd said. The word every man loved to hear from their partner. I almost relented, but forced myself to listen to my own logic. I'd make it up to Jess later.

Rourke shrugged. "Too bad. She's a remarkable young woman. A solid choice, if I may say so. Can I expect a wedding invitation soon?"

"I'll see what I can do." I met his gently mocking but flinty-eyed gaze while our server brought water and took our order. I practiced my breathing. "Let me get straight to the point. I asked for this meeting because we want your help. I have two requests of you."

He looked at me in silence for a few moments, then nodded. "Let's hear them."

"One of the nutcases in the Scales of Equilibrium has threatened my family. I can take care of myself, but Fiona and Mary both have small children, and Mary's a single mom. My stepfather struggles to walk from one end of his bungalow to the other. I've warned them, and they're being careful. I've alerted the City PD to the threat, but they don't have the manpower, and neither do I, short of bundling them all into the same house, and no one wants that."

"Yeah, I can imagine. What do you want me to do about it? I'm not really in the protection business."

"No, but you have eyes and ears, likely in places where the police don't. The scumbag's name is Lyall Morrison, although I guess he might use an alias if he comes to town. But any warning you can give us would help, and I'd appreciate it."

His eyes glittered, then he inclined his head. "And your second request?"

"We - myself, Jess, Jamal, as well as the FBI and other law enforcement types - are looking for Allen Weston, the guy who started the Scales of Equilibrium, who's running this shitshow. You told me about him once, at mom's wake. I suspect you had a hand in sending me and Jess to see him at a bookstore in Chicago in the spring. I want you to help us find him before he and his thugs find us."

"Good heavens, D," he said, shaking his head in affected despair. "I do believe I warned you to be careful. You appear to have stirred up a hornet's nest."

"The nest has been restless for some time," Jamal interrupted. "Ever since D did a favor for a friend and, by coincidence, ran into a fellow ex-con working a Scales of Equilibrium community cleanup detail. I worked with you long enough, Steven, to know you thoroughly vet your potential business partners. I don't doubt you know things about the Henry Lyons Foundation that I don't. If you even know the name Allen Weston, I suspect you have amassed a considerable dossier on him, one to rival or surpass any the FBI possesses."

Rourke smiled with satisfaction. "I enjoyed our partnership, even though we failed to achieve all our mutual goals." He shot me a scowl, and I allowed myself to look smug. "But what makes you think I know anything about Allen Weston beyond his name, his past association with the HLF, and his current status as a dangerous lunatic? What makes you assume I care about anything else, or have such a dossier as you describe?"

"Because that's your real business these days," I said. "Someone once told me that information is the real currency. I've known you since you started as a small-time drug dealer, and you weren't so small by the time I went to jail for you. You may not be 'in the protection business', but you learned to throw your weight around, either through political or judicial influence, or by employing goons to do so. You diversified into real estate a decade ago, and own more property than anyone realizes. But all of that is just a distraction from your core business: the acquisition, trade, and sale of information. You see, I have a dossier on you too."

I tapped myself on the forehead for emphasis.

"Very good," he murmured with approval. He sat back in his bench seat and set his linked hands on the table. I couldn't miss the glint in his eye. "You'd have made a great lieutenant, D. Still could, if you were interested."

That was not something I ever expected to hear. I tried to keep my expression neutral. "I'm just trying to make it day to day, Steven. Can you help us find Weston or not?"

Our server, a gangly youngster I didn't recognize, tattoos scribed on every visible inch of his dark skin, chose that moment to bring our food. Rourke and I had both ordered the brisket; I wanted to see if he thought it was an improvement over my effort from his first visit here. He took a bite, and chewed with a thoughtful expression, capped off with a slight grimace. "What do I get in return?"

I dabbed at my lips with my napkin. Not bad, just a little over-seasoned. "You help me take him down."

He cocked his head. "What do you mean?"

"I can't imagine his Scales of Equilibrium are good for business," I said. "They're spreading chaos around the world, despite the best efforts of the FBI and other agencies. They've spared St. Louis so far, but that could change tomorrow. You've got a good thing going here. You're comfortable with the status quo. I dare say you'd survive an attack like North Point, but it would cripple your accustomed lifestyle. I think that's one reason you keep pointing us in Weston's direction. Fine, mission accepted. Now give us your intel."

"And what makes you think you can do what the FBI and others cannot?"

"Weston's appeal to his followers is that he has Gaia on his side, some mythical personification of our planet that seeks retribution for the injuries and indignities humanity has foisted upon it. It's not total bullshit. There *is* something out there, something Jess and I have encountered often over the last few months. Jamal can vouch for that."

Rourke's skeptical gaze switched to Jamal, who finished his mouthful of pork steak without hurry. "As incredible as it sounds, D is right. I am no longer in denial, and neither are those within the HLF most hostile to Allen Weston's Agency Theory. You understood what I was doing when we worked together. You didn't bat an eye when you watched me teach Donovan and Lana how to tether an Intrusion, how to manipulate memories of past lives with our minds, in such a way that disturbed sensitive people. I couldn't fault your skepticism that there may be some vast, unknown intelligence behind it all, or at least taking advantage of the phenomena. I assure you it is true. D and Rosalind Hill are the only people I know who have successfully fended it off."

"We need to know what Weston knows," I said, lowering my voice as I got more animated. "What exactly is his relationship to this intelligence? What does he know about its capabilities? If we can understand our enemy, we have a better shot at taking it down. And if we can take down The Presence, I think the Scales of Equilibrium collapses. And you get your city back."

Rourke planted his elbows on the table and laced his fingers together under his chin. There was a time when I'd welcomed his intense regard, another when I'd flinched from it, and, more recently, disdained it. Now I simply endured his cool, calculating gaze. "This sounds... incredible. A little over two years ago, I would have laughed you out of my restaurant. Now, though, well. It might be worth it just to watch you try. What makes you think Weston will tell you anything?"

Jamal snorted. "All we need to do is get him talking. Believe me, from my personal experience, once the man starts, you can't shut him up. He wants to tell us, or at least to tell D, Jess, and Rosalind: those who have encountered The Presence too. We just want the conversation to be on our terms."

"Good idea," Rourke agreed. He dug out a phone from his jeans pocket and started tapping on its screen. Since there was already one phone next to his place setting, I assumed he used this one for less direct means of communication. Sure enough, moments after he finished tapping, my phone buzzed with a message from a five-digit number.

I gawked at the screen for several long seconds before raising my eyes to meet his. "You're joking. What is this?"

"I suspect Allen Weston also wishes to dictate the terms of your conversation," he said, unable to keep the smugness out of his voice. "This is an address at which there has been a confirmed sighting within the last forty-eight hours. I feel I should repeat my earlier warning. Be careful, D."

I showed my phone screen to Jamal, and his raised eyebrows showed his surprise. He opened his mouth to speak, but then we heard an ominous mechanical thud, and all the lights and TVs went out.

The low buzz of background conversation died as everyone held their breath, waiting in vain for power to be restored. Hickory wasn't alone: the street outside the windows looked just as dark and mournful. Inside, the gloom was interrupted only by the glow from people's phones, and its eerie reflection from their owners' confused faces. Emi was one such owner, and with a Jamal-like display of extreme emotion, widened her eyes as she tilted her device towards Rourke.

I couldn't make out his initial reaction, but Rourke's voice was grim when he finally spoke. "Show them."

The hair on my arms stood at attention as Emi swiveled her phone for us to see the image on its screen. I was all too familiar with the image, though mostly from seeing it tattooed behind someone's left ear. I stared at a set of monochrome scales, the lower side of which supported an image of the Earth.

"That's the home page of the Midwest Power website," Rourke confirmed. "It looks like the Scales of Equilibrium didn't wait until tomorrow to bring their chaos to St. Louis. Good luck, D."

Chapter Sixteen

WE'RE HERE TO TALK

The power didn't come back on that night, or the next day. The outage appeared to be widespread, reaching deep into rural Missouri, west and a little south of the city.

Jess made a habit of keeping at least one portable power bank charged, as did Martin, so with care, we maintained charge on our phones. Rosalind dug out her old battery-powered boom box and a plastic tub of CDs, which Jess rifled through like a treasure chest. She treated us all to the fruits of her exploration, including bands I'd heard of, like New Order and The Cure, as well as many I hadn't like The Sundays or All About Eve. Martin and Rosalind became quite nostalgic, especially once candlelight dominated after sunset.

The few businesses with power generators and public Wi-Fi suddenly reclaimed much of the business that had ebbed over the last month, as people overcame their anxiety over public places in order to sate their addiction to connectivity. Tempers ran high.

"I'm surprised the Scales haven't sabotaged any cell or broadband networks," I observed the following day, during a gloomy lunch of salad and fresh fruit at the Hill's kitchen table.

"They're using them for their cyberattacks, like this one," Jess said, frowning at her phone screen, thumbs poised above it. "Companies like Midwest Power make mistakes, leave gaps in their defenses. Although, you'd have hoped their internal network wasn't so wide open that anyone breaching those defenses could cause so much havoc."

"I'm not sure they want to dismantle all the trappings of civilization," Rosalind added, her voice much duller than usual. She looked by far the most exhausted of us, her weary, unfocused eyes withdrawn within dark shadow. She'd had a "difficult" conversation with Daniel the previous night, and clearly hadn't slept well. "They're targeting cities, the urban centers they believe symbolize, and are activity responsible for, environmental degradation. Perhaps they believe we should all revert to pastoralism, just with Wi-Fi."

Martin snorted. "I'd love to see that business plan, should such a thing exist. Society just doesn't work that way. We'd descend into anarchy, and likely open warfare, long before recreating some mythical agrarian paradise."

Rosalind tried a weak smile. "Perhaps I'll ask Allen Weston to show us the plan, if we ever meet him. Jess, my phone is upstairs. Can you bring up the street view of that address, please? Something about it is nagging at me."

"I still can't believe we traipsed all over the Midwest, and the asshole's been lurking in St. Louis the whole time," Jess grumbled, tapping and swiping, then passing her phone to Rosalind.

"I suppose Wildwood counts as St. Louis," Rosalind murmured, squinting at the screen. She pinched, swiped, and rotated the image, blinking slowly. I wondered if her post-Presence headaches lingered, as mine had. "I'm not sure, but I might have been here before."

"Seriously?" I said, before the penny dropped. "Was it a social event, or were you erasing an Imprint?"

"I never was very social, especially after Daniel left. No, I'm thinking this was an Erasure, before I met you. I remember that patio, to the right of the double front door. It looks lifted directly from a street cafe in Rome."

"Do you remember anything about the inside of the house?"

She frowned, then shook her head. "No. I can't even recall who brought me in, and I should. I didn't get too many jobs that far out of the city."

"Well, maybe you'll remember more when we go there," said Jess with unexpected ferocity. "Because you are joining us, right?"

Martin opened his mouth to speak, but Rosalind covered his hand with hers, and held his gaze as she replied.

"I think I should. Jamal and Izzy are capable, but I agree with him: we really don't know what to expect if we just show up on the doorstep. We don't know if Weston lives there, if he's visiting a friend or sympathizer, or if it's a decoy. But if the house once had an Imprint, we now understand there's a possibility other Intrusions will have occurred because of my Erasure. And if there's a chance he somehow uses those Intrusions to attract or communicate with The Presence, then - and I say this with all humility - we need to bring all the HLF's best and brightest."

"I still worry you're all walking into a trap," Martin protested. "And you're hurting, Rosa. I know you're trying to hide it, but I'm worried about you. Are you sure I shouldn't call Agent Jones and bring the FBI down on him?"

If anything could have roused Rosalind, it was mention of Carmella Jones. She withdrew her hand and straightened up in her chair, narrowing her eyes and pursing her lips.

"I am quite certain of that, love. Although, I do think it might be prudent to have her on speed dial. But if we leave Allen Weston to the FBI, it may be days, weeks, or even months before we get a chance to talk to him, if at all. We can't take that risk. Taking him into custody might hamper the Scales' mundane operations, but we need his intelligence on The Presence, especially if what Jamal fears is true."

Martin stared at her, and Jess and I watched in wary silence. "This eruption you spoke of?"

She nodded. "Daniel thinks one is coming too, although he refused to explain why he believes so. And, of course, he thinks we should let it. He's excited by the prospect, although he couldn't tell me what he thinks will happen. Our son may have taken a step towards us, love, but he's still a true believer."

Martin grimaced, then reached out to cover her hand again, and she let him. "I still think it's a mistake. One hint of trouble, call me and we'll bring down the wrath of the FBI."

"For what it's worth," I said, "I doubt we'll be walking into a trap, not blindly at least. I'm sure Weston knows we're all back in St. Louis, and probably that we're looking for him. But I doubt he knows we have this address. As long as we're careful, we should be able to get what we need from him and then get out. The Feds can have him then."

"And you trust Rourke not to sell us out?" Jess asked, not for the first time.

I shrugged. "Not if it was just about me. But I trust his self-interest. Any short-term gain he might achieve by betraying us will be more than offset by long-term losses if the Scales of Equilibrium drag us all down into chaos. Besides, what else can we do? If anyone has a better idea, now's the time to mention it."

Rosalind shook her head. "No, I think this is our best shot. Let's see how long it takes Jamal to 'make arrangements'."

It took less than a day, as it turned out. Jamal messaged us at what seemed like midnight in the Hills' candlelit living room, although the clear evening wasn't that old. We were to rendezvous the following afternoon at a small bed-and-breakfast just over a mile from our target, with him, Izzy, and "other agents".

"Who else has he found that he thinks will be able to help?" I wondered.

Our recent trip to England had forever spoiled the meaning of the word "cottage" for me. It now evoked a thatched roof over venerable brown stone, vines, and flowers tangling around a weathered oak door and lead-mullioned windows, nestled amid rolling wooded hills. By that standard, I wouldn't have looked twice at Grays Cottage, a plain white clapboard house set deep in a lot of patchy grass, next to a creek that burrowed under the two-lane highway. Paint peeled from the clapboard, and at least one plank of the wooden picnic table looked rotten. An expansive covered porch spanned the entire front of the house, a half dozen rocking chairs nestling amidst a riot of garland and Christmas lights, already shining as the sun sank behind the treeline.

I braced myself for Jess's rant about Christmas decorations in early November, but she'd just recognized the woman sitting in the chair to Izzy's right.

"Lana fucking Gunderson," she muttered, as we clambered out of Rosalind's Mini. I swear the damn thing shrank every time I rode in it. Jess's eyes were better than mine, and I had to squint before I recognized the smiling blonde we'd last seen at the Chouteau Village condos just over a year before. That was the day we'd learned people could create Imprints, that Jess discovered her own sensitivity to the phenomena, and, although we didn't realize it at the time, we'd first connected our wills to erase one. I'd barely managed to erase the Imprint that Lana and her boyfriend Donovan had created as we watched.

"Let's be professional," said Rosalind, straightening her skirt suit. She certainly looked the part. Jess and I had fallen back on T-shirts and jeans, making the most of the near seventy degree afternoon temperature.

Jamal and Izzy met us at the bottom of the porch steps, while Lana and two older men I didn't recognize hung back. Dark brown roots showed underneath the bubblegum pink of Izzy's hair, and her makeup was minimal. Maybe that was why she looked so disgruntled as we greeted each other.

"You're not seeing St. Louis at its best," I assured her.

She scowled and waved away the comment. "I like my cities the same way I like my men: bigger, and with power." Jess guffawed, which at least brought the hint of a smile to Izzy's face. "And preferably not radioactive. But this isn't even the city. It's the boonies. It's like being in Wisconsin. Are you sure You-Know-Who is out here?"

"So it seems," Jess confirmed. "Him, and probably some of his Death Eaters too." Jess never could pass up a Harry Potter reference.

"D, Jess, Rosalind, you remember Lana," said Jamal, beckoning to our former adversary. Lana's smile was uncertain. Rosalind shook her hand, and it seemed churlish not to return her hug.

"I'm sorry about Donovan," I told her, with some honesty. My former college buddy may have sold his services to Steven Rourke, and, honestly, been a bit of a prick, but Jamal claimed he'd also done some good. He certainly hadn't deserved to be attacked by his HLF handlers, the infamous Alice and Robert Harrington, or to be in a coma. "Any improvement?"

"Not that I've heard," she said. "I've only seen him once, after it happened. His parents don't approve of me. I'm grateful Maria keeps me posted."

"Maria?"

"Maria Gomez," interjected Jamal. "A top field agent for the Henry Lyons Foundation, and currently running things in St. Louis."

"But not here," observed Rosalind. "Unless she's inside?"

Jamal shook his head. "I have a lot of respect for Maria. But she's always been a stickler for the rules. I doubt she would approve of our operation here today without clearing it with HQ first."

"And you're a forgiveness over permission kinda guy?" Jess said, with a smirk.

"Sometimes. But the more people who learn about this, the more chance someone will warn Weston. I'm hoping I can trust these three, at least until after the fact."

He introduced us to the other agents, white-haired Brett and bald-headed Samuel. Both shook my hand, but neither said much, treating me with respect bordering on awe that made me uncomfortable.

"So what's the plan?" I asked Jamal, eyeing them and Lana dubiously. "I thought we were going to keep this small, just you and the three of us, with Izzy as lookout from the street."

"Yeah, cos I'm nice and inconspicuous in small-town America," grumbled Izzy.

"The address Rourke gave us is on record as a past Intrusion site," said Jamal, with an apologetic glance at Rosalind. She gave him a wintry smile. "That means it's a relapse candidate. Should Weston, or any other residents, attempt to bring that into play, I wanted backup. Lana was scheduled to tether an Intrusion at this bed-and-breakfast, demonstrating the technique to Brett and Samuel. Instead, Izzy will hang back here. If she hears from any of us, she can lead the others into forming a remote connection to help us out."

A dozen questions popped into my mind, and judging from the dubious looks on Jess and Rosalind's faces, they had their own doubts.

"That's a long way to form a connection," Rosalind observed. "Especially with agents we've never met."

Izzy folded her arms and raised her head in defiance. "Leave that to me. We proved the concept in England. D knows what to look for. He knows my 'shape'." Her eyes twinkled with mischief. Jess laughed, but she also took my hand and squeezed hard.

I cleared my throat. "Hopefully we won't need it, but I appreciate the help, from all of you. Is there anything else we need to discuss? No? Then let's do this."

Jamal offered use of his RAV4 and, no disrespect to Rosalind, my back thanked him. He drove under the speed limit down the winding county highway, in shadows from the already westering sun. Despite that, we almost missed the entrance to the driveway, protected by a cluster of mostly leafless oak trees. The gravel surface had deteriorated enough to toss us around vigorously despite our seatbelts, and we were all grateful after he parked on the semi-circular concrete pad in front of the house. No other vehicles were in sight.

I shielded my eyes against the sun and stared. It was the kind of sprawling mishmash of luxury typical of the far suburbs, where costs were half those in Clayton or Ladue. Dozens of windows punctuated the pale stone facade, taller and wider than usual, and there were so many gables that the jagged roofline looked fit to conceal a small army of medieval archers. The Italian street cafe style patio Rosalind remembered included a marble fountain, whose soft burbling was the only sound other than our cautious footsteps towards the double front doors. The house had power, possibly a generator.

I didn't realize I was holding my breath until we stood under the shallow porch, looking at each other and waiting to see who would ring the doorbell. I'm sure I wasn't the only one to notice the security cameras nestled in every crevice.

"You want to do the honors, D?" Jamal asked.

I shrugged. What difference did it make? Still, it was not without trepidation that I reached out and pressed the button. Inside, chimes fit to rouse a small village announced our arrival. Then we waited.

And waited.

After a full minute of awkward silence, Jess suggested I press it again.

"You don't think they would've heard that?" I protested, but did it anyway, with the same result. Jamal stepped back so he could watch the windows, but Rosalind placed her ear against the front doors, furrowing her brow in concentration.

"I'm certain I can hear something," she said. "Music. Classical. Vivaldi, I think."

"So either someone's home and ignoring us," said Jess, "or they're too lazy to turn off the music when they leave the house." She grabbed the right door handle and turned it experimentally. The door cracked open, and she froze, then looked at me in silent inquiry. I could hear the music too.

"The Four Seasons," murmured Jamal. "Spring, if I'm not mistaken."

"We don't seem to have triggered any alarms," I said, impatient and uninterested in the musical selection. "We might as well go in."

Jess hesitated. "Should we stay together? Or should some of us go around the back?"

Rosalind chuckled. "I don't think we split up this time. We're here to talk, not to burglarize."

Jess glanced at me, then pushed the door open wider, and we all stepped into a towering two-story entrance foyer. From what we could see of the great room, dining room, plus a glimpse of kitchen, the interior was as tastelessly lavish as the exterior of the house. Multiple wireless speakers sitting on shelves or in alcoves provided the soundtrack. Other than that, there were no signs of life.

"Hello?" I called. "The door was open. We rang, but no one answered. Is anyone home?"

No response. Jamal cocked his head, closed his eyes, and then reopened them. "Do you all feel that?"

I tried closing my own eyes, annoyed that I'd abandoned my usual first instinct to detect any Imprints when entering a new building. A wave of cloying heat lapped at my right side, possibly coming from the open staircase leading to the second floor. I sniffed, and caught a faint scent of antiseptic, as if the house had just been deep-cleaned. And maybe that's all it was, but when I looked around, I could see Jess's nostrils flaring with revulsion and Rosalind cupping an ear, listening to something that I doubted was Vivaldi.

I took a hesitant step towards the stairs. "Yeah, we feel it. There's an Imprint here, and a shitty one at that."

"I think we can rule out coincidence," said Rosalind. "Assuming we are not betrayed, this could just be for contingency."

"Or it could be bait," suggested Jess, with a dark glance at the staircase.

Jamal looked up from his phone, where he'd tapped out a brief message, presumably to Izzy. "Unless the occupants of this house take very deep naps, it's almost certain they know we are here and are choosing not to introduce themselves. We have a decision to make. Do we intrude further, hoping to find Weston and getting him to talk? Or do we retreat, perhaps to return later or pursue another approach?"

"What other approach?" I demanded. "Call the FBI to this house and hope Weston is here? This is the only lead we have. We've been chasing ghosts so far, and almost fallen into one trap. But we're prepared this time, and we have numbers. I say we explore."

"Me too," said Jess, taking my hand again. She was trembling, although whether from excitement or apprehension, I couldn't tell. Maybe both.

Jamal looked at Rosalind, who nodded. "I remember this place now. The Imprint was of a young woman giving birth, unmedicated, in one of the upstairs bedrooms. The sensations I experienced back then are almost identical to those I'm experiencing now. I'm really quite curious. But I'm sure I don't have to tell any of you to be on your guard and prepared for anything."

Her tone was measured, and her stance even. She was the shortest and lightest person in the room, yet she radiated power and control. I pulled myself together, and after one deep breath, nodded. Her eyes twinkled. "After you, D."

We crept up the stairs - me, Jess, Rosalind, and Jamal at the rear. The sickly heat and bleach odor intensified as we emerged onto a balcony, overlooking the empty great room, leading to a carpeted hallway. Three doors on the left, one at the end, all closed. I was fairly certain the Imprint was behind that last door, but it was strong enough to engage from where I stood. Not that I had any intention of doing so.

We flanked the first door, two on each side, and I rapped on the solid core wood twice before opening it. The bedroom, of a teenage Swiftie judging by the decor, was empty. So was the adjacent bathroom. Jamal frowned as we peered into the impersonal second bedroom. He held his finger to his lips, then shuffled back down the corridor. I couldn't understand why we'd try to be quiet now, after we'd so clearly announced our-selves, but said nothing.

One more door to go. We all looked back at Jamal, who stood at the balcony rail gazing down at the great room, and didn't acknowledge us.

"Here goes nothing," I muttered, and turned the handle.

A king bed dominated the master suite. Its solid oak head-board stood almost as tall as Rosalind. Blankets, sheets, and pillows tumbled together in chaos, evidence of light sleeping or, more likely, other uses of the bed. But the source of the Imprint was further on, in the bathroom whose door, on the far wall, was a few inches ajar. Unless someone was hiding in the massive wardrobe, which might have come straight from Shotcombe House, the bedroom itself was empty.

"I suppose we should check the bathroom," whispered Ros-alind doubtfully. Jess followed her, but I stayed on the thresh-old, one hand resting on the door handle.

Sweat beaded on my forehead, and I grew more nauseous by the second. This was a bad one. I associated the fever heat and bleach smell with memories of pain, which the Henry Lyons Foundation classified as a Level Two Intrusion. I should be able to tether such a memory by myself with a Single Point Lock. But, as Jamal often pointed out, each Level had its own range of difficulty. I wanted no part of this.

Jess choked as Rosalind pushed the bathroom door wider open with a strange creak, almost half a thud. The older woman's face was impassive as she stared inside, but Jess turned away, covering her mouth as she coughed. The sudden alarm on her face was my only warning before a hand clamped over my own on the door handle.

"Welcome home, motherfucker," hissed Lyall Morrison, and he brought his other fist down on my forearm like a hammer.

CHAPTER SEVENTEEN
A PART TO PLAY

The gravel road was murder.

I cradled my broken arm against my chest, desperate to keep it as immobile as possible until someone took pity on me and splinted it. The sudden, piercing pain of the break had ebbed to a dull throb. We'd been bundled into a pair of black SUVs, then driven down a series of winding rural roads as the daylight faded. When our vehicle turned off the last of these, I couldn't help but cry out at every bounce. I braced myself against the door and the seat in front of me, as the bumpy surface tossed us around like a ship's unsecured cargo during a storm. Tears streamed down my face, tears of agony and frustration.

We'd walked straight into a trap. We'd gambled, and lost.

Lyall gloated over me from the passenger seat, maintaining his gun's aim at my chest. He favored his left arm, the one I'd broken in similar fashion three months before, holding it flat against his stomach, slowly flexing his fingers. There'd been nothing wrong with his fist, though.

Despite his taunts, I refused to waste words on him. I sought my inner calm and allowed his mockery to wash over me, immediately forgotten. Sensei Ryuichi would be proud. Of course, I also devised several plans to give Lyall's ass a proper kicking in the near future. I had to do something, anything, to take my mind off the pain and the fear of what would happen next.

Darkness fell before the car rolled to a merciful stop. I had no idea where we were. We'd driven for at least half an hour, and could be anywhere in eastern Missouri. Perhaps, in a next level fuck you, they'd taken me to the doorsteps of Missouri Eastern Correctional. All I could see through the front windshield was what looked like a simple two-story farmhouse, flickering yellow light bleeding around the drawn curtains of one downstairs room.

Lyall climbed out of the car and yanked open my door, gesturing with his gun. "Out you get, asshole. Nice and slow."

I glanced at my backseat companion. Jamal lolled within the restraint of his seatbelt, still unconscious. I hadn't seen any bumps or bruises. Maybe they'd shot him with some sort of tranquilizer, but I wouldn't give Lyall the satisfaction by asking.

"Don't worry about him," Lyall said, sounding entirely too pleased with himself. "Let's get you inside first. We've got a guest room just for you. Need help with your bags? Oh, that's right: you don't have any."

A comedian, too. I hated him more every second.

"Where's Jess?" I demanded, my voice much hoarser than I would've liked. "Where's Rosalind?"

"Don't worry about them either. The only person you should worry about right now is you. How's the arm, Rodriguez? You should really see a doctor about that."

"Fuck you, Lyall."

He laughed at my pitiful rejoinder, and sped me on my way with a solid push in the back. I bit back another grunt of pain and stole covert glances around me as I stumbled towards the farmhouse. I couldn't see any more headlights, nor hear another engine. The disinterested chirping of insects or tree frogs was my dejection's only soundtrack.

Lyall hadn't been alone when he jumped me, and his three Scales-tattooed companions had wielded enough firepower to offset any martial art response Rosalind and Jess could conjure up. The Scales had confiscated their phones and zipped their wrists, before marching them downstairs into the second vehicle. Jess gave our captors several pieces of her mind before the car door thumped closed behind her, but Rosalind remained silent, regarding the thugs with every ounce of cool contempt she possessed. They didn't want to get near her, but she'd ended up in the backseat of the SUV all the same.

A short, middle-aged woman sporting a blonde pixie cut and a severe expression opened the front door. She gazed up at me with curiosity as Lyall prodded me inside, but said nothing. I wasn't in a conversational mood either. To my right, what looked like an oil lamp squatted on a kitchen table, providing the only illumination.

Lyall turned on his phone's flashlight and guided me up the creaking, straight staircase. My 'guest room' proved to be a corner room no more than ten feet on a side, furnished only with a twin bed without sheets or pillows. The single window looked as if it had been painted shut some time ago.

"Sit," Lyall commanded, so I sat as carefully as I could. The mattress was soft and uneven, but I doubted I'd be lying down anytime soon.

"Now what?" I asked.

"Now you wait. Don't go anywhere."

With a smirk, he shut the door behind him and slid home a deadbolt. Pale moonlight leaked through the window, wrestling unenthusiastically with the gloom. I listened to Lyall's footsteps recede, blending with the unintelligible murmur of downstairs conversation.

I waited, stewing over this turn of events. What could or should we have done differently? Had Rourke sold us out after all? As easy as it was to blame him for all my misfortune, I didn't think so. Whether or not he gave two shits for my personal well-being, I couldn't imagine him aligning with the Scales and what they represented.

Had we been too rash to enter the Wildwood house uninvited? Should we have tipped off the FBI instead? I worried over these questions, as if probing an aching tooth with my tongue. Their answers didn't change my current situation, didn't stop me worrying about Jess, or Rosalind, or Jamal. The key question in my mind was whether Izzy and her team had any idea what happened to us. Because if not, we were on our own.

Despite the pain, my eyelids had started to droop when I heard louder voices downstairs. I only caught a handful of words, like "upstairs", "necessary", and "for your safety". None of the voices sounded like Jamal. I hadn't heard them bring him upstairs; was he still in the car, unconscious? Or had they driven him somewhere else? Finally, I heard someone climbing the stairs, and composed myself. There was a moment of silence after the footsteps stopped, broken by two sharp knocks on the door. Then the deadbolt was withdrawn, the door opened, and in walked Allen Weston, carrying the oil lamp.

Life on the run didn't appear to have fazed him much. His silvering hair and short beard were still neatly trimmed, his eyes bright and lively behind glasses he might have bought from the same store as Jamal. The checkered button-down shirt and jeans looked fresh and clean. His brow furrowed in annoyance as he surveyed the room, possibly noting the absence of a chair. Then he sighed and closed the door behind him.

"D Rodriguez," he said, in the rich, melodious tones I remembered from the Chicago bookstore. He gazed at me with a hungry curiosity that was far more disquieting than Lyall's vicious enmity. "I assume you know who I am."

"Allen Weston," I said promptly. "I've been looking for you."

"So I gather. And having adventures in the process. May I see your arm?"

I hesitated, but he didn't have the air of a sadist. I lifted my visibly swollen forearm, and he stepped forward to inspect it. Careful fingers probed my skin, and I remembered how surprisingly small they were. I winced when they found the site of the break, where Lyall's vengeful fist had slammed down, and he withdrew.

"Bad, but not terrible. No skin break. We'll give you some pain meds and work up a field splint until you see a proper doctor. I do apologize. My instructions were to bring you to me unharmed, but I underestimated Lyall's grudge."

"Every boss needs his muscle," I spat. "Even if they try to distance themselves from it."

His eyes flashed, then he grimaced. "I can't fault you for looking at it that way, and I'm sure your current opinion of me is very much a negative one. But I hope to change that."

I snorted. "Good luck with that. You and your merry maniacs are killing people. You're terrorists. You claim you're trying to save the planet, but you're no better than any of the far right mobs trying to make their countries great again."

If I thought that would rile him up, put him on the defensive, I was disappointed. Instead, he sighed and nodded, then gestured to the end of the bed. "May I sit? I've been on my feet all day."

I shrugged, ignoring the resulting twinge of pain.

He perched on a corner of the mattress, his free hand brushing down his jeans as he settled on its lumpy surface. "I don't doubt we can both find much to dislike about each other. We can dwell on that if you wish, but it won't bring either of us closer to profiting from our conversation, to achieving our goals. And I don't think our goals are so very different."

"You must be joking."

"I'm not. We both wish to understand Gaia."

So there it was. The very topic I'd hunted him down to discuss. I sensed I could ply him with questions, perhaps sate my curiosity, and learn enough to protect myself and others from The Presence. But I wasn't in this alone, and I didn't care to abandon my fiancée and friends in the quest for personal knowledge.

"Not just us," I said.

He dismissed them with a wave of his hand. "I hear you managed to get heads out of the sand back in jolly old England. All those who ridiculed me for years, ignoring the mountain of evidence that an Agency is behind Echoes, now acknowledge the truth. Even dear old Astbury had to admit she was wrong. I wish I'd seen the look on her face! Such a brilliant mind, but the history of science is littered with brilliant minds closed to discoveries that would revolutionize their disciplines. For every Darwin or Einstein, there are dozens of forgotten establishment voices deriding new ideas. The Henry Lyons Foundation was once a noble enterprise, but it's been corrupted by zealots, those who wish only to destroy what they don't understand. I commend you for escaping their dogma."

This was the Allen Weston I remembered from the book store, passionate and eloquent, with a sprinkle of manic intensity. My own opinions of the HLF remained complicated. I wasn't ready to defend them, but I certainly wasn't going to condemn them either, not to him. I wondered at the source of his information and then remembered what Kara had told us of Carson Livingston's defection. Could I use that somehow?

"Sure, the HLF are interested, but I was thinking of Jess, Rosalind, and Jamal. You know, the other people your pet thugs kidnapped. What have you done with them? They deserve a seat at the table too."

Weston's lip curled. "Do they? Jamal Peters is a dangerous ally. Always on the periphery, never quite sure of himself, always happy for others to take the risks and face the consequences. Ask Carson about Jamal sometime, if you wish to learn the truth about the man."

"Carson's a friend of yours, is he?"

"A friend? No. I don't believe Carson has any friends, merely an ever evolving set of acquaintances, who merit his attention and favor based on what they can do for him. He's an ally, but an important one. Carson was one of the first to listen to my ideas, back when I began to understand what Echoes truly were."

I frowned. The persistent throb of pain from my arm was making it hard to think. "Echoes? Are you talking about Intrusions?"

"No. 'Intrusion' is the zealot's term, born from fear of the unknown. It's borderline bigotry and has no place in science. What else are these memories we manipulate, but echoes of events that once happened, either in our timeline's past or its future?"

"But you think they're more than that, don't you? That's what Agency theory is all about, right?"

He levered himself off the bed, and for a moment I thought he was going to storm out. Instead, he strode over to the window, peering outside at I could only guess what.

"How old were you when you encountered your first Echo?" he asked, without turning around.

"I'm not sure," I said, recalling my sometimes drug-addled college escapades and twelve year prison sentence. There had been many times I'd felt strange, singularly uncomfortable with my environment, but had any of those been caused by an Imprint, or Echo? "Definitely by the time I returned to St. Louis, a little over three years ago."

"I was sixteen, so not long after you were born. I stayed over at a friend's house, three months after I discovered my sister's body, dead from a heroin overdose in her own bedroom. His parents let me sleep in their basement, all ghastly pine paneling and a drop ceiling that was too low. I thought it was claustrophobia keeping me awake, but something in my subconscious mind recognized the phenomenon and knew what to do. What I saw there was disturbing. I tried to make myself believe it was the overstimulated imaginings of a pubescent boy, but it felt real in a way that wet dreams did not. My instincts took over, and I made the memory disappear, channeled it away somehow. Sound familiar?"

"You erased the Imprint."

He cocked his head, then turned back to face me, the room's shadows dancing as the lamp moved. "Imprint. Yes, I remember hearing you use that term. I told no one, of course. Who would believe something so outlandish, especially coming from an awkward, grieving kid? I might have made myself forget it, as I tried to reinvent a life torn to shreds, as I took up Angel's passion for saving the world, one animal and recycling container at a time. But it happened again, two months later in a New York subway station, and that time I wasn't so lucky. My coma lasted three days. I woke up in hospital, to my parents' immense relief. The doctors feared some brain injury, although they didn't understand the cause. All I know is I spent that time in dreamless sleep until I was called back."

I scratched my arm, then wished I hadn't. I considered demanding the pain meds and splint he'd offered, but Weston was talking freely. Perhaps he'd actually say something useful if I didn't interrupt his train of thought. "Called back?" I coaxed.

His eyes gazed into the distance over my head. "I heard my name. I thought it was my father at the time, or maybe one of the doctors. But I believe otherwise now. A few days after we returned home, a man from Harvard visited our dairy farm. He offered me a full scholarship to study environmental law and the services of a private tutor to ensure my high school grades were good enough to qualify. His name was John Livingston. You can probably guess who he really worked for."

"The HLF has a college scholarship program?"

"Not one you can apply for. He never did say exactly how he'd learned about me, but one thing I continue to credit the Foundation for is their ability and capacity to discover and monitor people sensitive to Echoes. It's been very useful, although now that Carson's masquerade is over, I'll have to make do with what he knows and is willing to share. And what I know, of course."

I shifted on the bed until I could rest my back against the wall. I needed him to get to the point. "What does this have to do with Agency theory?"

He blinked, and his convivial expression cooled. "Is my life story boring you? Did you think you could just stop by, get what you wanted from me, and leave, calling the FBI on your way out?"

"No. But I'm worried about Jess and Rosalind, and my fucking arm hurts."

"The ladies are fine," he snapped. "I'm going to talk to them too, but I'm starting with you, because you're the most important."

"Why?"

"Because Gaia knows you. You have a part to play. I've seen it."

My head thunked against the wall, harder than I intended. "What have you seen?"

"Echoes. Echoes of the future. I hear others see them now, memories downstream from our current vantage point in time. But I've always seen them. I've seen things that made me despair. I've championed environmental causes, tried to educate students and colleagues and friends alike that humanity is destroying our planet. Our species is causing a sixth mass extinction in record time, possibly one life on Earth can't recover from. Few listen, or even care. I've seen what will happen if we don't. Astbury never believed, always explained them away as events from our past. She refused to enter the data into her sacred model correctly, or maybe she would have understood. But I soon realized what Echoes were: warnings and a cry for help. I decided to listen."

I heard the buzz of a vibrating phone. He dug one out of his pocket, scanned its screen, then replaced it without acknowledgement.

"I was terrified at first," he continued, adopting a reverential tone. "I knew something was out there, in the background of these memories. Astbury wasn't the only one who refused to believe me, and soon I kept my encounters to myself. Or mostly to myself. A precious few also nurtured suspicions of an Agency. Others, such as Carson, were receptive. But even I wasn't sure exactly what this Agency was until I learned about the 'visions' of a young American drug addict in Denver, Colorado. It took time for him to open up to me, but after he did, there was no longer doubt in my mind. Not only had he encountered the Agency, he had communicated with it! And I could put a name to the Agency, a human name, but one rooted in ancient mythology that personified the planet to whose defense I'd committed my life's work: Gaia."

Most of this I knew, or had suspected. I sensed I was close to some of the answers I wanted, but also to some other peril. I latched onto the one piece of truly new information. "Speaking of names, would this young American drug addict be Daniel Hill?"

He nodded in satisfaction. "Daniel was in bad shape when I first met him, struggling with the latest attempt to kick his habit. Few paid attention to his withdrawal-incited ravings. Were it not for my own experience, I would've dismissed him as just another brain-fried junkie. But he was clearly sensitive to Echoes, and I proved that even though it left him a gibbering wreck for hours afterward. I needed answers, so I gave him what he craved. And at our next Echo... There are moments in our lives when everything changes, when all that happened before is relegated to the garage of history. Only moving forward matters. Only the new paradigm has relevance. Through the boy, I could communicate with Gaia! I emerged from that Echo with a new mission, a crystallization of what my life's work really meant."

"Wait. You gave Daniel drugs? You got him hooked again?"

"It was necessary," he said, with another dismissive gesture. "As I'm sure you know, clarity of thought is essential when embracing an Echo. If it makes you feel any better, once I got what I needed, I placed him in one of the best drug rehab facilities in the country. He's clean now. His devotion to Gaia replaced any of his old cravings."

"Yeah, much better, thanks. And was it you who prevented Rosalind and Martin from seeing him all those years?"

"No. That was all Daniel. I turned out to be a better parent than they ever were."

I wanted to hit him then, broken arm and all. I winced as I rocked forward, trying to stand, stabs of agony reaching all the way up to my shoulder. Weston watched me without emotion, and that stopped me as much as the pain. I took a deep, if ragged, breath, and added him to the list of people who needed their ass kicked.

"I am interested in his mother, of course," he went on. "From what Carson and others have shared, she's a remarkable woman, powerful and clever. There's something to the genetics after all. Daniel clearly derives his talent from her, in considerably less polished form. But I can't work with her. She has declared herself an enemy of Gaia."

"Why, because she keeps whipping the ass of all the Scales thugs you send against her?"

"Because she destroys Echoes. Twice now, instead of nurturing their energy, Gaia's energy, she has cut off that energy at the source. It's as if she amputated and cauterized a limb, instead of tending a shallow cut, allowing the blood to clot naturally. She cannot be allowed to do so again."

I wanted to ask how he intended to stop her, but for all that she was "remarkable, powerful and clever", she was one woman at the mercy of I didn't know how many Lyall-like thugs. I knew what men could do when confronted with a woman better than they were. *Jess, you and Rosalind take care of each other*, I prayed. "I did that once too, you know."

"Because of her tutelage. You didn't know any better. And you won't do it again. I have seen it."

"What have you seen? Cut to the chase here, Weston. You know I want answers - more answers - about Gaia. But what do you want from me?"

He gave me a grim smile. "I want answers too. Why does Gaia want to talk to you so badly? I'm going to find out tonight."

The skin on my arms, that wasn't throbbing in pain, prickled with foreboding instead. "And how will you do that?"

"Earlier this summer, a supporter of mine encountered an Echo here, in this very house. Instead of releasing its energy, he held it so I could see it for myself. It showed a future memory, one at which I was also present, in commune with Gaia. And so were you, D Rodriguez."

He opened the bedroom door, then paused before leaving. "I'll send someone to take care of your arm and give you something for the pain. But nothing too strong. I want you clear-headed. We're going to see Gaia together, and we're going to find out why it thinks you're so damn important."

CHAPTER EIGHTEEN
SALVATION

The pixie cut woman, who I guessed was the owner of the farmhouse, fixed up my arm. By which I mean she braced my forearm with a strip of scrap wood, wrapped it in gauze from a first aid kit, then fashioned a sling from what looked like an old bedsheet.

She avoided eye contact and stayed silent except for an occasional command to "hold still" or "lift". She refused to even acknowledge my demands to know where Jess, Rosalind, or Jamal were, but did, with reluctance, allow me to use the bathroom.

Before exiting the bedroom and locking the door behind her, she dropped two pain tablets into my palm. Since no one had given me anything to drink, I dry swallowed the pills, leaving a bitter taste in their wake. They didn't help much.

I tried to distract myself from the throbbing pain by pacing back and forth, seven steps one way, seven steps back. I'd done this in my first cell at Missouri Eastern Correctional, unwilling to accept my imprisonment by sitting or lying down. At least, I'd paced until my cell mate told me to knock it off. "It gets better," he'd promised. It really hadn't, and now I fought a simmering panic at being incarcerated again.

I called Jamal's name several times, to no avail. Either he was still unconscious, or they'd taken him somewhere else. I hoped he and Izzy had thought of something clever, a way he could alert her to our whereabouts despite having our phones confiscated. But did Izzy even know about our abduction? It had only been a couple of hours.

How long did Weston plan to hold us? Long enough for me to meet Gaia, or The Presence, again. Every time I returned to this thought, I paused and shuddered, forced myself to breathe. I didn't know how Weston communicated with the enigmatic, menacing entity without compelling Daniel, but I'd yet to enjoy any of my own encounters.

Lyall came to get me just after I'd slumped down on the mattress, resting from my relentless pacing. He wasn't waving a gun this time, nor did he bother with insults or anything but a single word command: "Move." Our brief, unpleasant acquaintance had given me little time to pick up on his character cues, but he appeared preoccupied, almost sulky.

Weston awaited me in the lamplit kitchen, alone. He sat at an old wooden table, huddled over a sleek gray laptop, frowning at a screen I couldn't see. He closed the lid as he rose to his feet. "Thank you, Lyall. You can wait outside."

"Is that wise? Surely—"

"Lyall." The two men locked gazes, and for all that Lyall was much bigger than Weston, he looked away first. "D is damaged, thanks to you. I don't believe he is a threat."

"Don't underestimate him," Lyall muttered, giving me the side eye.

"Oh, I don't. Not at all. But we need to do this alone. Besides, I want you to check in with Jamal for me. I don't want Carson getting carried away."

"Why's Carson even here? Doesn't he have better things to do than carry out his personal vendetta?"

"Yes, he does," said Weston, bitterness creeping into his voice. "I have told him so. Perhaps your reminder will be effective."

"Fine." Lyall turned, scowled at me one last time, then left the kitchen. Moments later, I heard the front door slam.

Weston sighed. "We can't always choose our comrades in arms, can we, D?"

"Maybe not, but it helps if you start with good friends."

He glowered at me. "Don't antagonize me. I don't have the time." He paused, then took a deep, stabilizing breath. "I talked to Rosalind and Jess. Remarkable, both of them. I understand now why you've been so successful. And your fiancée... well, I wish you long lives of happiness together, I truly do. But you must help her understand that will only happen if she aligns with our cause. Perhaps then, Rosalind may too, and Gaia may forgive her for the injuries she inflicted."

"What do you mean, 'our cause'? I'm not aligned with you or your Scales of Equilibrium crap."

"Not yet, perhaps. But you will be."

"Oh right, because you've 'seen it'."

"Scoff all you like. Let's see what Gaia has to say."

Weston took an almost reverential three steps towards the enormous stainless steel kitchen sink. At the end of that third step, his entire body shivered, and he closed his eyes in what looked like ecstasy. "Come here," he breathed. "Feel it!"

I recoiled. It was like walking in on someone watching porn. I wanted to be anywhere but there.

"This one is... powerful," he said. He half-opened his eyes, squinting as if trying to watch two things at once. "Echoes occur where Gaia's presence is the strongest, where its healing energy can do most good to the world and save us from ourselves. Come, join me, and heal yourself!"

Every instinct told me to flee. Weston's almost religious veneration of The Presence, and what he thought it represented, smothered whatever science he once possessed.

I wasn't sure how "releasing Gaia's healing energies" lined up with global urban sabotage, and how that combination was supposed to ensure our planet's survival and future prosperity. Maybe he thought it would wipe us out, humanity and all our endeavors, and that he was a latter day Jim Jones, presiding over a species-wide suicide. No thanks. I never had liked Kool-Aid.

I took another step back, then turned towards the doorway, not sure where I was going, just needing out of that kitchen. Carson Livingston blocked my way. One hand nestled casually in his rain jacket pocket, which bulged with what I suspected was a gun. Raindrops sprinkled his gray hair and trickled over the scar on his cheek. A burn scar. Daniel's Burned Man.

"I see you took my advice," he said in a pleasant tone. He gestured towards Weston with his free hand. "It would be a shame not to get the answers you came all this way to find."

Cornered. Shit. Even without the broken arm, I doubted I could bull rush Carson before he shot me, and I was too far from reaching the lamp or anything to throw. It looked like I might be visiting The Presence again after all. And this time neither Rosalind nor Jess were with me.

I didn't waste words. I just breathed, and reached for the inner calm that eighteen months of martial arts discipline had taught me. Weston extended his hand as I rounded the table, but I ignored it, stepping slowly but resolutely into the space where the Intrusion, his Echo, had to be.

Even prepared, the gut punch almost floored me. My lungs seized up, and the almost nauseating reek of smoke was probably my stomach burning, stabbed by what felt like a red hot poker. I wanted no part of this, but I managed not to flinch, determined not to show either of these assholes any weakness. I met Weston's intense gaze and refused to blink.

"They said you were strong," he murmured. "They were right. Are you ready?"

"Sure. After you."

His lips twitched, then he closed his eyes again. I tried to keep mine partly open, watching a self-satisfied Carson as he drifted closer, gun pointed at me. Then I embraced the Intrusion, my mind sliding through an unseen dimension into the memory.

I thought I'd gotten used to the dislocation, of my mind traveling to witness an event at the same location in a different time, sometimes decades or even centuries removed. I thought

I was prepared for the unexpected, knowing nothing about this farmhouse or its history, or even where it was. What I wasn't prepared for was a fly on the wall view of the very tableau I was part of.

I stood in the kitchen, wearing the same black T-shirt and jeans, left arm dangling in its makeshift sling, eyes closed and lips moving silently. Weston stood next to me, not quite touching, wearing the same preppy collared shirt, white with thin blue stripes. Carson stood off to the side, watching with ironic curiosity as Weston flinched, so hard he almost lost his balance. I swayed, almost enough to topple over, and sank to my knees, face twisted in a grotesque expression of pure terror. "No!" I couldn't hear myself, but I could see the word form on my trembling lips.

:: ALLEN WESTON ::

The Presence arrived with all the warning of a prehistoric solar eclipse. Inky blackness smothered the barely future memory, and the primitive humans - well, me - cowered in fear before a force so terrible and powerful it could eat up the very light of the world.

My only solace was that its attention was not fixed on me, not yet. I could sense Weston's consciousness near mine, a strangely jagged and fitful thing, nothing like the assured fanatic I'd just met in real life. I wasn't connected to him - nor did I want to be - so I could only assume that the irregular pulses I sensed from his consciousness represented his communication with The Presence. With Gaia, his Agency, and to all intents and purposes, his god.

:: YET I AM NO CLOSER ::

It's hard to detect emotion in a voice you don't so much hear as perceive as a thermonuclear detonation inside your skull. But somehow I sensed its disdain, its dissatisfaction, and Weston's spirit cringing. I might, given time, have enjoyed a moment of spiteful pleasure, but then The Presence turned its indefatigable attention toward me, like a black hole swiveling in space.

:: SALVATION! ::

I'm walking through a redwood grove...

Oh shit, not this again.

I descend into a dell, its red-brown earth scooped from the forest...

Please! No, I can't!

In the center of the dell is a door...

Amid my terror, speared by the regard of an omnipotent being, I sensed another's panic, another's rage. Weston?

In the door there is a reflection...

No! Please, no!

The reflection is not me. It could be me, if you lengthened my nose and slicked back my hair with gel, instead of constraining it with a ponytail. But it's not me. And it couldn't be, it just couldn't.

The panic I'd done so well to suppress bubbled up, threatening to overflow the banks. I needed Jess and Rosalind. I needed Jess, especially our connection, the way our spirits fit together, far more powerful together than we each were alone. *Are you out there, Jess? Help me, please!*

:: JESS ::

"Noooo!" I heard my plaintive wail, devoid of any power. I recoiled, but The Presence and the entire universe washed over me, a brain-devouring flood of incomprehensible magnitude. I felt like flotsam, caught up in the torrent like a dead branch dragged over whitewater rapids. The door and the dell disappeared, replaced with featureless, roaring darkness. I couldn't sense Weston or The Presence, or anything but the ringing in my ears. I couldn't open my eyes, I couldn't make myself move, I couldn't feel any part of my body. Was this what falling into a coma was like?

Sudden agony jarred me loose, and I came to, retching and writhing on the unforgiving wood floor of the farmhouse kitchen. I'd fallen and landed on my broken arm, and it screamed in protest. I rolled over, enough to free it and not cause further damage, but not to stop the pain. My vision blurred through watering eyes. My mouth felt impossibly parched, and my skull rang like a bell. The Presence had swallowed me whole and spat me out again. I twitched like a fish tossed on the floor of a rowboat.

"I'm fine. Dammit, Carson, I'm fine!"

The words seeped into my ears, as if spoken underwater. I could make no sense of what was happening. I barely remembered who I was. Something about a house. Was that the farmhouse, or some other house? Why did my arm hurt so much? Who was speaking? Who were they speaking to?

Gods, just let me sleep. Take away the pain for a while. Let me sleep.

"Help me," said a voice, less burbly and echoing than the first. Should I recognize this voice?

"Why?" asked another. My blurred vision identified two darker blurs looming over me.

"Because we're not savages, Allen." One of the blurs grew closer - it was a man. I could see that now. A man with a scar on his face, livid in yellow lamplight. I felt an arm coil around my shoulders, and with a grunt of exertion, he tried to lift me. I whimpered at the renewed jolt of pain from my arm.

"Are we not? As I've been reminded more than once this evening, we are killing people."

"Be that as it may, this one is valuable, or so you keep telling me. Help get him onto a chair at least. My back is killing me."

The bearded man - Allen Weston, I remembered now - stooped to help haul me to my feet, at least long enough to drop my helpless ass onto a chair. I slumped precariously, but managed to prop my arm on the surface of the kitchen table. The room shivered back into focus. Weston and the guy with the gun - Carson, that's right - remained on their feet, flanking me. Carson gazed at me with curiosity. Weston's face was expressionless.

"Well?" said Carson at last. "What did you learn? What does Gaia want with him?"

Weston didn't answer, simply stared as if he'd never seen me before. Then he turned, opened a cooler on the countertop, and extracted a plastic bottle of spring water. He didn't offer me one, and I was damned if I was gonna ask.

"We have a problem," he said at last, after a long drink.

"Which is?" Carson prompted.

"Our loyalty to Gaia does not appear to be reciprocated. We're not doing enough to restore balance."

Carson's lip curled, his burn scar twisting it into a sinister leer. "Reversing centuries of Industrial Revolution takes time. Rome wasn't burned in a day."

"Nonetheless, Gaia appears to be considering other options." Weston's eyes bore into mine, and his face flooded with emotion. Anger, confusion, but mostly jealousy. It was as if he'd just introduced me to his girlfriend, and she wanted to jump into my bed instead. *SALVATION.*

"I don't know what it thinks I can do," I croaked. *It's your insanely powerful pet spiritual monster, not mine.*

"Nor do I. But I cannot allow you to derail what it's taken me years to build, what men like me and Carson have pledged our lives to achieve. I cannot."

I heard the click of a safety. Carson had rounded the table and aimed his gun at my heart. I formed and discarded a half dozen plans to fight back, but none of them had much chance, even if I'd had two working arms.

"Do you want me to be a savage now?" he asked softly.

I stared back at him. If this was how it was going to end, I would look death straight in the eyes.

"Gaia wanted the girl," Weston murmured. "I don't know why. I'm too tired to think about it tonight. We have more important matters to discuss. Lock him in his room, and we'll figure it out in the morning."

"You heard the man." Carson gestured with his free hand, and I struggled to my feet. He at least had the decency to fetch me a bottle of water. I was grateful for it, and for the reprieve, but I feared for Jess anew. As I stumbled back up the stairs, demoralized and fighting exhaustion with every step, I resolved to find a way out of here. For all of us.

Chapter Nineteen
Fifteen Minutes

Easier said than done.

I figured I could break through the deadbolt on the bedroom door if I threw my full weight at it. But, even assuming my momentum didn't send me tumbling headlong down the stairs, what then? Everyone but Weston was likely packing heat, and I suspected any "special" status I'd possessed had worn off. From a fringe asset, I was at best a curiosity, and more probably a liability.

I also had no idea where I was. Even if I could somehow evade gunfire as I fled the farmhouse, and make it all the way down its gravel driveway, what then? Pick a direction on whatever paved road it took me to? Flag down a passing car? Who would be driving out here this late at night? My captors would catch up long before that.

Could I avoid the roads and go cross-country, disappear into the fields and woodland between here and the suburbs? That risked worse injury, and not just the frontier retribution of rural property owners against trespassers. I was a city boy. I'd gotten turned around in Forest Park.

Most important, all these harebrained ideas involved only myself. I was no longer sure they held Jamal in this same building, and I had no idea where Jess and Rosalind were. I dared not leave without finding that out.

Eventually, my body took matters into its own hands. Slumped on the bed, back against the wall, and cradling my arm, I drifted off into an uncomfortable and fitful sleep.

A rooster's crowing awakened me, accompanying the weak November dawn. It helped me remember where I was, a farmhouse somewhere in rural Missouri. Not for the first time, I longed for the bed in my Chicago apartment, the one I shared with Jess. Would I ever see it again?

My broken arm throbbed with pain. With exaggerated care, I stood and stretched, then examined the window. As I'd suspected, someone had painted it shut, or otherwise jammed the sash. I'd have to break the glass and survive a twelve foot jump onto hard packed dirt. That didn't make it to Plan B, probably languishing mid-alphabet.

The modest and almost grassless backyard huddled between the house and a short line of oak trees, which I guessed had been planted for privacy more than anything else. A decrepit children's playset squatted in its midst. Rusted bolts studded the sun-bleached plastic slide, and one of its two swings dangled forlornly from a single chain. The sight saddened me, despite my own woes.

I waited for the first sounds of movement in the house, a door closing and the murmur of conversation. Then I banged on my own door with a plea to use the bathroom. I'd just started wondering where I'd pee if no one let me out when the staircase creaked.

"Morning, Rodriguez," said Lyall as he opened my door. His eyes were almost feverish in his intensity. "Be quick now. I'm needed back downstairs. The gloves are coming off!"

I didn't bother replying, but took as much time as I dared slouching to the bathroom. I could hear many voices in, I guessed, the kitchen, but only snatches of the conversation before I closed the door behind me. "More reliable", "risky", "elevation", and "Gaia" didn't tell me much, other than we'd riled up the hornets' nest. Now, we just needed a way to escape before they stung us all to death.

Lyall hustled me back inside the bedroom, impatient to rejoin the discussion. I tried to listen through the door, but its solid oak muffled most sound. Then I noticed someone had cut the worn blue carpet almost an inch from the bottom of the door. Carefully, I lay down and pressed my ear to the gap.

"...population centers at once."

That was Weston's voice, clear, loud and used to public speaking. I couldn't make out more than an occasional word from the quiet reply. "Logistics" was one of them, and I was pretty sure it was Carson.

"Because that's your job," snapped Weston. "That's why you're sitting at this table, instead of playing jailer with Jamal Peters."

More sulky murmuring.

"I don't care. I can only show you so much gratitude for all the money, people, equipment, and other resources you've contributed to the cause. Thank you. One last fucking time, thank you. Now, do your fucking job."

There was a pause, and then a door slammed. I flinched despite myself.

"Shall I go after him?" asked Lyall.

"No. I'm done with his privileged temper tantrums. Let him cool off. We'll move forward with what we have. Did you get your New York tickets yet?"

"Yeah, but they're not direct. Layover in Atlanta."

"Dammit, I hate provincial airports. We'll be rid of them all soon, but right now, it's a major pain in the ass. I assume you're already packed?"

"Yeah. What about Rodriguez and the others?"

"I'll worry about them. I've got it, Lyall. You do your job, and let me do mine. Kathy, Blake, can I have a minute?"

Another door closed, and then the house lapsed into an uneasy silence. It took a long time to climb to my feet without jarring my broken arm. Now what? Lyall going to New York sounded ominous. Well, everything sounded ominous, but this was concrete information that people like Special Agent Jones would love to have. How the hell could I get it to them?

I resorted to pacing back and forth, wearing out the carpet with an all-too-familiar trail. Door to window, window to door. Seven steps one way, seven steps back. I peeked outside every time I approached the glass, but wherever everyone had gone, it wasn't the backyard. My action, born of frustration, grew calming, almost hypnotic. I found I could go a long time between cracking open my eyelids. My feet knew the distance, my body understood when and how to turn. Seven steps, turn. Seven steps, turn. Seven steps—

What the hell was that?

For a moment, I thought it was my imagination, that I'd wandered into a daydream during my soporific prowl. A current of air tugged at my scalp, followed by a familiar punch low in my gut.

An Intrusion, here? I would've bet everything I owned it hadn't been there thirty seconds before. My pointless traipsing had not varied by more than a few inches either side for what felt like at least half an hour, and I'd followed the same route last night too.

Had I just witnessed the birth of a brand new Intrusion, the phenomenon that had plagued my life for three years?

What a coincidence.

I could imagine Rosalind's quiet disdain and Jess's open scoffing at such a "coincidence". I didn't know what the odds were of being close enough to detect the creation of an Intrusion, but they had to be pretty low. Kara had warned us of a recent upsurge in activity. Could that have improved the odds enough?

No. I couldn't make myself believe that. It was too convenient. Because an Intrusion wasn't just a window into the past, or sometimes the near future. It was a potential escape route.

I wondered what Izzy, Lana, and the others were doing. When had they realized something was wrong? What did they think had happened?

Izzy must have tried using the Grays Cottage Imprint to connect with us, and likely investigated the house when that failed. If she suspected our capture by the Scales of Equilibrium, she would have alerted Martin, who would relay that to Special Agent Jones. Someone was out there looking for us, but I couldn't guess what leads or resources they had. Izzy wouldn't sit still, especially not in this provincial town. I reckoned there was a chance she'd engage her Imprint regularly, releasing the Lock, trying to connect with me and the others, then tethering it again. It must be a hell of a long way to establish such a connection, but what was the harm in trying? We didn't really understand the limits of what was mostly a mental exercise.

The harm, of course, was the possibility of facing The Presence again, alone. Was it truly responsible for all Intrusions? Had it set a trap for me?

Did it matter? What choice did I have?

I prepared myself as best I could. I was weary and worried about Jess and my friends. No one had bothered to give me any more pain medication, and every movement of my arm was agony. Too bad. Pucker up, buttercup! I closed my eyes and pretended I was back at my Chicago dojo, as Sensei Ryuichi led us through the kata. My pain, fear, and exhaustion were real, but unimportant. My purpose was clear. I stepped sideways through the dimensions and embraced the Intrusion.

Oh my, what did they get up to out in the country? I considered myself a broad-minded guy, so the sight of two hairy naked men writhing on the bed didn't especially shock me. It did distract me, however, along with a powerful, musky scent, strong enough to make my eyes water. *Focus, D.* The good news was that this type of memory usually indicated a Level One Intrusion, the easiest to control. I'd last longer searching for Izzy, or any other sensitive for that matter. As long as The Presence didn't crash the party; I didn't have a plan for dealing with that.

I extended my awareness, trying to ignore the physical distance involved. I thought of my consciousness as an expanding sphere, in whatever dimensions the memory occupied. I was a bubble, but a bubble with a particular shape. A bubble, in search of other bubbles with which it could connect, like a bizarre metaphysical dating app. Jess would kill me, ha ha!

Focus, dammit! You're losing control.

Sure enough, my hold on the memory of the silent, forbidden lovers reaching their inevitable climax began to fray. Just because it was Level One didn't mean it wasn't dangerous. I could still lose myself in this Intrusion, and then I'd be no use to anyone. *Fuck.*

While I still could, I folded the memory into a tight sphere and sealed the Single Point Lock. I was too discouraged to celebrate how easy it now was. I hadn't found anyone. I was still a prisoner, right back where I started.

Well, not quite. I had a tool, something I could reuse, for as long as I was locked up in this room. And as long as my strength held up. Connecting with anyone on the first attempt would have stretched coincidence to breaking point. I just had to keep trying.

As soon as I thought I was ready, I picked my own Lock and immersed myself in the Imprint again. Ignoring the grunting and groaning of gay sex, I hunted for other sensitives, engaged with other Intrusions. They might not all be HLF agents - and I might be in trouble if they were Scales or one of Carson's recent defectors - but I just needed one. Preferably Izzy, but any HLF agent would do. I embraced the memory as long as I dared, then reluctantly tethered it again.

I found someone on the third attempt. Not Izzy, but I wasn't sorry. It was Jess.

D? Is that you?

You know it's me! Are you okay? What about Rosalind and Jamal?

I'm fine. Rosalind's fine. We're seriously pissed off, and hungry, and worried about you. No idea about Jamal. How are you? Your arm...

Hurts like a motherfucker, but I'm dealing. When did you find your Intrusion?

An hour ago? They took our phones, so that's a guess. Rosalind's guess. She says she doesn't need newfangled technology to keep track of time. She's getting on my nerves.

An hour sounds about right. This is the third time I've engaged the memory.

Fourth for us. We're alternating. Don't burn yourself out, love. Remember, now we've connected, it's just a matter of time before The Presence shows up.

I strained to stay connected. The Imprint sapped my strength, and maybe hers too. There wasn't time to tell her everything.

We need to find Izzy or another HLF agent. Give them whatever info we can to help them or the Feds find us.

... our thought too... alone... easier when connected.... D?

Fifteen minutes! I sent, with as much strength as I could spare. Then, I tethered the memory and slumped down on the mattress.

Jess was okay! Rosalind too! I'd worry about Jamal later.

That left two problems. First, my temples pounded with a headache that rivaled the pain from my broken arm. My mouth was so dry, my tongue kept sticking to its roof. I sat as still and calm on the bed as I could, nurturing my body's reserves. Last night's bottle of water was still half full, and I spared myself a single mouthful.

My bigger problem was keeping track of time, without "newfangled technology". I resorted to whispered counting: "one Mississippi, two Mississippi..." Maybe Rosalind had a better way. I just hoped we wouldn't diverge too much over a fifteen minute time span.

We did better than I expected. Not long after I forced myself back into my Imprint, the consciousness that was unmistakably Rosalind reached out. We connected easily, with reverence and a touch of embarrassment on my part.

Happy to see you, D. How are you holding up?

Okay. Can't maintain for long. Need to find Izzy.

Agreed. Let's look together.

We tried. Maybe no one was out there after all. Maybe they were too far away for us to detect, with this bizarre mechanism none of us pretended we really understood. Rosalind made us stop before my struggles began.

Conserve your strength. Let's try again in half an hour.

She was gone before I could object. Thirty minutes would increase the margin of error for synchronizing our next attempt, but I knew I needed to rest. I couldn't do this many more times, not without pain meds, more water, and probably something to eat. Although, the very thought of food made me nauseous.

I lost count twice. The house brooded in silence. I forced myself to keep counting and hoped I hadn't strayed too far. When I decided the thirty minutes were up, I struggled to pick the Lock and wrangle the memory. I searched for Jess, or Rosalind, to no avail. The heartbeat-driven pain behind my temples thudded like the relentless bass drum of a dance floor, disturbing my focus. I refused to give up, terrified of losing contact with my friends. At the very last moment, as my grasp on the Imprint started slipping, Jess found me. She lent me her strength, succor to a drowning man.

Stay with me, babe.

Lost count. Can't do this... for long...

I sensed her alarm before she masked it. She offered me all her energy, all her will, and I struggled not to drink her dry, like some sort of vampire.

Fifteen minutes, I sent instead, taking just enough for the Tether before severing our connection. It was a sloppy Lock, and I was far from certain I could do even that again.

One problem at a time. Count. Drink. Breathe. If I only had one more attempt in me, I needed to maximize our connection time. Give us the best chance to find Izzy or anyone else.

As I embraced the Imprint again, I heard a door close below, followed by quiet voices. I ignored them. I had time for one last deep breath before the plunge.

Right on schedule!

Jess sounded impressed. I withheld a mock-offended retort when I realized Rosalind was there too.

I thought you guys were alternating?

Jess and I worry this will become difficult to sustain. We thought we'd pool our resources and increase our chances of finding someone as soon as possible. Our clock is ticking.

Agreed. I'm ready. Let's go.

We pooled our strength, and I was sometimes confused by whether a specific thought was mine or one of theirs. We pushed and pushed in every direction we could imagine, but had no idea how this space correlated with our own, with the geography of eastern Missouri. With no markers, nothing to guide us, we just hunted for lights in the darkness.

And, miraculously, we found one. The hint of a spark, a candle in an amphitheater, and then...

D! Jess, Rosalind, is that really you?

Izzy! Oh my god, I can't believe we've found you!

Same! We were hoping, trying every hour, but... Where's Jamal?

On this farm somewhere, but we've been separated. If we describe what we know of our location, can you pass that on to someone who can find us?

I hope so. Martin's making a pest of himself with the FBI.

Good. Okay, let's send what we know.

Judging from the ensuing kaleidoscope of images, Jess and Rosalind were confined to a dingy office next to the stables. They could see the gravel road, which crested a grassy hill on its way to the partially hidden white farmhouse. A dozen horses grazed peacefully, heedless of the drama playing out in the human world. I sent my view of the back yard, the neglected playset and the privacy trees. My strength faded fast, and after Izzy told us to hang tight, I pulled away.

I couldn't summon the energy or focus to tether the memory, so I erased it instead, allowing the body heat and leather cologne to pour through me. The Imprint may be gone, but I'd remember it forever.

Alone again, and bone weary. All I could do was wait. How long would it take to find a horse farm of that description within an hour's drive of St. Louis?

How long did we have?

I'd just shaken the last drops of water into my parched mouth when I heard footsteps on the stairs. Carson opened the door. He handed me another bottle of water and two more pain pills.

"Medicate," he said. "I don't know when, or if, you'll get to a hospital. We need to move, and you're coming with us."

"Moving where?"

"You don't need to know."

"Just me, or all of us?"

"All of you. We don't have time for questions. Out front, now."

"Can I at least use the bathroom?"

"Fine. Two minutes."

I took a lot longer than that. Every minute was precious, and I used at least fifteen pretending to take a dump. Impatient knocks on the door escalated to threats to break it down, while I yelled it wasn't my fault I had only one working hand. Carson almost pushed me down the stairs when I finally emerged.

The temperature had dropped overnight. Despite the bright sunlight, I shivered in my T-shirt as we joined the gathering throng in front of the farmhouse. Lyall waved in derision as he slipped into a dust-streaked red sedan, its spinning tires kicking up gravel as he accelerated towards the road. An irritated Weston barked instructions into a walkie-talkie, watched warily by the farmhouse owner and one of the men I recognized from our Wildwood misadventure. One of the black SUVs waited nearby, and through an open back door, I spotted Jamal. His seatbelt was fastened, but he was unconscious.

"What did you do to him?" I demanded.

Carson sneered. "Nothing he didn't deserve, I assure you. Allen, where the hell are the others?"

Weston shot him a venomous look. "Our female guests refuse to be rushed. I'm trying to convince your people that now is not the time for gallantry."

"Oh, they're my people now, are they?"

Weston opened his mouth, then reconsidered and stalked away. Carson muttered something that sounded insulting. I wondered how I could drive further wedges into their uneasy alliance.

Everyone was relieved when the second SUV rolled into sight. Although, my relief at seeing Jess and Rosalind again was tempered by a growing despair that our efforts to reveal this location to Izzy had been in vain. Had we told her about the two black SUVs? The highway patrol would be able to find us then, right? Right?

"Hey hon!" called Jess. A nervous young man with a mop of black hair hauled her out of the just-arrived SUV, then prodded her in the back with an AR15. My heart was in my mouth, but she ignored him, favoring me with an imperious smile. Her only evident concern was in her study of my arm in its makeshift sling.

"Hey, babe!" I replied. "How was your room?"

"Terrible. Stank of horse farts. Zero stars."

I chuckled, but Weston wheeled on her.

"Get in the car with Jamal," he barked, earning himself a contemptuous glare. There wasn't much else she could do with ziptied wrists. "D, you'll be riding with Rosalind."

I didn't move. "Why? Where are we going?"

"Carson."

The former head of logistics for the Henry Lyons Foundation rapped me on the arm with the barrel of his handgun. "All in good time. We'll have a nice chat on the way."

Jess paused before joining Jamal in the nearer SUV, and we exchanged helpless looks. I glanced at the other car, in which I could barely see Rosalind fuming in the back seat. And so I was probably the first to see Lyall's sedan roar into view, pursued by an endless parade of state police cruisers.

"What the fuck?" declared Weston, walkie-talkie dangling uselessly in his hand.

The sedan skidded to a broadside halt, blocking the driveway. Lyall scrambled out, clutching a handgun and shielding himself behind the front door. Someone liked watching cop shows. The police vehicles fanned out as best they could before stopping, disgorging at least a dozen brown-uniformed officers. They also protected themselves behind their doors, and trained the barrels of at least twelve weapons on the red sedan, and us.

We all held our breath.

"This is the Missouri State Police," one of the officers announced over their car's loudspeaker. "Weapons on the ground, and hands up."

"Get out of here, Allen!" Lyall yelled, staring back at Weston with all the righteous determination of a suicide bomber.

"I said weapons *down*, assholes!"

Carson and Jess's captor complied. Weston gaped at Lyall and dropped his walkie-talkie to the ground.

Lyall's eyes boggled, then he jumped to his feet. "Gaia!" he screamed, and opened fire.

A fusillade of gunfire erupted. I covered my head and dropped low, saw Jess do the same. I watched Lyall mown down by a hail of bullets. His lifeless body toppled to the gravel, blood oozing from a dozen wounds into the dust.

As the echoes faded, I uncovered and lifted my head. I met Jess's alarmed eyes under the chassis of Jamal's SUV. I raised a thumb, and so did she. Gods, I hoped Rosalind and Jamal were okay.

"Izzy did it," I said, and she nodded, a grin shining over her lovely face.

"Oh." To my right, Carson sprawled, awaiting the police officers who fanned out, weapons drawn, to secure the scene. He met my eyes, and I saw the realization dawn. "Oh, well played."

Chapter Twenty
GHOSTS AND STUFF

"I distinctly remember telling you to call me first, if you ever got a lead on Allen Weston."

Special Agent Jones stood with arms folded inside the doorway of the oddly musty treatment room, just off the busy ER at Missouri Baptist. The hospital still ran on generator power, with low light and minimal heating. I perched on the edge of the massive black vinyl patient chair, nursing my new air cast and sling. My arm throbbed anew from its professional examination. The exhausted but patient doctor had assured me the break was clean, and would heal completely given time and care.

Jess stood beside my chair, arms also folded in defiance. She'd refused to leave my side ever since our rescue from the horse farm.

"Don't do anything foolish, I said," Jones continued. "This is one reason you didn't ride along when we stormed the ranch in Montana. Not only did you put your own lives at risk, but you almost cost us the chance to find and capture the leaders of the Scales of Equilibrium!"

"We just handed them to you on a silver platter," Jess insisted. "Do you think they'd have shown themselves at that house in Wildwood if a bunch of Feds had stomped around it? We only got taken to meet Weston because he wanted to see us. You should be more grateful."

"But you had no plan! I'm still not sure I understand how Ms. Fisher could describe with such accuracy where y'all were being held. I've known for a while that there's something strange going on, with you lot and Daniel Hill. There's stuff you're not telling me."

"That makes two of us," I cut in, before Jess's pent up frustration boiled over. "You have your duties to the law, we have duties to something else. We're not above the law, but we're not obliged to reveal everything we know either."

Jones unfolded her arms, then didn't appear to know what to do with them, so folded them again.

"I assume you're talking about the Henry Lyons Foundation. Yes, of course we know about them. I spoke to David Taylor, your director, an hour ago. I understand there are connections between his organization and Weston, and his Scales of Equilibrium. I don't have to believe in your weird supernatural shit to accept that you do. But I'm surprised the HLF has your loyalty."

"I said nothing about loyalty, not to the HLF at least. But we're loyal to our friends, to Rosalind, to Jamal and Izzy too."

"How is Jamal, by the way?" Jess broke in. "They took him away in an ambulance."

"He's awake, but concussed," Jones said, her face grim. "Several bruises and a minor fracture of his left orbital bone. Someone roughed him up pretty bad."

"Carson," I spat.

Jones raised her eyebrows. "Really? What makes you say that?"

"There's bad blood between them. I'm not sure what. But I heard Lyall complaining to Weston that Carson seemed fixated on his personal vendetta with Jamal, out at the farm. I don't know if he landed the blows himself, or had someone else do it for him. But I'm sure he's responsible."

"Lyall Morrison? The perp the trigger-happy state police gunned down?"

"Couldn't happen to a nicer guy," I said. And I meant it. There were killers, and then there were murderers like Lyall. Death by firing squad was better than he deserved.

Jones exhaled and rubbed her tired eyes. "Well, I'm going to have a quick chat with the Hills, and then we'll see where we go from here." She turned to leave, then paused, her expression troubled. "Carson turned state's witness against Weston and The Scales of Equilibrium. He seems unreasonably pleased with himself. Can either of you tell me why?"

Jess and I gaped at her, and she sighed. "I guess not. I may let you have a word before we haul him off somewhere the sun don't shine. Let my people know if you need anything."

"I just wanna go home," I groaned, after Jones closed the door behind her. My head thudded against Jess's chest, and she cradled it, stroking my hair until she worked her way down to my ponytail.

"It's matted," she murmured. "You need a shower. Hell, I need a shower! I'm sure I stink of the barn."

"You smell perfect," I said, and she did. Sure, I picked up an animal tang and something that might have been wet straw, but they blended into the cocktail of Jess's intoxicating scent, sharp, floral, wild and powerful. I nuzzled her T-shirt, filling my nostrils with it, and she laughed, swatting me away.

"Now is not the place or time," she remonstrated, eyes twinkling. "Maybe we can take that shower together later."

"I want to do everything together later," I said, gazing up at her. "I was so worried about you. I mean, I know you can take care of yourself, and Rosalind, well, we know she's a force of nature. But still, there were a lot of them, and I didn't know where you were, or what was happening, and—"

She pressed a finger against my lips. "I'm fine. We're fine. They didn't touch us. They didn't even try. I think Weston was kind of in awe of us, to be honest."

"Him and me both."

A nurse arrived with my discharge forms, and we escaped to the main ER. Rosalind, huddled in a corner with Martin and Agent Jones, gave us a perfunctory wave before resuming what looked like an animated discussion. We gave them a wide berth.

I recognized Agent Levitz standing near the main entrance, studying the room, and he intercepted us on our way out.

"We need some fresh air," I protested. "We're not going anywhere. Martin's our ride."

"Fine. Just stay where I can see you."

A slab of cold air greeted us, carrying the threat of snow. Brooding clouds darkened the sky. A front must have gone through. Jess and I shivered in our T-shirts, clinging to each other as we contemplated heading straight back inside.

"Hey, lovebirds!"

Huddling against the wall to my right, blowing a stream of smoke from her lips and stubbing out a cigarette under her boot, was Izzy. She'd wrapped herself in a dark green jacket, adorned by dozens of patches that looked either military or musical in nature. The dark smudges around her eyes weren't eyeliner. She looked as tired as I felt.

"I didn't know you smoked," I said, suppressing my distaste at the odor of stale tobacco as we joined her.

She grimaced. "I don't. Not really. Just in emergencies. Lana and the guys went home to rest, but I wanted to make sure everyone was okay. How's the arm?"

"Hurts, but it'll heal. Thank you, Izzy. What you did... you saved us." I reached around her shoulders with my healthy arm and gave her an awkward hug. She froze for a moment and then responded with a fierce embrace.

"That's the second time you've thanked me," she whispered. "I could get used to it."

"D's very emotional today," Jess observed in a gentle, mocking tone. She drew Izzy away from me and into her own two-armed hug. "But thank you. We were running out of strength. You found us just in time. I can't believe we connected over all that distance!"

Izzy looked at Jess in wonder. "You guys and Rosalind are so strong together! I thought I was powerful, but that was beyond anything I ever dared imagine. Beyond anyone's imagination! You guys are fucking *stars*!"

"You're so powerful," I told her. "You had to be, to find us over that distance. Was Lana helping you, or was it all you?"

Izzy shook her head, clinging to Jess for a moment as she disengaged. "I connected with Lana easily enough. We share certain... similarities. Brett and Samuel aren't as strong, but they helped too. It was def a team effort. I'm still getting used to that."

A blast of frigid air tore through the parking lot and broke like a tidal wave against the front of the hospital building. We cringed and huddled together for protection.

"Fuck this," growled Jess. She took my free hand to lead me back inside, but Izzy grabbed both our shoulders.

"I need to tell you something. Maria Gomez was here earlier. She knows what happened, all of it. I think Lana spilled her guts - she's pretty loyal to Maria. It doesn't matter. The word is out. Maria knows about us, and what we did, and so do the HLF brass."

"Are we in trouble?" I asked through chattering teeth. "Because I don't care."

Izzy grinned. "Nah, we're not in trouble. Maria may be a rule follower, but she's not as much of a dick about it as Faustyn was up in Chicago." Her grin faded. "She's scared. She's scared, guys, and she's not the only one."

Her gaze flicked over my left shoulder, then she frowned and leaned closer, close enough that her bubblegum pink hair collided with my forehead. I could smell her, and it was far from unpleasant.

"Kara just called me," Izzy continued. "That's why I'm out here in the damn cold. They're coming to St. Louis, the day after tomorrow. Astbury's coming too, and Charli, I think. And David Taylor, presumably so he can yell at Carson."

"Why?" demanded Jess. "Did the internet stop working? What's wrong with a phone call?"

"Because shit's getting real, Jess. And I think they think we're the answer."

We hadn't even warmed up after scurrying back inside the ER, when the Hills marched up and asked, rhetorically, if me and Jess were ready to go home. Rosalind looked grim and Martin angry. Agent Jones glowered in their wake, then stabbed at her phone and turned away.

No one said a word until we found Martin's car - another damn black SUV - in the parking garage. He offered his arm for support as I climbed in. I'd need to adapt to doing things one handed for a while. The engine purred to life, drowned out by the radio volume, until Martin turned it down. Sounded like our boy listened to NPR.

"Is everything okay?" Jess ventured at last.

No one answered for a moment, then Rosalind sighed. "Martin is cross with us, and understandably so. We let our guards down and almost paid the price."

"I'm not cross with you," Martin protested, stabbing his parking ticket into the payment machine. Rosalind raised an eyebrow. "Well, maybe a little, when you first told me what happened. I told you I thought it was too much of a risk. But mostly, I was scared. Scared at what might have happened to you, Rosa. I lost my son years ago. I couldn't bear to lose you too."

Rosalind's face crumpled, and she reached for her husband's hand as she fought to compose herself. I looked away, embarrassed.

Jess stared at the road ahead with grim determination. "I think it was a risk we had to take," she said, almost to herself. "We'd be stuck, otherwise. And Weston would still be free to cause havoc. We got lucky, but we learned a lot."

"Do you call D's broken arm lucky, Jess?" Martin gazed back at her in his rearview mirror, but she didn't flinch.

"Of course not," she snapped, resting a tender hand on my arm, just above the cast. "But we brought the Feds down on them in the end. We decapitated the Scales of Equilibrium's leadership, and that's no small thing. Maybe Agent Jones will give you your life back now."

Martin snorted, but didn't get a chance to reply.

"I assume you're referring to our means of escape," Rosalind mused. "A pair of Intrusions conveniently manifested exactly where we could use them to connect, as we learned in Shotcombe House."

"Yeah, I don't think anyone's gonna claim that was a coincidence, right?" Jess turned to me, as if daring me to do so.

I cleared my throat. "I have a theory, but you're not going to like it."

As Martin turned south on I-270, I recounted my conversation with Weston, and the Echo we'd embraced to communicate with The Presence. I still shuddered, suppressing a latent panic that this menacing power recognized me, even knew my name. I described my vision of the dell in the redwood forest, but I omitted the reflection in the door or The Presence's mention of Jess.

"Salvation?" Rosalind interrupted. "You're sure that's what it said?"

"Positive. The word's practically carved into my brain. So I've been thinking. What if Weston's right about this at least, that Intrusions are manifestations of The Presence's power? We don't really know why - assuming his Gaia theories are horseshit - but what if it created these two Intrusions exactly so we could use them, to find Izzy, and escape?"

"Why would it want us to?" Jess asked. "Seems like it had us right where it wanted us."

"Why bother?" Martin jumped in. "If this thing, whatever it is, is as powerful as you all say, why would it mess with any of this crap? Why not just wipe us out, or enslave us, or whatever it wants to do?"

"I don't think it can," said Rosalind. "As powerful as it is - and love, please believe me when I say it's as powerful as any God I've ever imagined - I think it's constrained in our world. It's forced to act through human agents. It knows us now, and it thinks we're important, for reasons I'm too terrified to guess."

Jess hissed in frustration. "So why didn't it show up? We connected multiple times, for as long as our strength lasted. We connected across almost fifty miles with Izzy and those guys. The Presence has been lurking like a creeper for months. So where the hell was it?"

"Maybe it didn't want to interfere," I offered after a brief pause, but that sounded weak. I was about to elaborate, but Jess suddenly leaned forward as far as her seatbelt allowed. "Hey, can you turn that up?"

A clip of the Ghostbusters theme song faded even as Rosalind increased the volume on the car radio, to be replaced by the measured tones of a female reporter.

"Jason Hennessy has owned the Sunset Oaks apartment complex in Brookline, a thriving middle-class suburb of Boston, for seventeen years. In that time, his waitlist has always been in the double digits."

"I take good care of the place, always have," said a scratchy male voice. "Probably better than I take care of myself. Some tenants have lived here as long as I've owned it. They tell me 'Why would we leave, when you look after us so well, and keep rent so reasonable?' They're like family to me."

The female voice resumed. "But recently, the family has broken up. Jason's waitlist is empty for the first time, and a handful of Sunset Oaks apartments sit vacant. When Jason asked his former tenants why they were moving out, sometimes despite penalty clauses on their leases, he couldn't believe what he heard."

"I asked them, 'What did I do wrong? If it's a money issue, let me work with you.' But it didn't make any difference. Some wouldn't tell me, like they were embarrassed. Then an older resident, a widower, the first guy who rented from me after I took over the place, told me: 'Jason, my apartment's haunted.' I didn't know what to say to that. I wasn't gonna tell him he was crazy to his face. I don't really believe in that stuff, you know? Ghosts and stuff. His apartment seemed fine to me. But the young couple who moved in two weeks later left within a month and said the same thing. Then I heard it from another tenant. I'm like, what the hell's going on?"

"Jason's partner, Shannon, is an emergency room nurse at Massachusetts General Hospital. She says she started hearing odd stories from patients earlier this summer, but thought nothing of it, until Jason offered to show her the widower's ex-apartment."

"There was a spot in the corner of the bedroom," a younger woman said. "Just next to the window. I got real cold, and it felt like someone punched me in the stomach. Jason thought I was having a panic attack."

"Jason persuaded Shannon to check out one of the other vacant apartments, with similar results. Now, she refuses to even set foot on the grounds, and Jason's worried about her, and about his business. And he's not the only one, according to Nolan Jeffries of the Greater Boston Realtor Association."

"It's happening in single-family homes, in condo buildings, and apartment complexes," said a gruff male voice. "Tenants are breaking leases. Owners are selling below market value, as long as they can sell quick. I keep hearing stories, stories I wouldn't ordinarily believe. And it's not just happening here. I've got friends and colleagues in New York, in Philly, even in Chicago, before the North Point disaster. They're all saying the same thing. It's like every day is Halloween around here."

"It's an unsettling notion in already unsettled times," concluded the reporter. "Sociologists and psychologists have been reluctant to engage in the issue, but the sheer number of anecdotes have convinced some that a real problem exists. We don't yet understand it, but some are asking an unthinkable question."

Jason's voice again, nervous now. "Am I being haunted? What could I do about it if I am?"

"This is Priya Latha, for Boston Public Radio."

"Wow," I said, as burbling music segued into a donation request. Martin killed the volume and coasted our car down the exit ramp to Elm Avenue.

"I'm surprised," admitted Rosalind. "NPR is the last place I'd have expected to hear such a story."

"It might be the last place," Jess said grimly, swiping headlines on her phone as it charged from the USB port of the center console. She'd been the giddiest at reuniting with her device, after the state police recovered them from the farmhouse. Mine rested, brick-like, in my left jeans pocket. "I'm seeing related headlines from several major news outlets. Even Fox News, although their talking heads seem to think it's some kind of woke conspiracy."

"Those people have lived in their own fantasy world for years," Rosalind huffed. "But serious news agencies carrying such stories, however accurate, is ominous indeed. It's not just social media anymore, Jess. This supports the upsurge of Intrusions that Jamal described last week."

"The earthquakes before the big eruption," I muttered.

"Indeed. Oh!"

I didn't understand her surprise, until Martin pulled into their driveway, and I saw most of their front windows flooded with light.

The power was back on.

Chapter Twenty-One
BURN

Jess helped Rosalind clean out their refrigerator and freezer, while Martin and I reset clocks and checked circuits throughout their home. There was just enough hot water for the ladies to take showers, after which they announced their intention of braving the grocery store. The local Schnucks, which had survived the extended power outage with careful use of generators, had been comprehensively picked over the last time I'd visited, three days before.

"I need to cook," Rosalind declared. "There will be plenty of time to worry, analyze, and debate when our HLF friends arrive. Until then, I need to give my mind a rest, let it take a back seat to familiar, menial tasks."

Martin watched them leave with a doleful expression. I thought I detected lingering tension between him and Rosalind, but hesitated to mention it. Some things were private, even with good friends. And, honestly, I was more comfortable asking Rosalind about it than Martin.

"Fancy a glass of wine?" he asked suddenly. I didn't, but sensing an overture, I assented. He grabbed a bottle of red from the rack above one of their kitchen cabinets, which was where he kept their "everyday" wine. The good stuff was in the basement. He poured two glasses, and we sat at the kitchen table.

"Danny's coming back to St. Louis," he said, after taking his first sip. I twirled the stem of my glass where it rested on the table, delaying my drink. "Carmella... Agent Jones thinks he'll cooperate, help prosecute Allen Weston for enough felonies to put him away forever."

"Okay," I said, keeping my voice neutral. "When's this supposed to happen?"

"Tomorrow. Danny's flying in first thing in the morning. They're yanking him out of some high end, high security rehab program somewhere - he says he's not allowed to tell us where - just to throw him in front of that asshole."

"And you don't think they should?"

"No, I don't. No one wants to see Danny home again, or at least back in St. Louis, more than me. But I want him to be well, finally and truly well. And I want him to *want* to come back. To be with us, with me. I've gone out on a limb for the FBI, at risk to my career, but my opinion on this doesn't matter, apparently."

"That sucks." I took a sip and grimaced at the wine's acidity. "What does Rosalind think?"

He sighed and took a longer, larger sip. "She says it will be good for Danny. Cathartic. Confront those who misled and used him for their own ends. I think she just wants him home, at any cost."

Part of me yearned for a parent who had shown such unconditional love for their son. My mother had shunned me for years, and her deathbed reconciliation had only reinforced my longing for what might have been. True, I'd done bad things, just as Daniel had. I hadn't been "well". And, rather than wallow in my bitterness, maybe I should understand it as Mom giving me the time and space I needed to get well.

Parenting was hella hard.

"Make sure the Feds give the three of you time together," I said. "He's on his own journey. Just keep letting him know you're both there if he wants you."

Martin raised his glass. "I'll drink to that."

So did I.

Agent Jones summoned us to the nondescript FBI Field Office on Market Street the following morning. We drove in relative silence, each consumed by our own thoughts. Mine included regret that I'd drunk so much wine the previous night, but it'd been the perfect complement to Rosalind's incredible beef stew. Everyone was in better humor by the time we retired to our beds - especially Jess.

"Do you want to see Daniel first?" Agent Jones asked the Hills, as we waited for our visitor badges to print. They both nodded.

"What are me and D doing here, exactly?" asked Jess. "We told you everything we knew about the horse farm yesterday."

"So you said. If you've remembered any other details, I'd love to hear them. But the main reason you're here is because Carson Livingston wants to talk to you."

"Everyone wants to talk to D," grumbled Jess, but Jones shook her head.

"Both of you. Let me escort Martin and Rosalind back, then I'll take you to him."

Jess embraced me, nuzzling my cheek with her cold nose, while we waited by the visitor's desk. "Sorry, love. I get tired of being forgotten about."

I cupped her face and kissed her. "Anyone who forgets you is a moron and deserves what's coming to them."

"Good. Cause I've got some avenging to do."

Jones returned and led us to an elevator, which descended one level to the basement. She led us down an identical corridor before halting outside an unmarked steel door. She held up her badge to the key reader and scowled as it pondered its response. Finally, it flashed green, and I heard the solid clunk of a deadbolt withdrawing.

"Livingston has offered to tell us everything he knows about the Scales of Equilibrium," Jones said, her hand resting on the door handle. "I'm not sure why, other than to avoid prosecution. I want to know if I can trust him, or if I'm wasting my time."

She ushered us inside an almost featureless interrogation room, a dull gray square about twelve feet on a side with a steel table bolted to the center of the floor. I battled unpleasant flashbacks of my arrest fifteen years before; some memories were not so easily erased. Carson, still wearing his REI gear from the farm, sat on one side of the table, so me and Jess each took a chair opposite. He looked tired but content and favored us with a condescending smile.

"Thanks for coming," he said. "I wanted one last chance to see the couple who'll destroy the world."

"Nice to see you too, Carson," I said, taken aback but determined not to show it. "We heard you're ratting out Allen Weston and the rest of your scaly friends. Scared to go to jail? A handsome gentleman like yourself should be. They'd love you in there."

He scowled, lip curling with distaste. "You and I both know I won't see the inside of a real prison cell. One way or another. It doesn't matter. Who knows how long our prisons will last? Who knows how long any of it will last?"

"A lot longer now you're selling out the Scales of Equilibrium. What must Weston think of you?"

"I don't care what he thinks of me," he spat. "He's irrelevant."

"How do you figure that?" Jess asked, leaning forward.

Carson flinched, then attempted a smile. "He lost control of Gaia. He's out of favor and has no influence. I watched it happen, two nights ago, in that farmhouse kitchen." His gaze shifted to me, and the feverish intensity in his eyes unsettled me. "I saw Gaia switch allegiance to you, D. And to Jess."

I gaped at him.

"What the fuck are you talking about?" Jess's tone was even more belligerent, but this time Carson didn't seem to care, keeping his eyes on me.

"Did you know you echo Gaia's words when it speaks to you, D? 'Salvation. Jess.' Sound familiar?"

Jess glanced at me, and I licked my lips. I'd forgotten to tell her that part of the story.

"So what if it did?" I blustered. "It was aware of Jess already. It didn't forget her." That earned me a prod under the table, either gratitude or a warning for later.

"No, it did not. It's clear to me that Gaia thinks highly of the pair of you and is tired of Weston and his rabble of sociopaths. No, you're much better tools for its ends, should you wish to be. Although not strong enough to stop it if you wish otherwise."

"So, what, you think we're gonna help it destroy modern civilization?" Jess said. "You're delusional."

"Why?" I demanded. "You don't strike me as a zealot, not like Weston."

"Oh, but I am. For very different reasons."

"Which are?"

He sat back in his chair, as if gathering his thoughts. Uh oh. Monologue incoming. "Did Jamal ever explain our history to you? Why we despise each other?"

"No, not really. Is that why you spent time beating him up at the farm, instead of doing your job?"

His eyes flashed, then he regained his composure. "Fifteen years ago, Jamal's brother Kendrick and another HLF agent accomplished what you and Jess did this year. They established a connection with each other when manipulating Intrusions. They were young and reckless, and no one understood the risks, or tried to rein them in. One day, they tried their circus act with a Level Five that had defeated some of our most experienced agents. They failed. Kendrick fell into a coma, from which he's never emerged. His companion was not so lucky. Collapsing in the living room of the condo hosting the Intrusion, she cracked her skull on the edge of a glass coffee table. She died instantly."

He gazed expectantly at me, and then I remembered. I remembered our conversation on the grounds of Shotcombe House.

"She was your daughter," I said in hushed tones.

He nodded, emotion draining from his face. "My wife committed suicide less than a year later. Couldn't bear the pain of losing our only child. So you see, I don't really care about the Scales, or the environment, or holding back the tide of Intrusions, or really much of anything else. Humanity is fatally flawed. I want Gaia to succeed, because I want our whole fucking world to burn."

Chapter Twenty-Two
Ifs and Mays

The Hills suggested we spend some of our crisp late fall afternoon at the Missouri Botanical Garden. They were our ride, so it would've been churlish to object. Besides, after a recent night cooped up in various farm buildings, me and Jess were perfectly happy to savor the open air. Rosalind and Martin held hands and conferred in quiet voices as we wandered the autumnal pathways. Jess and I followed suit.

"We need to get in the proper headspace for The Council of Elrond tomorrow," she murmured, as we circled the Japanese garden.

"The Council of what?"

"Elrond. It's always been one of my favorite chapters of The Lord of the Rings. The books, not the movie. All these different dudes travel from all over Middle Earth to the house of Elrond, the elf, to figure out what to do with the One Ring, and how to defeat Sauron. That's what this feels like to me."

"It would, cos you're a nerd," I said with a chuckle, earning a playful swat of my good arm. I thought for a moment. "Didn't the big guns at that council decide to send one poor little hobbit to destroy Sauron all by himself?"

"Him and his best friends. They all played a part, even the guy who betrayed them."

"I'm not sure I like this analogy."

"Alright then. How about we get T-shirts made tonight? 'D and Jess: Destroyers of Worlds'. That should get the conversation going." She said it lightly, but set her lips in a tense line.

I slipped my good arm around her waist. "I'm sorry I didn't tell you The Presence mentioned your name. You deserved to know that."

She bumped my shoulder with hers. "It's not like it didn't know me already, like you said. Rosalind too. I'm scared, D."

"Me too. Let's just enjoy the day together. We can worry about all that tomorrow."

Easier said than done. We enjoyed a pleasant, if subdued, home-cooked meal with the Hills, then spaced out in front of a British murder mystery show on Netflix. The sets reminded me of the Cotswolds, and who we were meeting with the next day. I wondered how Madam Sophia was doing, wherever the HLF had sequestered her, and made a mental note to ask - nicely, this time.

Our visitors had piled out of Lambert Airport into the towering Three Rivers hotel just across the I-70. Maria Gomez, a cheerful Hispanic woman, greeted us in the lobby. She'd gathered her thick silver hair in a bun, and draped a thick shawl of colorful, geometric design over her ankle-length, forest-green dress. She hugged Rosalind, then turned to me and Jess with curiosity burning in her dark eyes.

"We meet at last. I'm sure you're tired of all the attention, D, but I have to ask. Did you really pick a Two Point Lock before you'd had any training?"

"*Any* training?" Rosalind said, raising a disdainful eyebrow. Maria blinked. "Where are we meeting the others?"

"Uh, we're in one of the event rooms. Follow me."

Maria led us down a corridor, round a couple corners, and into a room of a similar size and shape to where we'd spent our days at Shotcombe House. There, the resemblance ended. These walls were devoid of English country estate finery, or indeed anything else. Someone had hastily jammed three trestle tables together in place of the wooden monstrosity I remembered.

The people sitting around it were familiar, however. David, the affable Foundation director, rose from his folding chair and shook our hands, telling us to sit where we wanted, while coaxing us into three adjacent seats. Astbury regarded us over steepled hands from the other side of the table, and Kara inclined their head politely two seats down. Between them sat Charli, smothered in an amorphous navy blue sweatshirt that looked at least two sizes too big. She gave us a nervous smile, then returned to silent contemplation of her laptop. Izzy, on Kara's other side, looked like she'd had her pink hair color refreshed, and the elaborate patterns of her dark eyeliner looked immaculate. She hugged herself, obscuring the design of her black T-shirt, and scowled at no one in particular. I considered saying hi and asking what was bothering her, but in the adjacent seat, expressionless and hands folded on the table in front of him, sat Jamal.

"Hey!" I said, taking the closest seat. "How are you doing?"

He turned a grim smile on me and shrugged with his eyes. Stitches replaced half of his left eyebrow, and darker blotches discolored his cheek and chin. "Better now. Apologies, I wasn't careful enough at the house in Wildwood, and was too preoccupied being Carson's punching bag at the farm. I'm as impressed as anyone with what you guys did."

"It wasn't your fault," I insisted. "We all pushed our luck too far. We were fortunate at the farm, and thanks to Izzy, we made the most of that luck."

I glanced at her. She didn't raise her eyes, but her lips twitched. "More gratitude, D?"

David coughed the cough of someone bringing a meeting to order.

"Thanks to everyone for coming, and to Maria for organizing this on short notice. We'd rather have had this meeting back at HQ, but there were fewer obstacles to us flying than you." He glanced at my broken arm, and I shuddered at the thought of dealing with that on an international flight. "We flew over your Arch on the way in. The Gateway to the West, you call it? I hope this meeting will be a gateway of sorts, to a path forward."

"Spare us the poetry, David," growled Astbury, rapping the arm of her wheelchair. "There are several reasons I loathe flying, not just because of this damn thing. But we're here now, and we have problems to solve. Charli?"

The younger woman looked up, her gaze skating over us until settling on Rosalind. "The model's blowing up. We can't enter the field data fast enough. It's struggling to cope. It wasn't..." She hesitated, looking over at Astbury, who answered with an impatient gesture to continue. "Its design couldn't support such rapid changes, an order-of-magnitude increase in little over a month. The sheer volume of reported new Intrusions over-whelmed it."

"That doesn't sound good," I murmured, adding precious insight to the discussion.

"What is this model exactly?" Jess asked. "You guys never really answered me. It might be top secret or whatever, but we're past that now. Everything the HLF does depends on this magical model. What is it?"

"Think of it as machine learning," said Astbury. "Before everyone started calling machine learning 'artificial intelli-gence'. Don't get me started on the semantics. It's been an effec-tive tool, although I disagree that it's governed the Foundation's every move. But, as a predictor of Intrusion evolution in the current environment, it's effectively useless. And that should concern us."

"Our field agents are up against it worldwide," Kara put in. They looked the most exhausted of the four travelers. I won-dered if it was jet lag or something else. "I'm sure everyone's read or heard reports in the mainstream media. We can't respond fast enough. We can't train enough new agents. Maria can vouch for that."

Maria looked surprised to be called out. She glanced at Rosalind before answering. "Until a couple months ago, we were fine here in St. Louis. I had three senior agents, and had started training two more. But now, even were Rosalind not, um, unavailable, we'd still struggle to keep up with all the reports of new Intrusions. Two high school students and a cleaner at a downtown condo complex fell into comas last week. My agents are exhausted, troubled by memories of possible futures, and by a looming threat."

"We can't get to these people in time to help them, and deal with the Intrusions," Kara went on. "It's happening everywhere. Most people who pay attention to the news focus on the urban sabotage, and on the Scales of Equilibrium. The arrest of Allen Weston and his cronies still commands headlines. But some have noticed this uptick in coma victims, and of unexplained phenomena, and are starting to connect the dots. Few use words like 'paranormal' or 'supernatural', because they want to be taken seriously. They know something is there. Time is running out for keeping a lid on this thing."

There was a pause after this ominous statement, then Rosalind took a sip of water and cleared her throat. "What do we think will happen if we don't? What will happen if word gets out? Which, by the way, it already has. If NPR and the BBC are broadcasting unironic stories about hauntings, I'd say the cat is well out of the bag."

"It's not about the press." David had followed the conversation with a thoughtful expression. "I'm not worried about mass panic if more people start believing ghosts are real, or however they choose to interpret it. In some ways, it might help us. Perhaps others would take us seriously, and give us more and better resources, rather than treat us as a fringe group of quacks and conspiracy theorists. If this was merely a temporary upsurge in the Intrusion density, I doubt we'd have flown four thousand miles to have this conversation."

"You're worried about The Presence," I said.

The silence was deafening. David flashed an uneasy glance at Astbury, whose face remained impassive even as she gripped the arms of her wheelchair.

"I spoke to Carson yesterday," he went on. "He's not the man I thought I knew. Carissa's death hurt him deeply, of course. It hurt all of us." Next to me, Jamal stirred, but remained silent. "Carson may have allied himself with Weston, even lured other Foundation agents to a double life, to align with the Scales of Equilibrium and even attack their own. But he's no fanatic. Few men are as practical and capable as Carson, or have such a network of people and resources. And he believes the Agency, your Presence, is real, and every bit as powerful as you have maintained. He told me, calm as you like, that it's capable of 'knocking humanity off its pedestal'. That scared me."

"Weston may be a reprehensible human being," said Rosalind quietly, "and quite deluded in many respects, but he remains intelligent and articulate. I will loathe him forever for what he did to my son, but there is no doubt in my mind that, between them, they established a beachhead for interacting with this entity. Daniel believes they were the first to do so for centuries. Weston thinks he knows what it wants, and took considerable time to convince Jess and I that he did, and that we should honor it."

"So much time," yawned Jess. Rosalind's lips twitched into a grin that didn't quite succeed.

"Weston created a cult, a religion centered on himself as much as his Gaia," said Astbury, her voice dripping with derision. "If vestiges of his shrewd analytical mind remain, that almost saddens me more."

"He always respected you, Emma," said Rosalind. "Still does, I think."

"I don't want to hear it. What exactly does he think it wants? And how does it intend to get it?"

Rosalind poured herself a fresh glass of water, but didn't take a drink. "He thinks it wants to take a more direct hand in our affairs. He genuinely believes it is some sort of caretaker of the planet, a god by any other name. But it's a largely impotent god. Intrusions - what he calls 'Echoes' - are all it has to show for exerting its will on our material world. Until recently, at least. Until, through what kind of miracle I cannot fathom, it communicated with my son."

"And then with D," Jess whispered. All faces turned toward me, most expressing fascination sprinkled with an uncomfortable amount of dread.

I swallowed. "Rosalind, I hate to ask this. But shouldn't Daniel be here too? He probably knows more about The Presence than anyone, even Weston."

"No." Rosalind shook her head emphatically. "It's enough that he returned to St. Louis yesterday to meet with the FBI and, I believe, with Weston. I've spoken more with my son during these last two weeks than the entire prior eight years. For that, I am grateful, but also shocked and saddened. Daniel is sick, but he's healing - slowly but surely. It may take a lifetime for him to heal fully, if he ever does. I won't imperil that further, not for anything. Besides, I don't think he knows as much as you think. Heavy use of psychedelics and other illicit pharmaceuticals have taken their toll on his mind and his memory."

She gazed at me with steely-eyed defiance, and I raised my palms in acknowledgment. "I'm sorry."

"So am I, D. So am I."

Astbury sniffed with impatience. "So, anecdotal evidence suggests The Presence, which is as good a name as any other, is responsible for creating Intrusions. Or, at least, it takes advantage of another phenomenon driven by human activity, particularly in cities and other densely populated areas. The model, when the damn thing worked properly, detected and projected patterns on a regional scale, but not globally. There's no evidence of a grand plan. Are we sure we're not ascribing godlike intelligence purely because of its perceived godlike power? This recent spate of Intrusions reminds me more of my grandniece's temper tantrums."

"Then how do you explain the Intrusions at the farm?" Jess asked. "Two Intrusions, far from the city, appearing at precisely the right place and time for me, Rosalind, and D to connect with each other and then with Izzy. Explain that."

Astbury shrugged. "I can't. When it comes to unseen primal powers, I'm out of my depth."

"We all are," said David, his voice grim. "This Presence appears to be gaining control and flexing its muscles. That does not bode well. Aside from the hazards to our own operations, we don't know what might happen if the escalation continues, or even accelerates. Dare we take the risk? And if not, what can we do to stop it?"

His questions hung heavy over the table. My arm itched fiercely, and I craved more coffee, but I dared not leave my place. Jess fidgeted, but remained quiet. Rosalind caught my eye, but her expression was inscrutable.

Jamal broke the silence. "The fact that D, Jess, and Rosalind have seats at this table, and that four of you flew over from England to meet them, suggests you already have some idea. What Izzy did yesterday, with myself as a sidelined observer, only confirms it. Perhaps you can just ask them."

"What did you do yesterday?" I asked Izzy.

She looked up from intent study of her close-bitten, black-painted fingernails. For a moment, I saw a hint of her usual mocking arrogance. "I was practicing."

"Practicing what?"

"What do you think? Long range connections with other agents. I know how to do it now. You and Jess showed me, and now I've got the trick of it. It's knowing where to look, and truly understanding people. Some of us find that harder than others." Her voice trailed off with a note of bitterness.

"How long range?" Jess asked.

"Chicago."

"You connected with someone in Chicago?" I couldn't keep the disbelief from my voice. "Wait, there are people back in Chicago?"

"Some never left," Izzy said, eyes glinting. "Some couldn't afford to, or had nowhere to go. I know a guy who's still in his South Side rental. We dated once. So yeah, we connected. And then we connected with others in Detroit and Buffalo. The more of us there are, the more it boosts the signal, and our range. It's incredible!"

"Wow," said Jess. I was speechless. Buffalo was hundreds of miles away. This was crazy!

"And then?" prompted Jamal quietly.

Izzy grimaced. "And then The Presence came, and we broke it off just in time. We're strong, but not strong enough for that. Not yet. Not without you guys."

"Very flattering," said Jess, eyebrow raised. "But what difference do you really think we'd have made?"

"Don't you see?" Rosalind continued to look straight at me, expectant. And I thought I saw.

"They think we can excise it," I said, returning Rosalind's gaze but turning towards Jess. "They think that if you, me, and Rosalind are part of the connection, we'd be strong enough to excise The Presence and all its Intrusions. That we'd prevent it from entering our world."

David, Astbury, and Kara sat in silent confirmation. Only Charli had the grace to look embarrassed, shrinking down in her seat as if she could hide behind her laptop screen.

"You've got to be fucking kidding me," said Jess at last. "I mean, it's wonderful what Izzy did, truly. But what you're all suggesting would take agents connecting all over the world, engaging every Intrusion there is. That's just not possible."

"Even if it were," I said, my voice shaking more than I would have wished, "the cost of such an attempt would be brutal. You saw what happened to Rosalind when she excised one Intrusion at Shotcombe House, and me caught in the crossfire. Some saw what it did to me up in Bloomington. I still get headaches, and forget things I know I shouldn't." Rosalind's expression turned mournful, and she nodded. "If we tried an excision on that scale, even if it succeeded... I can't imagine how damaging the blowback would be."

"We understand what we're asking," David said solemnly. "Believe me, we - I - don't do so lightly, and we will force no one. We're not conscripting an army. We're asking everyone in the Foundation to step up and face the greatest threat we've known since Henry Lyons first studied these phenomena."

"And the organization won't be as daunting as you believe, Jess," said Kara, earning a disbelieving stare. "Between Jamal, Maria, and myself, we know most of the world's top agents personally, and all city heads report to me. Jamal's been working the phones already. Yes, we've operated in careful isolation over the decades, but we have the means to band together if necessary."

"Really?" scoffed Jess. "You have agents everywhere, who can engage every Intrusion on the planet simultaneously? I call bullshit."

"We may not need them all," said Astbury, gesturing at Charli's laptop. "We're still running simulations, and of course there's much we're uncertain of. But if we believe the early results, they support the idea of a 'critical mass'. We think there may be a threshold percentage of excised Intrusions, sufficient to destabilize the entire system. If we throw everything we've got at it, that may be enough."

"That's a lot of 'ifs' and 'mays', Emma," Rosalind put in mildly. "I thought your model was overwhelmed."

Astbury threw up her hands. "It's what you get at short notice, Rosalind. I had decades to refine the model - which isn't one single thing by the way, it's a set of tools and algorithms, each with their own purpose. I've barely had weeks to adapt to this new data, and frame it into a new hypothesis. If you all believe you can hold this thing back for a few more years, I can give you a more definitive answer."

Jamal shook his head. "I don't think anyone here believes that's possible. But I think Rosalind may be right. Whatever The Presence is, it's powerful but not omnipotent."

Silence descended, broken only by the clink of ice as David poured himself another glass of water. It was early, and I'm not a big drinker, but suddenly I longed for a beer. A kernel of panic stirred within me, the primal fear of a prey animal stalked, not yet trapped, but with the trap in sight.

Rosalind rubbed her temples wearily, but I caught Jess's determined eye. She wouldn't be bullied, and she refused to let others be bullied either. But she also wouldn't back down from responsibility, from a fight worth fighting. She looked lovelier in that moment than I'd ever seen her.

"Let's say we do this," I said, turning back to face David. "What about all these Echoes of future memories? Weston said he's always seen them, did you know that? Now all of us are. If they're true predictions, don't they mean whatever we try will fail? That, despite the personal cost, it won't make a difference?"

He grimaced. "The interesting thing about these future memories is that, as far as we can tell, they all take place in the very near future. Some imprinted memories have already happened, as you know. Nothing we've heard suggests glimpses of a future beyond the next few weeks, perhaps not even days."

"Well, that's comforting," muttered Jess.

CHAPTER TWENTY-THREE
ROLL OF THE DICE

For all Kara's confidence, organizing the simultaneous engagement of Intrusions by every active field agent around the world couldn't happen overnight. Hell, we struggled to figure out the logistics in St. Louis alone.

"We have thirteen HLF personnel in the area," Maria summarized at the end of a tense and weary day. "That includes the four travelers from HQ."

"I can step up in a pinch," Kara said. "But, given that St. Louis is essentially battle command for this exercise, the four of us think it best if we monitor things. We'll preserve conventional connection between teams of agents here."

"Why bother?" I asked. "Can't we all just use the same Imprint?"

Jamal shook his head. "That might not give us the strength to make long-range connections. Remember what Izzy described: each established connection bolstered their ability to find and make others."

"So we all find our own Imprint, and connect with each other?" Jess sounded dubious.

"You could, but we think the sweet spot will be teams of two. They can connect using their own Imprint, then combine with other local teams before reaching further afield. We've got to build this global network as fast as we can, before The Presence can react and disrupt it all."

"I'm with Jess," I said immediately, taking her hand. She gave mine a contented squeeze in return.

Kara grinned, one of the warmest expressions I'd ever seen on their face. It suited them. "I didn't doubt that for a moment. Otherwise, I think we should pair junior agents with more experienced ones."

Rosalind coughed. "I may teach English, and not Mathematics, but if my calculations are correct, five agents do not divide evenly by two."

"Brett is the newest, and is really feeling the strain of recent days," said Maria. "I was hoping you'd help me with him."

Oh no. "We want Rosalind," I demanded, echoed a fraction of a second later by Jess. Rosalind beamed. "If you guys believe we three hold the key to this insane gamble, then we should be together. We need to be able to communicate face-to-face, if necessary."

"Just like old times, eh?" Rosalind said, but her smile grew wistful and her eyes troubled.

"I think that's fair," interjected Jamal, before either Maria or Kara could object. "I'll take Samuel while Maria works with Brett, and Izzy with Lana. Now, we just have to find Intrusions for each team."

Charli broke her long silence. "There's one in this hotel," her voice little more than a whisper. She stared at her hands, clasped together on the table surface, laptop forgotten.

"We don't have to use it," Izzy said, low and fierce. "We can find another."

Charli shook her head, then met Izzy's eyes with a mournful expression. "No. We'll see it through."

Izzy bit her lip as everyone held their breath. Then she gave the faintest of nods.

"There are two more on my radar," said Maria, breaking the awkward silence. "My contacts are looking for a fourth. These days, it shouldn't take long."

"Would one of those happen to be in South City?" I asked. She shook her head. "Then I may be able to help."

It took two days for the HLF to make their arrangements. More unseasonal warmth blanketed the St. Louis region during the weekend before Thanksgiving. While Scales of Equilibrium attacks hadn't ceased entirely, the diminished threat encouraged more people out of their homes and back into their normal routines. Tales of hauntings preserved an undercurrent of unease, but it appeared most were thankful for the reprieve, and determined to celebrate.

Mine and Jess's families agreed, and we spent the day after the council fending off torrents of messages and phone calls about food and timing. It was both an irritating and welcome distraction.

Despite the tension, Martin appeared faintly amused by it all. "We don't celebrate ourselves," he told me. "We've joined friends and colleagues in the past, but I prefer my roast turkey dinner at Christmas."

Rosalind rolled her eyes fondly, but she didn't appear inclined to celebrate anything. She had said little since the council. Her brief phone call with Daniel the following morning had done nothing to lift her spirits. I couldn't recall seeing her so dispirited. After Jess cried "Oh my God!" at another family text, storming from the living room to make a call, I asked Rosalind what was bothering her.

"I've never been one for fatalism," she said, after a long pause to gather her thoughts. "I've had my share of dark times, my own and with Martin. I've never given up, never lost hope, and I'm trying not to do so now. But it's very, very hard, when the little we know is stacked so heavily against us."

"You don't think we can pull this off?"

"I think it's a calculated move, but a desperate one. My grandfather fought in World War 2. Have you heard of D-Day? He was there, on a Normandy beach, with over a hundred thousand other Allied soldiers, prepared to sacrifice his life in a war-changing roll of the dice. He never forgot his resignation, his terror, and then the simple joy of survival. The Allies understood their enemy. They understood what was at stake and what they needed to do. I don't believe we do. But we know the risks - to ourselves and all who join us in our own roll of the dice. I watch you and Jess make holiday and wedding plans, but I fear - both Martin and I fear - that none of us will be in a position to celebrate anything. Even if our gambit succeeds."

I rubbed my forehead above the right eye where the headaches normally began. "You worry our minds won't survive so many excisions at once, even with the combined strength of every willing HLF agent?"

"I think it is all too likely. Excision is a violent act, even if primarily a defensive one. Something on the scale we're planning may result in more than just a headache, nosebleed, and memory loss."

"Perhaps that's what we have to do though."

I jumped. Jess had crept back in to stand behind my armchair.

"You're okay with that?" I asked her, turning in my seat. "To sacrifice yourself, ourselves? This is serious shit, Jess."

She covered my hand with hers, fingers interlacing. Her expression was grim, but with a fierce glint in her eyes. "I know how serious it is, love. I know what we're being asked to do. I don't want to do it. But if the worst happens, and The Presence enters our world to wreak untold havoc, I couldn't live with myself if I'd spurned a chance to stop it."

Rosalind gave a heavy sigh. "Unfortunately, I agree with Jess. With no clearer idea of this entity's motives, I think we have to fear the worst."

The clinking of dishes in the kitchen, as Martin prepared dinner, accompanied a brooding silence. I rubbed my eyes. Another headache was definitely on the way.

"And how does Martin feel about it?" I asked at last.

"Frightened, for me," Rosalind said evenly, as if she didn't trust herself with any specific emotion. "Angry at the situation, even though he understands my decision. Helpless, because he thinks he can't contribute, that he can't protect me." Her voice hitched at the end, and she lowered her eyes.

I steeled myself. "There's one thing I haven't mentioned. It may be nothing."

"Nothing is nothing," Rosalind said with a wintry smile. "Out with it."

"I told you about this recurring vision of a dell in a redwood grove, right?"

"Recurring?" Jess interrupted. "You mentioned it once."

"Well, it's happened several times, the last few times I've interacted with The Presence. Do you remember that night after we first met Jamal, Jess? After he saved us from being trapped in the Imprint in that high school gym? We both had nightmares, vivid ones. Mine was of that redwood grove, and of a dell with an infinite succession of glass doors."

"That's interesting," said Rosalind, as Jess frowned. "The Presence wasn't there that time, I take it? Nor would it have been in your apartment. I wonder if it has seized on your memory of that nightmare somehow."

"To communicate, you mean?" Jess twirled strands of her hair in her fingers as she considered this.

I soldiered on. "That last time, with Weston at the horse farm, I saw something else. Someone else. A reflection in the glass door. But it wasn't me."

Rosalind gave me a shrewd look, but didn't elaborate. I still wasn't ready to speculate on exactly what, or who, I'd seen.

"It sounds like it wants to talk to you," said Jess. "Properly. Does that change anything?"

"Talking is almost always better than not," Rosalind declared. "I can't imagine what The Presence could say to change our plans, but if it invites you back to that dell, D, I would go. What do we have to lose?"

"Ah, the famous Rosalind! D kept you under wraps longer than his engagement to Jess!"

Fiona studied the other woman with interest while holding open the front door to Mary's bungalow. Rosalind returned her inspection with a placid smile, the first such emotion I'd seen since her private farewell with Martin earlier that morning. I began regretting my choice of Imprint for the big event. The last thing anyone needed now was any of my family drama.

"D talks about you often," said Rosalind. "He's grateful to be back in the fold, and believe me, I know how important that is."

"He's my big brother," Fiona said simply, pushing a teal strand of hair behind one ear. "Sorry, I'm being rude. Come in, please."

She ushered us inside the entrance foyer, kicking a pair of child's tennis shoes into the pile in one corner. It was tight, but we managed to shed our jackets and hang them on hooks, already supporting winter coats and school backpacks. Jess helped with mine, then Fiona fussed over my arm, only stopping when I introduced her to Astbury. The HLF lead researcher navigated her wheelchair up the short ramp Mary had installed for mom's last few visits, and hadn't had the heart to remove.

Mary rose from her couch as we entered the living room, wringing her hands under a rose-colored shawl. She wasn't used to visitors and had only agreed to our visit when Fiona promised to come over and help tidy up. In many ways, the decor reminded me of our childhood bungalow a half-dozen blocks away, just with more evidence of small children. The corner of an iPad poked out from under the couch, and I wondered how many tantrums it would take to find it.

"Thank you for doing this," I told her. My hug was awkward, not only because of its one-armed nature. "I wish I were here under different circumstances."

"You said it was important," she replied, uncomfortable, but obviously trying her best to erase over two decades of sibling enmity. "Besides, if you really take care of whatever's going on in my guest bedroom, I'll be grateful."

She'd met Jess before, so I introduced Rosalind and Astbury. Mary shook Rosalind's hand gravely, but Astbury appeared to intimidate her. "And you traveled all the way from England?"

"Indeed," Astbury confirmed, similarly ill at ease. Although, that was also due to her discomfort with our mission. "D told me about your mother and your husband. I'm sorry for your losses."

Mary's breath caught, then she offered a shaky smile. "Thank you. He... It's nice to be on better terms with my big brother."

She glanced at me, and I nodded. "I'm happy to try and help."

"How dangerous is this?" Fiona interrupted. She looked from Rosalind to Jess, then to me. "You said there were risks. What kind of risks?"

I met her steely gaze with what I hoped was the reassurance I needed myself. "Mostly those that come with unknown territory. That's why there's four of us, and not just me." I could tell that didn't satisfy her, but then it didn't really satisfy anyone. "Perhaps someone could show us to the guest room?"

Mary glanced at Fiona in silent appeal. "Follow me," Fiona said, heading for the hallway.

I was last in line, sharing one last moment with Mary. We'd done our research on her house, turning up nothing suspicious in its history before she and her husband, Bill, bought it eight years ago. When Fiona confided in me that Bill had died in the guest bedroom, isolating from his family in late 2020 while COVID stole his health and then his life, I thought I knew what to expect. This would be tough enough, without giving Mary any hint of what we might witness. Whether or not she suspected what the cold spot in that bedroom represented, she wanted no part of it, and I couldn't blame her. It was bad enough that others would endure what she'd gone through.

"Go," she whispered. "Do your thing, big brother."

I tried to find the words, failed, and simply nodded. Then I followed the others down the hall.

Peach-colored walls and a musty smell greeted me as I slid past Astbury's wheelchair into the bedroom. Stacks of clear plastic totes and cardboard boxes lined the walls and covered the unmade full-size bed. The drawn floral drapes blocked most of the daylight and threatened a dust storm if we so much as touched them. The ancient frosted lampshades of the ceiling fixture leaked pallid yellow light onto the depressing and crowded tableau. We huddled underneath, all staring at the corner of the room above the scratched wooden headboard.

Rosalind and I shivered, and she and Jess cocked their heads, as if listening to sounds I couldn't hear. I blinked unseen snowflakes from my eyes and took Jess's hand. She gripped mine and wrinkled her nose.

"Looks like we've got ourselves a Level Five," Astbury murmured, thumbs tapping slowly on her phone screen.

Fiona stared at her in curiosity. "What does that mean?"

"It means nothing is ever easy," sighed Rosalind.

"Oh. Well, sorry this room's a bit of a mess. I don't feel what Mary feels, but it still gives me the creeps. I tried to at least create some floor space for y'all."

"Thanks, Fi," I said. I would've given her a hug if I'd had two working arms, but I wasn't letting go of Jess's hand for any reason.

She lingered on the threshold. "I left bottles of water on the end table. Can I get you anything else?"

"We're good, thanks."

"Okay. Well, good luck, I guess." She turned and left, each creak from her receding footfalls sounding ominous to me.

"David wants to know if we're ready," said Astbury, bringing me back to the task at hand. She held her phone to her ear, poised to join the conference call they'd agreed upon.

I turned to Jess, who gave me a determined nod and reached for Rosalind's hand. Our friend peered up at us, and this smile was genuine. "Who thought it would come to this, when we first met in your friend Colton's apartment last spring?"

I grinned, even as I steeled myself for what was to come. "Saving the world? Yeah, that wasn't on my bingo card."

"We wouldn't have it any other way," said Jess. "Okay, we're ready. Let's do this!"

I heard the faint sound of a dial tone from Astbury's phone, then a click and David's tinny voice. "Hello Astbury. What's your status?"

"Team Rosalind is ready to go," she said, lips twitching in a dry smile. She listened for a few more moments, then her expression sobered as she focused on me.

"Whenever you're ready. Other teams are engaging with their Intrusions now. 'Good luck' is the traditional thing to say, but I don't believe in luck. Do what I know you're all capable of doing, and do it well."

I nodded, then clasped Jess's hand tighter as I caught her eye. "I love you."

She exhaled, then rewarded me with a radiant smile. "Love you too!"

I closed my eyes, reaching for her consciousness with my own. It was as easy as falling. We savored those first instants, then sought and found Rosalind, her polished and potent shape melding easily with our own.

So far, so good. To connect with others, we had to embrace the Imprint, and I unlocked it reluctantly. I'd never met Bill, Mary's former husband, and would likely have loathed him. But the memory we tapped into was less about Bill than about my sobbing half-sister, holding the hand of a dying man, pleading with him to go to a hospital. I didn't want to watch, but I couldn't look away. The sorrow and despair wrenched my heart.

"D. D, come back to us." Jess spoke aloud, rather than through our connection.

I snapped out of my reverie and took a deep breath. "Sorry. Okay, I'm good."

We expanded our sphere of consciousness in much the same way as we'd done at the horse farm, and almost immediately found Izzy and Lana. Izzy's essence radiated triumph as she flexed her own considerable strength, and we let her carry our search forward. Within moments, we'd recognized and made connection with a resolute Jamal and Samuel, then an uncertain Maria and Brett.

On the edge of my awareness, I heard Astbury say, "All spearhead teams connected."

It was an incredible rush, a far more intimate commune than sitting around a meeting table, and for the first time I understood Izzy's thirst for it. The power we wielded, at least in whatever plane of existence Imprints inhabited, was intoxicating. I could even detect fragments of those other memories, rage and joy, pain and sorrow.

Further.

The thought was likely Izzy's, although it was increasingly difficult to tell. Astbury fired off terse comments in the background as the rest of us discovered another group of connected consciousnesses, and then another.

I lost track of time, although somewhere a clock was ticking. I lost track of my own self, but that was important, wasn't it? Weren't there decisions to be made, and someone who needed to make them? The more agents that connected, across distances too vast for us to truly comprehend, the more I struggled to think for myself. A hundred voices yammered inside my head, more than a hundred, a thousand maybe, astounded, enraptured, terrified. Terrified: yes, there was a reason for fear, wasn't there? What were we all so afraid of?

The Presence arrived with a soundless explosion. A dull ring-ing smothered the babel of thoughts and voices, and our web of consciousness buckled. A thousand alarmed recoils spat with the fury of a downed power line.

Hold firm, dammit!

The thought wasn't mine, but I didn't know how I knew. I was still part of something, part of a plan, part of an un-precedented psychic connection faced with a poorly defined and almost impossible task. But I struggled to remember what that task was, even who I was connected with.

Jess. There was Jess. Her hand trembled in mine, or was mine trembling in hers?

It was getting so hard to think.

:: D. JESS. ::

Oh no! The Presence. I remembered The Presence, our mys-terious adversary. That's what we were here for, right? We had to do something. We had to stop it.

"...you okay?" Someone was speaking to me. Someone... No, that was too much.

"Jess," I croaked.

I heard or imagined a whispered "D" in return.

I only retained a dim sense of where I was, where my physical body stood. My mind, joined with more than a thousand oth-ers, was trapped in some sort of stasis. I knew I was connected, but my thoughts felt like they were swimming in morphine, back in the hospital where they'd reset my broken arm. All the strength people like me, Izzy, and Rosalind wielded was for nothing. I couldn't even sense them any longer. And as for Jess...

She was there. Faint, indistinct, her lithe warmth blurred and muted, but she was still there. And, deep within, a fire, a furious candle set against the nothing that wasn't even darkness.

— *trapped* —

—*Jess?* —

— *knew we were coming* —

—*Jess!* —

Jess!

I'm walking through a redwood grove...

Something! Something other than the pitiless void.

I descend into a dell, its red-brown earth scooped from the forest...

This is important, isn't it? Why is this important?

In the center of the dell is a door...

A door? Why is this so familiar?

In the door there is a reflection...

The reflection. The reflection that is not me. And a voice from my recent past: "It sounds like it wants to talk to you."

I face the reflection and remember. I face the image of a man I've only seen once before, in an almost forty-year-old photograph now stashed in the bottom of my travel backpack. My father, Ramon Rodriguez.

I stand before the door, in a featureless scoop of red-brown earth, in what was once a redwood forest. But probably not, not really. I face the image of my father on the other side of the glass. Also, probably not. That man is as dead to me as the mother who gave me that photograph.

"You're not him," I say. My hushed voice echoes around the dell.

The image of my father cocks his head, but doesn't change expression. He doesn't even blink.

I fight both revulsion and a smoldering fear. "Who are you?"

"D." His lips twitch, but they don't form the word I hear.

"You're not D. I am." My father stares back at me, with all the animation of a department store mannequin. An idea strikes me, and I tap my temple with my right hand. My arm is unbroken. "Are you a memory?"

"Memory?" His mouth moves better now, and there's a glimmer of what might be recognition in his dark eyes. Slowly, he raises his hand and taps his own forehead in eerie mimicry, and I shudder. "No. Not memory."

"Then what? What are you? Who are you?"

I can see him struggle, as if possessed by an entity unfamiliar with human anatomy, doing a crash course in the heat of the action.

"Watcher."

"Watcher? Watching me?"

He shakes his head, and finally blinks, once, twice. He spreads his arms wide enough to hug the doorframe. "All of it. Watcher of all this world."

Holy crap, was Allen Weston right after all? I shy away from the idea and latch on to the one tangible thing in front of me.

"Why do you look like my father? I've never even met the man, and probably never will."

His slow smile is almost wistful. "Regret. We all regret, D Rodriguez."

"How do you know my name?"

"You answered my call."

"Call? What call? I'm not one of Weston's followers."

"No. You are not." He grimaces at me through the glass door, and suddenly I feel the weight of ages and infinite space. I stagger and almost fall. "You are strong, D Rodriguez. Stronger than most. Once, many had your strength. Many could hear us. Now, your kind dwindles, even as you consume all in your path."

The image on the other side of the door may not be my father, but The Presence is rapidly improving its impersonation of another human being. It's trying to talk to me, and I'm listening. Just not understanding very much.

"Us? There are more of you?"

"Once. I am the last. As, perhaps, are you."

Icy fear grips my heart. "What do you mean?"

I see a glint of anger in his eyes. "Soon, it will be too late. Soon, no one will have the strength. No one will listen. No one will answer my call. You will do as you will with this world, heedless of consequences. You will sow, and you will reap. There will be no Daniel Hill, no Allen Weston. No D Rodriguez. No one will answer my call." The desolation in his voice terrifies me.

"What do you want?" I blurt. "Are you out for revenge? Do you want to knock humanity down a peg, stop us from ruining the planet? Or do you want to enslave us, make us worship you?"

"I could." Again, a dizzying impression of near infinite power almost overwhelms me. "You answered my call. You brought me others, many others. Jess. And..." It hesitates, then my father's image frowns. "And Rosalind."

"Yeah, you think I'm strong? Rosalind's kicked your ass twice, motherfucker." I'm frightened and angry, and it knows Rosalind's name now. It may not matter, but dammit, D!

"Rosalind is strong," my father's image acknowledges, expression serene once more. "She did what no other has done in many an age. She resisted me. You once did also. It doesn't matter. Those were but the stings of frightened insects to one such as I. Stings bought at great cost. And now you bring a swarm of insects against me, not understanding that you bring them *to* me."

Oh shit. The realization hits home, hard. This is what it wanted all along: a multitude of connected sensitives delivered to its door. *Oh shit, oh shit, oh shit!*

"We won't do it," I declare, summoning every ounce of confidence I have left.

It's not enough. He smiles tolerantly, and I'm dislocated, a child throwing a tantrum, refusing to do his father's bidding. He lowers his voice, his tones calm and chilling. "I could use your strength, yours and Jess's and Rosalind's, and the strength of all the other insects. I could compel you, chain you to my will. Though it goes against my original task, through you I could undermine your species, as Allen Weston foresaw. We could not repair the damage, but we could prevent humanity from inflicting more. You could not stop me."

"We could resist you. I *will* resist you. I won't be someone's pawn, not again."

"You are trapped, D Rodriguez. You, and all your fellow insects, trapped as if in amber. Just like the others." Sudden sadness floods his face. "We are all trapped. All alone. Yes, you could resist, and pay with your sanity, or your life. You have that choice. I envy it. But would others make that choice? Would Jess? Would Rosalind? Would the thousands of others sacrifice themselves to stop me, to keep me in chains? Can you ask them to?"

Could I? Isn't that what the Henry Lyons Foundation has already asked of its agents, to rally together in this last desperate roll of the dice? Are we asking them to storm a Normandy beach, hoping to mount a well-orchestrated counterattack? Or are we asking them to go over the top into trench-scarred no-man's-land, because it's the only way we can think of to fight back?

"What chains?" I ask, buying time, because these questions are too terrible to answer.

He sighs, and his breath stirs a wind that rustles through the long vanished redwood trees surrounding the dell. "The chains of power and impotence. The chains of purpose and futility. The chains of desire and honor. If I compel you, I become that which I am not. If I compel you, and you resist, I lose those who are my only hope of salvation. If I do nothing, I remain where I have dwelt for so long: in the dark." He fixes me with a mournful gaze. "It is so lonely here, in the dark."

The weight of ages settles over me, a shroud of burden and despair. A kernel of pity stirs, and I fight to suppress it. How can I pity this thing that holds so many lives in its hands?

"What do you want?" I ask again.

Absolute silence descends. Silence, but for the thudding of the heart in my chest, and the roaring of blood in my ears. With almost infinite slowness, the image of my father closes his eyes and rests his weary forehead against the glass door. "Release. I want release. Let me go, D Rodriguez."

And I understand. I know what it wants. I stare at him, every instinct screaming this is a lie, a ruse to lure me into unleashing this entity on the world. Instincts served my ancestors well, when they first roamed the African plains and post-glacial forests of Europe. Yet we'd evolved since then. We were more than just our instincts now.

I can forgive my father. I can let go of my decades of resentment, my unquenched thirst to know why he abandoned me and my mother. Perhaps he'd had no choice. Perhaps he'd died. She'd never said. I can let him go.

And I understand why The Presence chose the memory of my father to make its appeal. It wants humanity to let it go too. It wants me to let it go. Yet, I waver.

He opens his eyes and looks deep into mine, deep into my soul. "You, of all people, know what it is to live in a cage."

There was an abrupt release of pressure, and I was back in Mary's guest bedroom. I held hands with Jess and looked into Rosalind's alarmed eyes. No, that wasn't quite right. I could still see the glass door, and the image of my father behind, but I could also see the bedroom, and the memory of Mary weeping at her dying husband's bedside. I could still sense The Presence, but it waited now. I could sense a swarm of other consciousnesses through our connection, reeling and terrified, released temporarily from thrall. I could sense Izzy and Jamal. I could sense Rosalind. And I could sense Jess.

D... Is that you? Rosalind! Jess almost squeezed my hand in half.

I'm here. We're all here. It's let us go, for now. It's given us a choice.

What choice?

Between the HLF way, and our way. Rosalind's way.

And what is my way, D?

The way you taught us from the beginning. Let these memories go. Let them pass. And with it, The Presence. It wants release.

Time passed. Stars wheeled across the heedless sky. Our strength dwindled. Everyone held their breath.

It always felt right to me. It was Rosalind's thought, but our own too. All those connected understood and consented. *And maybe it's right now too.*

"What's going on?" Astbury demanded, her voice low but urgent. "People are struggling to stay connected. Are you ready to execute the plan?"

"New plan," I stated. "With new information. Excision won't work. We need to let it go."

"What? That wasn't... how do you know?"

Straining through the torrent of sensation, dream, memory, and reality, I could see Astbury's alarm. A hint of outrage too, outrage of authority defied. "I don't know," I admitted. "But trust me. Trust us."

The moment hung, suspended in spacetime while the universe watched.

"Very well," Astbury whispered at last. "Show us how it's done."

And Rosalind did. I let her guide me, and by extension the collected consciousnesses of all Henry Lyons Foundation agents, as we embraced the memories in as many Imprints across the world. We started with our own, and I offered reassurance to the half-sister I'd once loathed that we loved her, that her family would help her through her grief. While doing so, I glimpsed other memories, memories of other sorrows, of fear and terror, of rage and murderous anger, of terrible pain, of lust and profound joy. Rosalind's example, true to her nature and vocation, guided us through our initial confusion and reluctance. By engaging with those memories, empathizing, listening, and speaking without voices, we released those emotions and broke each link in the chain of imprisonment.

Then something even stranger happened. As we gained momentum, as the number of memories pouring through our collective will snowballed, threatening to overwhelm us, other consciousnesses joined us. Other minds, aware of us, but dis-oriented and afraid, bringing memories of memories, memories of Imprints that no longer were, and memories of their own. Amid the bewildering flashes of sensation, I saw a marauding three-year-old girl with wild ginger hair, and two brothers, in-cluding a younger Jamal, comparing snappy-looking tuxedos in a mirror. I thought I understood then, but I couldn't cope with the cacophony. I was losing focus, my strength failing, fearful of being washed away in the avalanche of released memories.

I've got you. I've got you all. Come to me!

It was Jess's thought, but it wasn't for me. She made herself a beacon for all those lost souls, and they flocked to her without hesitation. She was the one thing in all this madness that made sense to them, and they clung to her for dear life. Just like I did. Just like I always would.

But there was something else I had to do. One final task.

I'm still standing in the dell, amid the long-vanished redwood forest of my dream. The image of my father, the avatar of The Presence, watches me from the other side of the glass door. His eyes are full of wonder and hope, but also fear. Fear that I won't do what I'm resolved to do.

I open the door. It makes no sound and swings easily towards me. I step back and wait.

"Thank you, D Rodriguez," The Presence says, and crosses the threshold. From nowhere, a warm breeze strikes up, and my father's face turns up to meet it, already looking paler, thinner, less substantial. With every thud of my heart, my father's image grows more translucent, fading away from this and maybe every reality. At last, when only a hint of an outline of the man who sired me remains, I hear an echo on the breeze.

:: you're all on your own now ::

Chapter Twenty-Four
Our Own Story

"I do."

And with those words, echoed moments later by Jess Evans, the woman of my dreams, my light, and my life, I became a married man.

"You may now kiss the bride," said the smiling celebrant. I let go of Jess's hands, and she clung to my neck as I swept her almost literally off her feet. We kissed with undisguised passion. Our guests' roar of approval carried across Tower Grove Park.

"Later, husband," she purred. Her grin promised mischief, and her emerald eyes outshone the afternoon sun.

Husband. I still only half-believed it, even as I stood before a hundred friends and family in a rented tuxedo.

The string quartet struck up the theme from Game of Thrones, by Jess's design. She clung to my arm, and we smiled and waved, acknowledging the standing ovation as we walked between rows of white folding chairs towards my trusty Hyundai. As we approached, I saw that, besides scrawling "Just Married" over the rear windshield, someone had covered almost every inch of paintwork with retro Ghostbusters decals. We drove to our reception at a Clayton hotel in a demented, polka-dotted sedan.

"Who was it?" I demanded, confronting Fiona, Izzy, and Sharelle as we took our seats at the head table. "Were you all in on it? I hope you're planning to take the damn things off yourselves before I have to drive to the airport."

"Why assume it was us?" Fiona countered, eyebrow raised. "I'd look to your side of the table if I were you, big brother."

I whirled to face Jamal, Eric, and Kioko, and it was Jess's younger brother who gave the game away, dissolving into fits of laughter. Of everyone at that table, he was the last I'd suspected. I laughed too.

Calvin and Zawida Evans spared no expense on the reception, providing a first class meal and an open bar. Zawida frequently burst into tears - of happiness, she assured everyone - and hugged me the hardest and longest. Calvin allowed himself more than one wistful glance at the perfectly cooked steaks most of us enjoyed, but honored his new vegetarian diet.

"If I can't set a good example for my patients, what kind of doctor am I?" he told me, shaking my hand yet again.

Jonathan, their oldest child, clapped me on the back and asked me, poker-faced, if I'd counted the decals thoroughly. I gaped at him, then shook my head as he sniggered and gave Kioko a thumbs up. These were good people. And now they were family, for real.

Speaking of family, Jess and I stopped by Mary and Patrick's table first. Mary looked flustered, and still hadn't touched much of her own food as she tried to wrangle Fiona's two kids plus her own three. My stepfather, whose plate was clean, watched with bemusement and helplessness. I shared my sisters' worries for him. He'd gone downhill after my mom died, almost a year ago now, and showed little sign of recovery. We'd only had one conversation in the days leading up to the wedding, but I'd had it several times. However, he rewarded us with a genuine smile and a firm handshake of his own.

"Siobhan would be so proud," he said, a tear welling in his eye.

"I know," was all I could think of to reply. "We'll come and say 'Hi' before we leave. Give Mary a hand, would you?"

Mary's snort revealed how likely or effective she thought that would be. "I'm happy for you, D. I really am. Take good care of Jess, you hear?"

"I will," I promised.

"At this rate, I need to be the one taking care of him," said Jess. Here we go. "No sooner does he get the cast off his arm and start training again, than he breaks his toe walking out of the dojo!"

"That wasn't my fault!" She and Mary laughed as I shifted the weight off my left foot. These dress shoes were killing me, and not just because of my broken big toe.

"Did you see who else showed up?" Mary asked quietly, gesturing towards the bar. "I didn't think you'd sent him an invitation."

I sighed. "We didn't. Not an official one. I'm not that tone deaf. But it didn't feel right to ignore him either, so I texted him. I supposed we'd better go say hello."

Steven Rourke stood alone at one end of the bar, nursing what looked like scotch straight up. I didn't see Emi, his usual companion/minder, but that didn't mean she wasn't around. He beamed as we approached and kissed Jess's hand with a flourish. She looked like she couldn't decide if she was amused or annoyed.

"I confess I never thought I'd see the day," Rourke said, shaking my hand with his usual crushing grip. "But then, it took a special woman to lure you into marital bliss. To Jess!"

I'd been nursing the same glass of champagne for a while, and Jess had already switched to water, but he didn't seem to mind. We clinked glasses, and he drank half his scotch with relish.

"I wasn't sure you'd come," I said, sensing family eyes on us.

He grinned, like that affable uncle at the holiday dinner table you hoped wouldn't go off on some bigoted rant. "How could I turn down your kind invitation, unorthodox though it was? Not to mention more of Hickory's fabulous food."

He toasted someone behind me, and I turned to see Mike Szemis, sitting at a table with TJ and others I once worked with. Mike returned the gesture half-heartedly, but was more enthusiastic when I raised my glass, empty though it was.

"Mike tells me further congratulations are in order," Rourke went on, relieving me of my empty glass, and thrusting another scotch into my protesting hand. Jess narrowed her eyes, but remained silent. "I believe I'm talking to Trattoria Capelli's new sous chef? I may make the trek up to Chicago for that!"

Out of politeness, I took the tiniest sip of my scotch and still almost sprayed him with it. How did anyone drink this stuff?

"Chicago's getting closer to normal, to what it was before. But not everyone chose to come back, including Tamsyn, the previous sous chef. I wasn't sure Luca would open back up. I'm nervous, but excited. Excited to have a normal job again." Another clink of glass on glass, but this time I didn't drink.

"You'll do great. I'm genuinely happy for you, for both of you. Even happier than I am to see that lunatic Allen Weston finally put away for life, even if a handful of his followers are still causing trouble."

"They're just terrorists without a cause now," Jess said, with a sniff of disdain. "Everyone knows them for what they are, even if they try to get their tattoos removed. The Feds will round 'em up."

"I hope so. They were bad for business," said Rourke. A gleam entered his eye. "Speaking of which, you rather scuppered my hauntings-to-order business plan. Lana's had to turn to other means of employment."

"I heard she just became a sensei at our old dojo," I said. "Donovan's still in recovery."

With some reluctance, we'd invited them to the wedding. They'd declined, but sent a gift, a matching pair of Gateway to the West Karate headbands.

"Good for her. Well, newlyweds, I'll take my leave and allow you to celebrate properly. I understand my effect on social engagements. Before I go, there's the small matter of my wedding gift."

He handed me a plain white envelope. "D and Jess" was laser-printed on the front, in the same font as the "Stop" note I once received from him. This envelope contained the key fob to a car. I stared at it, then at Jess, and then at Rourke, who smirked with satisfaction.

"It's parked in the valet lot, and they have the second key fob. I've taken care of all the paperwork. You'll be driving back to Chicago in style!"

"Thank you," Jess said, as I struggled with conflicting emotions. I'd given up twelve years of my freedom for this man, only to receive ignorance and contempt in return. We'd scuppered his biggest ever real estate deal, erasing all the Imprints he'd had made to scare off existing Chouteau Village tenants, and temporarily devalue the property. It had taken my mother's death, the death of a woman he'd once respected, and possibly loved, for him to repent even a little. He'd helped put us on Weston's scent, and now he was giving us a car?

"Tell me, Steven," I said, looking him dead in the eye. "When you gave me the address of that house in Wildwood, did you know the Scales would ambush us there? Were you in on it?"

He held my gaze for a long time, then smiled and saluted. "Enjoy the car, guys."

Then he walked out without a backwards glance.

"Fucking prick," growled Jess. "I say we sell whatever piece of shit car he tried to buy us off with!"

I pocketed the key fob, took her in my arms, and kissed her. "Later, love. Don't give him another thought. This is our day."

She smiled, mollified, and pressed her body against mine. Damn, she looked fine in a wedding dress!

A hesitant cough prevented us from losing all sense of decorum. I turned to see Colton Lynn, holding hands with another, slightly taller man of Jess's complexion. I fumbled for his name, but fortunately, Colton spared me the indignity.

"Hey, D! Hi, Jess. Congratulations! This is my partner, Derrick."

"Good to meet you, Derrick," I said, shaking his hand. His smile was smooth and composed, unlike Colton's nervous one. Jess, unabashed, gave them both a big hug.

"Colton's told me a little about you," said Derrick, in a much deeper voice than I expected. "He said you're one of the good ones."

I shared a sheepish grin with my old high school buddy. "Yeah, he and I went through some of the same stuff. It helped me to see him work things out. In some ways, I wouldn't be here if it wasn't for Colton."

"Don't know about that, dude," Colton said, shaking his head. "But I recognize that cute British lady, who came to my apartment on Locust last spring. You remember that, D?"

"Oh, I remember."

"Guess you're still in touch, huh? That's cool. But I wouldn't have worked things out if it wasn't for Derrick. And, well, we wanted you to be one of the first to know."

He held up his left hand so I could see the black tungsten band encircling his ring finger. Derrick disengaged his own left hand and raised it to match.

Colton grinned. "We didn't do anything as fancy as this. Just went down to the courthouse, then ate a steak dinner with friends."

"That's awesome!" gushed Jess, hugging them both again. I settled for the half-hug, half-handshake combo.

"We don't want to steal your thunder," Derrick said cautiously. "But we're thrilled you invited us, so we can reflect in your glory!"

I laughed and gestured at the bar. "Can I get you guys a drink to celebrate?"

Colton grimaced. "We're both teetotal now. Trying to stay away from all that stuff."

"Oh, hey, no worries. Coke? Diet Coke? Two diets? Coming right up."

I grabbed their drinks from the bar and swapped out Rourke's scotch for another Diet Coke. I'd just handed over their glasses when a shriek of "Jessie! Jessie!" rang out, and a ginger-haired demon threw herself at Jess's dress.

"Hey, princess!" my new wife cried, picking the girl up and swinging her around. Colton and Derrick hastily backed away. "Are you mad because I haven't come to see you yet?"

"*I'm* not mad," Esmeralda objected, crossing her arms and pouting. "Daddy is. He says if you don't come see him soon, he'll fall asleep. And then we'll have to go back to the hotel room, and it's soooo boring!"

"We can't have that," Jess said gravely, setting the rampaging four-year-old back down on the floor. "Take us to your daddy."

I waved farewell to Colton and Derrick, then hurried to keep up with Esmeralda as she led us to the table nearest the door. Conor and Michelle McKee rose to greet us, Conor wobbling slightly and leaning on a cane. Across the table, Jamal rose too. The man sitting in a wheelchair next to him might, had he been less gaunt, have been his twin.

"Sorry about that," Conor said, giving Jess a careful hug. Although still recovering from almost three months in a coma, he'd retained his rakish good looks. Other than the cane, the only outward sign of his experience was a guarded, haunted look in his eye. "Es takes her responsibilities seriously." He ruffled his daughter's hair.

She beamed at him, then turned to his wife. "Can I get more cake now, mom? Please!"

"One more piece," said Michelle, her voice suggesting she'd reached the limits of such generosity. She hugged Jess and then me, whispering "Thank you" in my ear, before escorting her sugar-craving daughter towards the dessert buffet. Conor sat with a grimace and stretched out his left leg.

Jamal gave me a firm handshake and even cracked a smile. "D, Jess, I'd like to introduce you to my brother, Kenny."

"Kendrick, please," his brother said, with a long-suffering eye roll. "Jamal's the only one who persists in calling me Kenny. But hey, congratulations! I've been wanting to meet you ever since, well, ever since I woke up and remembered who I was. And what I did. It hasn't been easy." A spasm of horror crossed his face, then he chased it away with a grim smile. "From the sounds of it, you two perfected what Rissa and I tried all those years ago. And you brought me back. I can never thank you enough."

"None of us can," murmured Conor. "It's all so hard to comprehend. What happened to us, and our families, our loved ones... well, I'm just happy it's over. Thank you. Both of you."

I was glad my complexion was too dark for me to blush, but I'm sure I looked awkward.

"We're just happy you're back," Jess said simply. "We didn't expect it, but it was one of the best surprises I've ever had. Next to this goof going down on one knee in a crowded restaurant, of course."

Everyone laughed, and any embarrassment evaporated. "We're glad you're all on the mend," I added. "And that you could be here with us. We did invite some other Henry Lyons Foundation folks. We wanted to thank them for their gift in person. I'm not sure when we'll find time to make use of it, but an all-expenses-paid week in London sounds amazing."

Jamal nodded. "They all send their best wishes. The HLF is changing. We've detected no new Intrusions, and the evidence suggests what we did, what you did, really worked. Kara will retain a handful of field agents for a while, but most are moving on. Astbury's retired, although I'm sure she'll make a nuisance of herself somewhere."

"And what about you?"

"I'm staying, just switching responsibilities. The Foundation's public front has always been as a supporter of coma research. Now, that's our sole endeavor. Those whose comas resulted from Imprint encounters are back with us. But, they were only ever a fraction of worldwide coma victims. We've amassed skills and personnel that can help. Conor and Kenny - deal with it, little bro - will join us when they're ready. As, so I hear, will you, Jess."

"I'm excited!" Jess's face lit up anew. She'd only found out a few days ago. "I thought I was destined to work in corporate IT forever. Now, I can make a real difference. And I get to work with Charli too!"

"Yes, I've been meaning to touch base with her," mused Conor, with a sly wink in my direction. "She needs to understand how much trouble having you on her team can be."

Jess stuck out her tongue, and he grinned.

I glanced over at the head table. Only one person remained seated there. I poked Jess's arm and jerked my head. "Speaking of Charli..."

She followed my gaze and lost some of her good humor. "Great talking to you, guys. We'll try to catch you again before we leave."

She took my arm and led me back towards our seats, skirting the edge of the sparsely populated dance floor.

Izzy looked up from her phone and set it down as we approached, forcing a smile. Midnight black dye had replaced the bubblegum pink of last year, and she'd cropped her hair just above the shoulders. Her ever-present black eyeliner extended in delicate curls from the corner of her eyes, and her lipstick was as dark a shade of red as I'd ever seen. Despite all this, she was easily the second most beautiful woman in the room, and I couldn't believe she sat alone.

"Everything okay?" Jess asked. "I figured you'd be hanging out with Jamal and Conor."

Izzy's smile turned sad. "I was, but I don't think Conor's wife likes me much. I guess I have that effect on some people - I can be a lot."

"You're fine just the way you are," Jess insisted, laying a hand on her arm. "I mean, you were a little tough to take at first, but I've seen the real Izzy when you let your guard down."

"Oh darling, you have no idea," said Izzy, with a laugh and flirtatious wink. She glanced at me, then inspected her dress. "I still can't believe you asked me to be a bridesmaid. Or that I said yes. Although, black is def my color."

"Why wouldn't I ask you? You rescued me from captivity! I'll never forget that. We'll never forget it."

Their eyes met, and Izzy nodded. Her attention drifted to the dance floor, and she raised her eyebrows. "I see Rosalind's letting her hair down."

Turning, I saw Rosalind and Martin slow-dancing to The Cure's "Lovesong", her arms around his neck, his resting above the waist of her teal-colored dress. They gazed at each other as they swayed, not really in time to the music. If Jess still looked at me that way in thirty years' time, I'd know I was doing something right.

"I've never danced to that song," Izzy remarked. "Never really had anyone to dance with."

"We did invite Charli," I said. "I'm sorry she couldn't make it."

Izzy sighed. "Charli has her own life to lead. She's an amazing person, but she has her own hopes and dreams. I'm not gonna mess that up for her. I let her go. If I've learned anything from these last few months, it's humility. And maybe some self respect."

Someone coughed behind me. Daniel Hill, looking healthy but awkward in his white chef shirt, stood at my shoulder. He'd graduated from first stage rehab and had returned to St. Louis for work experience. Mike Szemis had taken a chance on him too.

"Excuse me," he said, nodding to me and Jess, but staring at Izzy. "Could I... would you like to dance with me?"

Izzy looked him over with cool curiosity, then her face erupted in a radiant smile as she got to her feet. "Why not, then?" She placed her hand in Daniel's, and he led her to the floor. Their dancing was at least in time with the music. They stayed for the next song, while his parents left to join us, but not without a glance at their son on the way.

"Before I forget, or it gets too late, I want us all to try that bottle of Bordeaux I've been saving for the occasion," Martin announced. "Let me go grab it, and some fresh glasses. What, Rosa?"

Rosalind pursed her lips as she stared back at the dance floor. "I'm not sure I approve of Daniel's choice of dance partner. She'll eat him alive."

Martin drew her into a side hug with a contented smile. "He's fine. Let him live a little, dance with a pretty woman. He wouldn't be the first male Hill to fall for a pretty goth girl."

"I wasn't that much of a goth," Rosalind retorted.

"I have photographs that prove otherwise."

"You know," I interjected. "I've never seen those photographs. You'll have to show us next time we're over."

Rosalind swiped at my arm, then fixed her husband with a steely glare. "Don't you dare, Martin Hill!"

"Of course not!" he protested. As soon as she looked away, he gave me a mischievous wink and walked off.

The three of us stood in silence for a while, watching more dancers take the floor. Izzy and Daniel looked to be enjoying themselves. Everyone was enjoying themselves. The tension and danger of the previous year might never have existed.

"Cute dress," Jess remarked at last, admiring Rosalind's figure.

"Thank you!" said Rosalind, beaming. "I bought it specially."

"And I see you're wearing a cross now."

I looked closer, and sure enough, a small gold cross dangled from a chain around Rosalind's slender neck.

She shrugged. "I never lost my faith. I just place it in different things these days. And people."

"I just worry sometimes, you know?" Jess bit her lip, leaving her thought unfinished.

I took her hand. "About what, hon?"

"What if we... did we kill God?"

I didn't know how to answer, and looked at Rosalind in silent appeal.

"Humans have tried doing that for years," Rosalind murmured, fingering her necklace. She dropped her hand back to her side. "I think the simple answer, Jess, is no. We don't know what The Presence is, or was, and I doubt we ever will. Nor do I think it's that important, quite honestly. We know what it was doing, and what happened to it at the end, perhaps even a little of what it wanted. Names confuse the issue. God, Gaia, even 'The Presence': they all impart their own meaning to something that may not apply, that may mislead us entirely. A name doesn't change the thing itself. But, it changes our perception of the thing. It's debatable, which is more important."

Jess and I absorbed this. For my part, I was happy not to know more. I couldn't separate thoughts of The Presence with the image of my father. That would haunt me for the rest of my life.

"Is it truly over?" I said. "Jamal said the HLF has detected no new Intrusions since last year. Are we done with Imprints and Erasures forever?"

Rosalind pondered the question. "Perhaps. Perhaps not. There will always be things we don't understand until science can explain them. We tell stories around the gaps, to help us make sense of it all. Telling stories is what makes us human. I'm content with that."

Martin returned with wine, and we all drank a toast, to long life and happiness. The DJ announced it was time for the happy couple to join the dance floor, so Jess and I walked out to raucous applause and the strumming guitar of The Sundays' "Wild

Horses". I wrapped her in my arms, and her body melted into mine, swaying along with the heartbreakingly beautiful tune.

"Are you content?" she whispered, her warm breath tickling my ear.

I gave her a gentle squeeze. "More than content. I'm with you. I love you, Jess."

"I love you too, D."

So we danced. Whatever had gone before, whatever had led us to this point, was done. Our lives had changed. We'd made wonderful friends, and we had a future together to look forward to.

It was time to tell our own story.

ACKNOWLEDGEMENTS

When I began writing *Imprints of the Past* I didn't know if the book would be more than a standalone. Once it became clear there was more of D's story to tell, I embraced the extra challenges of a series, especially for a debut author. Many readers, understandably, don't want to read an unfinished series from someone they've never heard of. I resisted many temptations to further explore the lore of Imprints and Erasures, of the Henry Lyons Foundation and The Presence. There's much more to tell, but I hope enough has been told where you, dear reader, can fill in some of the gaps yourself.

Many people have been generous with their time and opinions to help shape and complete the story. Rick Wurl read the first draft of every chapter hot off the printer, corrected and refined every fight scene, and made me rewrite the penultimate chapter after my first attempt fell far short of expectations. Geri Dreiling, Enrique Valle Serrano, Adriana Daniel, Aimee Keener and Tina Sellars all provided invaluable and complementary insight as beta readers, solving problems I knew I had and those I didn't. This book is only as good as it is because of your efforts on my behalf. Thank you!

Gareth Clegg again had the dubious privilege of copy editing and formatting the text. I appear to have lost all understanding of how many commas to use, where or when, and I'm glad he's been there to bail me out. Our email conversations are quite surreal, since we're both old enough to include salutations

("Hi Gareth") and signoffs ("Gareth") in each message. I would highly recommend Gareth to anyone needing an editor.

Also seeing the series through, Michele Guarnieri produced a wonderful third cover. I couldn't wait for Rosalind to join D and Jess, with Shotcombe House in the background. Rosalind looks exactly like I imagined! We've used purple and dark bronze accent colors on the prior covers, but green made sense here for many reasons. I'm excited to see the three books together!

Now that the fun part of writing a book is complete, I turn with trepidation to the slog of marketing the damn thing. But that trepidation is far less now due to Heather Mayers, my PA who stepped in to organize my chaos, and The Unusuals, my wonderful street team. They are part of an incredible, supportive indie author and reader community, primarily on Instagram, that already feels like home to me. A special thanks to Jacki and Mehdi Fakhrahmad, leading lights of this community, who convinced me to join after I met them at the ScaresThatCare AuthorCon IV in St. Louis last year.

Targeted online marketing is one thing, word of mouth is another. I am forever grateful to all my family and friends who have read my books and/or recommended them. There are so many amazing stories out there, and for others to take time to read mine, to write a review, or mention them to others, truly humbles me. Again, thank you.

My wife Sherri not only indulges my writing habit, but actively supports me. She beta reads my work with unvarnished and invaluable criticism, and even allows anniversary trips to coincide with author conventions! She truly is my rock in times that grow more uncertain by the day. I dropped occasional love notes into the story for you, hon. I hope you found them all.

About the Author

Gareth Ian Davies was born and raised in the south of London , during which time he wrote many terrible things and dreamed of becoming a novelist. Instead, he earned a degree in Physics from the University of Bristol and didn't quite know what to do with it. After moving to the American Midwest he flirted with a career in nuclear engineering before taking the somewhat safer path as a software architect. He spent the next three decades writing code and technical documentation, before finally realizing his dream by publishing his first novel.

Gareth lives in St. Louis with his wife, two cats, and a cockatiel. Where have all the fish gone?

ALSO BY GARETH

OF IMPRINT AND ERASURE
Book 1 – Imprints of the Past
Book 2 – Tethers of the Present
Book 3 – Echoes of the Future

Dark Fairytales for the Unloved (Volume 1) - anthology
Nourishment

k Fairytales for the Unloved (Volume 2) - anthology
The Path

STAY CONNECTED

Want to be one of the first to get all the latest news? Check out Gareth's socials and sign up for upcoming announcements, first looks, and more!

Facebook:
Gareth Ian Davies

Instagram
@author.garethiandavies

TikTok
@garethdaviesauthor

Website
garethiandavies.com